BERT AND MAMIE TAKE A CRUISE

Also by John Keyse-Walker

The Teddy Creque mysteries

SUN, SAND, MURDER
BEACH, BREEZE, BLOODSHED
PALMS, PARADISE, POISON *

The Cuban Noir series

HAVANA HIGHWIRE *

* *available from Severn House*

BERT AND MAMIE TAKE A CRUISE

John Keyse-Walker

SEVERN HOUSE

First world edition published in Great Britain and the USA in 2023
by Severn House, an imprint of Canongate Books Ltd,
14 High Street, Edinburgh EH1 1TE.

Trade paperback edition first published in Great Britain and the USA in 2023
by Severn House, an imprint of Canongate Books Ltd.

severnhouse.com

British Library Cataloguing-in-Publication Data
A CIP catalogue record for this title is available from the British Library.

ISBN-13: 978-1-4483-1015-9 (cased)
ISBN-13: 978-1-4483-1017-3 (trade paper)
ISBN-13: 978-1-4483-1016-6 (e-book)

All Severn House titles are printed on acid-free paper.

FSC www.fsc.org MIX Paper from responsible sources FSC® C013056

Typeset by Palimpsest Book Production Ltd.,
Falkirk, Stirlingshire, Scotland.
Printed and bound in Great Britain by
TJ Books Ltd, Padstow, Cornwall.

To my grandparents, A.R. (Bert) Keyse and Mary Jane (Mamie) Keyse

NOTE ON CRUISE BROCHURE QUOTES

The Round Africa Cruise brochure quotes found at the beginning of each chapter are taken directly from the original Raymond Whitcomb brochure for the sixty-three-day Round Africa Cruise of the S.S. Columbus from February 1939 to April 1939

ONE

> The Round Africa Cruise of 1939 will sail from New York on February 4, on the North German Lloyd Liner *Columbus*, and will return to New York on April 8, sixty-three days later.
>
> – *Round Africa Cruise brochure*

Mamie – February 8, 1939 – At sea

No one was more surprised than me when Bert shot the purser. You could have knocked me over with a feather. Here we were, just meeting some nice people like Jack and Bunky Olsen from Minneapolis, and the Waynes from Dubuque, and that handsome Baron Schmitz, and Bert has to go and ruin it all with gunfire.

I didn't even know he had that funny little gun along with him or I never would have permitted it. You don't need a gun on an ocean liner, even if you are on a voyage around a place as wild and untamed as darkest Africa. At least Bert says it is wild and untamed. Oh, you should have heard him go on about the lions, and the gorillas, and the Zulus, and the Watusis. You would have thought that we would be in daily peril.

But so far I haven't encountered much wild and untamed on this cruise, other than Bert himself. And he was even doing pretty well until he pulled the gun, but things went downhill fast from there. And I do have to give Bert the benefit of the doubt. The purser had reached into his tuxedo jacket pocket and yanked out a pea shooter of his own, a shiny silver pistol I think they call an automatic. He was waving it around, demanding that the ship put him off at the Azores, and threatening to shoot anybody who tried to prevent him from leaving when Bert fired.

Still, I thought there was something phony about what was happening at dinner. Here we were, the Olsens, the Waynes, and that tubby man from Detroit and his blinky-eyed wife whose name I can't seem to keep in my mind – Hinkley, Huntley, Hurley? – in the chi-chi main dining room, just finishing our hors d'oeuvre of boiled lobster, with the waiters about to serve the consommé Julienne, when the band started up with the dinner music. They had just wrapped up a kippy little version of Artie Shaw's 'Back Bay Shuffle', which is my kind of music and which had everyone swaying in their seats. It must be a German thing that you can't have jazz when you get beyond the hors d'oeuvres, so they drifted into something the band leader said was '*Vagner*'. I think he meant Wagner. I like to think of myself as being as classy as the next dame, but that stuff just gives me indigestion. And puts me to sleep.

No sooner did the band spit out the first few bars of that Wagner snoozer than one of the wine waiters pipes up that he sees someone lying on the ground behind the bandstand. The band stopped mid-note, and a general hubbub ensued in the dining room until Herr Pfennig, the second officer, ran in from the deck. I'd met Pfennig two days before, when we were about midway between New York and Casablanca, and he was all smiles and smooth charm then. But when he rushed behind the bandstand where the wine waiters had all gathered in a semi-circle around the unseen person on the ground, he was dead serious. Pun intended.

'Everyone, please be quiet and remain seated,' he said. Then aside, to the wine waiter nearest him, 'Go fetch Herr Doktor Ehring, and be quick about it.'

Herr Doktor Ehring appeared in mere seconds, black medical bag in hand, and immediately bent over the person behind the stage. While the doctor conducted his examination, Herr Lau, the ship's first officer, bustled into the room, his great salt-and-pepper beard puffed up like an angry porcupine from the wind on deck. He was followed shortly by Herr Kletz, the third officer, and Herr Blanck, the purser, both rushing in through opposite entrances and converging together a discreet distance from where Doctor Ehring now knelt, sadly shaking his head.

While this was going on, the waiters continued serving, a bizarre mix of German efficiency and 'the show must go on'.

Wine for the fish course was poured, and the sole meunière marched forth, while Herr Lau and the doctor consulted in hushed tones at the rear of the bandstand. Unfortunately, the acoustics were good and the words '*tot*' and '*die Stewardess Ella Althane*' could be heard. Third Officer Kletz, his trim mustache quivering, began to sob. He was guided to a chair by one of the waiters, where he sat hanging his head.

Everyone had stopped eating by now. The waiters, done serving the fish course, remained scattered among the diners, not moving. Except for the crying Herr Kletz, the room was a silent tableau.

Then Captain Dane entered at the far end of the dining hall, striding rapidly toward the bandstand and the sober cluster of officers gathered at its rear. His gait was the gait of a seaman, balanced and rolling, despite the fact that the ship sailed on calm seas. Of medium height and slight build, he could have been called ordinary or even nondescript on any street in America or Europe. That is, until partway along his passage to the stage, when he removed his peaked cap, revealing a high, intelligent forehead, and those eyes. A man might call those eyes wise or knowing or intelligent. To a woman, even a woman on the north side of – though I'll never admit it – a half-century, those cornflower blue eyes said 'bedroom'. I think I even heard a woman give a swooning sigh as the captain passed near our table. I think the woman may have been me.

Captain Dane stopped just short of his first officer and spoke in English, tinged with a mild accent that declared itself to be continental, rather than the guttural Teutonic cadence of most of the officers and crew. 'What seems to be the trouble here, Herr Lau?'

Taking his cue from Captain Dane, the first officer switched to English. 'Fräulein Althane, the A Deck stewardess, was found back there.' He gestured toward the curtained rear of the bandstand. 'Dead.'

A collective gasp emerged from the diners. I looked to Bert beside me, but he was as impassive as the Sphinx of Egypt we hoped to see later in the trip. The chief waiter roused the wine waiters into action; a river of Veltliner splashed into goblets.

'Has a cause of death been established, Herr Doktor Ehring?' the captain said.

'The preliminary appearance is strangulation.' Herr Doktor Ehring spoke the words slowly, with emphasis on the last.

Another, louder sob issued from the third officer, followed by '*Meine* Ella!' as he buried his head in his arms.

The captain turned to the seated diners and asked, 'Did anyone see what happened?'

There was only silence as a response.

'Did anyone see Fräulein Althane before she was found injured?'

No response again.

The captain tilted his head back slightly, and scanned the room with those eyes. They seemed to fall on me but when I glanced aside I could tell that every woman in the room older than twelve and younger than dead felt the same way.

A birdlike woman at a table near the band flitted her hand into the air like a schoolgirl who knew the right answer. 'Yes, madam?' the captain intoned.

'I saw one of the officers near there,' the bird-woman said. 'Right where the young lady was found. He seemed flushed.'

'Which officer, my dear lady?' Such a suave interrogation.

'Herr Blanck, the purser.'

The mention of the purser's name shattered the unreal calm that had enveloped the dining room to that point. Herr Blanck stepped back from the tight knot of his fellow officers and looked about, for a friend, or an alibi, or a way out, I don't know which. At the same time the third officer did a switch-eroo from milquetoast mourner to raving maniac.

'You killed her,' Herr Kletz screamed. 'You couldn't have her and so you killed her. You crushed her; she was a flower, a delicate flower, and you crushed the life from her with your dirty, brutish hands. I'll kill you now, I will. I've no reason to live without her.' The third officer stood and clawed toward the retreating Herr Blanck, restrained by Herr Lau and Herr Pfennig.

Captain Dane pointed to the purser. 'Arrest that man.' The first officer, a busboy, the chief waiter and several of the musicians in the band moved warily in the direction of the accused Blanck who, surrounded on three sides, backed toward the diners. Several of the gentlemen passengers rose partway from their seats, as if to close the box around the purser. I noticed my Bert, not exactly the picture of courage, sat stone still, casually watching the commotion.

Herr Blanck brought the advance on him to a halt when he drew a silvery automatic from his coat pocket and said, 'Stay back. I'll shoot. I have nothing to lose now that I can't have her.'

Several of the ladies screamed as Herr Kletz rushed Herr Blanck. The purser leveled the pistol at the heart of the sobbing third officer and two shots snapped out. The shots rang loudly in my ear. My left ear, only, I realized, though I was facing the two combatants directly on. Then I smelled an acrid smell, gunpowder I supposed, again from my left.

Herr Blanck dropped to one knee, clutched his chest, rolled slowly to his side and lay motionless. The shiny automatic clattered across the floor. After it stopped moving, you could have heard a pin drop in a basket of cotton balls.

I turned, with everybody else in the room, in the direction of the sound and the smell from the shots. There was Bert, as calm as could be, arm extended, cradling that odd little gun in his palm, with smoke still issuing, not from the muzzle but from two of the chambers in the cylinder.

Bert turned toward me and started to laugh his great, uproarious horselaugh of a laugh, while the rest of the people just stared.

TWO

> This is truly an African cruise: except for the final three calls in the Mediterranean, it is devoted entirely to Africa, and the islands off the African shores.
>
> – *Round Africa Cruise brochure*

Bert – February 8, 1939 – At sea

Maybe it broke the mood too soon but I really couldn't help but laugh after I shot the purser. It was the expression on Mamie's face – the absolutely incredulous, is-this-the-man-I've-been-married-to-for-thirty-years look – that broke me up. That and the fact that we hadn't touched land and were nowhere near to Africa yet and I was already having the time of my life.

Adventure and Africa had called to me for years, even when I was a small boy back on the Shaaf Road farm. Now I was finally headed for the untamed continent and even the sea travel was turning out to be fun. After all, how often do you get to shoot ship's officers in front of a crowd, even if the cartridges are blanks and the gun is a starter's pistol.

The purser rolled to his feet, quickly joined by Herr Keltz, the third officer, in a smiling handshake. A ruckus arose among the passengers seated at the dining tables.

Captain Dane stepped just in front of the two officers and raised his hands for silence. 'Ladies and gentlemen, I hope you were amused by the crew's modest vignette. Over the years, we have found that the occasional murder relieves the boredom of a long sea voyage and, occurring at the dinner hour, sharpens the appetite. This is now the tenth crossing of the Atlantic during which these talented thespian-crewmen have provided a faux crime, in lieu of the real thing, for our passengers' amusement. Please join me in congratulating them on another wonderful performance.'

Slow realization stole across the faces of Mamie and the other passengers, and they smiled and applauded as the crew members from wine waiters to the resurrected Fräulein Althane formed a line in front of the bandstand, joined hands, and took a theatrical bow.

As the applause continued, the purser broke free from his compatriots and gestured with his arm in my direction. 'Please also recognize the deadliest shot in the house and our only co-conspirator among the passengers, Mr Bert Mason.'

There was more polite applause all around except from Mamie, who shot me one of her patented you-will-pay-for-this-later-Adelbert-Russell-Mason looks. I thought I might as well enjoy myself since I knew what was coming later in our stateroom, so I stood to acknowledge the applause and hand over the popgun to the purser.

Make no mistake about it, though, I didn't bring any of this on myself. My role began on the second day out of New York. Mamie was in our cabin, napping in an effort to catch up on thirty years of sleep she had missed while raising three kids and running the domestic side of our life together. I went up for a stroll on the Promenade Deck. I was at the rail, taking in the empty horizon and enjoying the roll of the following sea, when Herr Blanck appeared at my side.

'Excuse me, Mr Mason,' he said. 'Are you by any chance from the western United States perhaps? I have read of your cowherds there and thought you have the look of such a man.'

'Nope, Herr Blanck, never been west of the Indiana line, though I have rode plenty of workhorses. I have two that I use to work the ground in the greenhouse right now. As for my rugged good looks, you'll have to talk to my ma and pa.'

'Still, Mr Mason, you look the part, rangy and strong. Can you handle a gun?' he asked.

'I was a Tuscarawas County Sheriff's deputy for a year.' I didn't tell him that I'd never had occasion to draw my gun on duty and there wasn't even enough money in the county budget to buy ammunition for target practice. Next thing I know, he shoves this odd little bean shooter into my hand and fills me in on the crew's playact to come. I thought the idea was aces, and that was how I ended up shooting him a few days later.

Things finally settled down in the dining room and at our table. Old Jack Olsen joked with me about unwisely gunning down crew members before we'd been served our full meal, while Mamie chatted with his wife, Bunky, which boded well for me because she stopped firing daggers at me with her eyes for a minute or two. The waiters collected the remains of the sole meunière and brought around the entrée, something they explained was vol-au-vent Toulousaine. That sure didn't let a fellow know what it was but it was tasty in an unrecognizable kind of way. And I did come for the adventure.

We were on to the roast chicken and potatoes, something I could identify and understand, when Captain Dane appeared at our table-side. The ladies collectively flushed and fanned themselves. I guess it's the uniform. Or the authority. Or the soft, assured accent. I swear that Martha Wayne was ready to toss old Lyle over on the spot if the captain had so much as crooked his pinkie in her direction. Not that Mamie was much more collected. But I shouldn't complain because what the captain did made my shooting stunt OK in Mamie's eyes. He invited us to dine with him at his table the very next evening.

THREE

> With the Moorish countries in the northwest, the primitive sections, the progressive South African Union, the old Portuguese settlements in the East, the extraordinary Big Game Reserves, and the wonders of Egypt, Africa offers the traveler a dazzling variety.
>
> – *Round Africa Cruise brochure*

Mamie – February 9, 1939 – At sea

What possessed Bert to travel to Africa is beyond me. Oh, sure, he always talked about going out and seeing the world outside Hills Corners, Ohio. Whenever we went to the moving pictures in New Philadelphia, Bert always wanted the B feature to be John Wayne as one of *The Three Musketeers*, followed by a newsreel of Berbers riding through the desert in Tunisia, or Tutsi tribesmen dancing in the Belgian Congo, and then close the evening with Tarzan and Cheeta. Not that he didn't like Jane, too. He liked her maybe a little more than I felt comfortable with, but I wasn't about to give him the satisfaction of saying anything. The last one we saw, *Tarzan's Revenge,* was not that good anyway, with that dim Eleanor Holm as Jane instead of Maureen O'Sullivan. At least O'Sullivan had some red-headed moxie, even if she did reveal a whiff too much skin in the swimming scenes.

All those moving pictures must have made more of an impression on my hubby than I thought because once our youngest son Lee graduated from Hills Corners High School – a lazy last in his class of twelve, and he is smarter than that, the little . . . ah, never mind – Bert started getting these cruise brochures in the mail. And reading them in the evenings when he used to be satisfied with the *New Philadelphia Daily Times* after a hard day planting tomatoes in the greenhouse. Next thing I know, he starts reading the brochures aloud to me, and I knew then he had a bee in his bonnet about something.

'Take a gander at this one, Mamie. Round Africa Cruise on the SS *Columbus*, of the North German Lloyd line. Port calls in Casablanca, Dakar, Cape Town, Madagascar, Zanzibar, Egypt. The Kasbah in Rabat, the Cape of Good Hope, Mombasa, Nossi-Be, the Pyramids of Giza. Mummies. The mighty Nile. The Sphinx, Mamie, the Sphinx with its nose shot off by one of Napoleon's cannons. And look here, first-class accommodations, a swimming pool right on the deck that converts to an outdoor dance floor at night. Think of it, Mamie, the two of us dancing under the stars south of the Tropic of Capricorn, the coast of the Dark Continent gliding by in the moonlight.'

'I think I sense something gliding by me right now,' I said.

'Aw, c'mon, Mamie, don't you ever wonder about it? Don't you want to see the place before it gets all civilized and ruined?'

'I like civilization. I like hot water, ice cubes, toilet paper, and underwear under my overwear. I like overwear, too.'

'Don't you want to see the wild side?' Bert said. What I was seeing right then was Bert's wild side. Where did he get this?

I tried changing tactics. 'We can't afford it, Bert. Didn't you hear, we just got out of the Great Depression?' As soon as the words escaped my lips, I knew I was defeated.

'The Depression is over, Mamie. And if anyone can afford this trip, we can.'

He gave me the long, earnest, why-can't-I look he probably learned begging cookies from Ma Mason. It worked on me. It always works on me, whether he wants another helping of mashed spuds or to make whoopee. And he was right; we could afford it. Who would have thought that a great way to make money in a Depression was to raise tomatoes in a greenhouse? But it was. While farmers in the Dust Bowl pulled up stakes for California, Bert shipped thousands of baskets of winter tomatoes to New York, Philadelphia and Boston. A fresh tomato in February was one of the few luxuries most of the once-wealthy of those cities could still afford. Bert and I prospered, to the extent that we now had money to rub elbows with some of those same once-wealthy, and now merely well-to-do, individuals on a cruise.

'C'mon, Mamie, Polish Katie and Otto can keep an eye on the crop and make sure everything runs smoothly in the greenhouse for a couple months. And, look here, we can go in style. A double cabin on A Deck for $1,005 each, with food and drink and shipboard activities included. Whadda ya say, old girl?'

You can guess what I said because I'm writing this on a green baize writing table in the wide corridor between the social hall, which spreads from one side of the SS *Columbus* to the other, and the carpeted quiet of the ship's library.

I have to admit, Bert was right. Traveling on the *Columbus* is traveling in style. The way I heard, the ship was in the midst of construction at the outbreak of the Great War, originally to be named *Hindenburg*. When her sister ship, also under construction and originally named *Columbus,* was given to the White Star Line as part of war reparations after the Huns were defeated, she took the explorer's name and became the pride of the post-war German merchant fleet. One of the English passengers aboard told me that she's Germany's answer to the *Queen Mary*, only to be corrected by a German passenger who informed her that the *Queen Mary* was built in 1936, in response to the completion of the *Columbus* and her North German Lloyd line sister ships. The *Queen Mary*, he said, was England's pitiful effort to match the splendor and luxury of the *Columbus*.

I don't know what the *Queen Mary* has since I've never set foot on her, this being my first time out of the US of A and my first ever cruise. But I do know it would need to be pretty exceptional to beat what this tub has going for it. There's the pool, for one thing, up on what they call the Beach Club Deck. It's got tiled walls and dressing rooms and showers nearby. It seems a little discombobulating, the thought of swimming in a pool of water that's on the deck of a ship that is resting on an ocean of water. It's not like skinny-dipping in the muddy Tuscarawas River where I learned to swim as a little girl. I haven't been swimming since, but I bought my first bathing outfit for this trip and I plan to try out that pool when we get out of the North Atlantic and the weather warms up some.

I have tried out some of what Purser Blanck calls the 'amenities'. The deck tennis and the golf putting were a snap. I have always been athletic. The dining room, which is hardly a room at all, more like a barn, being two decks tall and the full width of the ship, is wonderful, with its fancy oak tables and plush chairs. Bert and I danced last night in the Marine Garden, with its potted palm trees and parquet floors. Well, I danced and Bert clomped along. At least he only stepped on my feet twice. I'm sure he would rather have been squirreled away in the smoking room with Jack Olsen, sitting in the leather club chairs, smoking cigars in front of the fireplace. It was supposed to be open to the ladies, but it was already clear a couple of days into the voyage that it was really the men's hideout from their wives. I stuck my head in the door of the place once, to find Bert for some shuffleboard, and all eyes turned to me. There wasn't a skirt in the place. Bert hustled over and moved me out the door, which was what I wanted, anyway.

But what I like best is to be out on deck, with the scent of the sea, in the wild wind. The polished teak decks are wide, with room for oodles of deck chairs, and they have them, with deck stewards, all nice German boys, to supply you with cushions and blankets and steaming cups of bullion and coffee. I swear I could bask on deck the entire trip, just crooking my finger to the nearest Fritz or Hermann when I needed sustenance or a bit of pampering.

Oh, my stars, where has the time gone? I have to get dressed. We are at the captain's table tonight, thanks to Bert's shoot-em-up. I want to look my best. I wouldn't want to disappoint that dreamy Captain Dane.

FOUR

> The North German Lloyd Liner *Columbus* which has been engaged for the Cruise will be the largest and fastest ship to ever encircle Africa.
>
> – *Round Africa Cruise brochure*

Bert – February 9, 1939 – At sea

Fifty-two years and I never owned one of these monkey suits and now here I am wearing one every night. Not that I don't look smart in it, the cat's pajamas, except saying that makes me sound old-fashioned. But I cut a decent figure for fifty-two – no pot belly, still most of my hair, and there's not too much gray in the red yet.

'You, sir, look right handsome for a man of fifty-two years,' our bedroom steward, Paul Grap, said as he brushed the back and shoulders of my jacket with a palmetto whisk which he had produced from the pocket of his uniform jacket. Steward Grap seemed to be able to produce everything a man could need from his jacket pockets. Or thin air, if necessary. I never had a servant before but I could see where a man could get used to it. 'The cat's pajamas, my old mum would say,' Grap grinned.

The cabin door opened. 'You don't look too bad for fifty-two,' Mamie said as she paused inside the door.

'Just been thinkin' that myself,' I said. 'But does everybody have to say "for fifty-two"? Will they be saying that when they look down into my coffin – "he doesn't look too bad for a man of eighty years and in his condition"?'

'I'd better get ready, too. We don't want to be late for the captain's table,' Mamie said. She popped open the narrow closet, completely filled with the four new dresses she had traveled all the way to Halle Brothers in Cleveland to buy for the trip.

Steward Grap melted noiselessly from the room, an eerie skill only slightly less unsettling than his ability to appear whenever needed, though not summoned, at any hour of the day or night.

'That Grap fellow should really give me the creeps,' Mamie said. 'The way he just . . . materializes and dematerializes. But I like him. So polite but not aloof, like most of the Germans.'

'He told me he's half English, on his father's side,' I said.

Mamie pondered, then drew out a dress. 'What do you think, the red one?'

'I thought you were going to hold that one back until the party when we cross the equator.'

'That was before we had an invitation to dine with the captain.'

I put my arms around her. 'Out to impress Captain Dane like every other woman on the cruise?'

'A girl just likes to look her best for special occasions.'

'Does this mean I'm forgiven for shooting the purser with that popgun?'

'Don't press your luck, Bert. Now, zip me up.'

The wine waiters were already orbiting the tables when we entered the main dining room. More or less half of the seating had arrived, and the purl of conversation drifted and echoed through the elegant two-story space. The captain's table was nestled in an alcove of its own, with a lower ceiling making the space more intimate.

'No Tarzan stories, Bert,' Mamie said under her breath as we approached the table. Does she think I have no couth?

Captain Dane, in a spotless blue uniform jacket with gleaning brass buttons and white pants pressed to a knife edge, was engaged listening to an intense, black-haired woman to his left. Neither he nor the woman was seated, and she punctuated whatever she was saying with short, sharp jabs of her finger in his direction. Dane calmly took in her statements without comment.

To the captain's right, First Officer Lau and a gentleman in a white tuxedo jacket, both also standing due to the presence of an unseated lady, smiled and chatted, holding their glasses of white wine to the light and then swirling, sipping and holding the glasses to the light again. I might have thought the wine was bad, the way they were examining it, if I hadn't seen how to drink wine in the moving pictures.

Captain Dane, no doubt hoping to avoid more finger jabbing, seized the opportunity for introductions. 'Ah, Mr and Mrs Mason, so good to see you. May I introduce Señora Pia de Ribera of Torremolinos and, more recently, of your United States of America.'

The lady held out her hand to Mamie, who shook it, and then to me, a bit differently, with the back of her hand facing up. I realized she expected me to kiss it. There was a brief moment where I couldn't think of anything to do but just that, but a nudge in the ribs from Mamie told me I would only get to do something like that once before I died, probably at Mamie's own hand. I opted for the safe route and gave the señora a one-pump shake.

'Charmed,' I said. Saw that in the movies, too. I think it was Franchot Tone, or maybe Cary Grant, said it. From the expression on Señora de Ribera's face, that went about halfway toward making up for the lack of a hand kiss.

'And you know Herr Lau, of course,' the captain said.

The first officer fairly crushed my hand in his big paw. Mamie, taking a cue from Señora de Ribera, held out her hand with the back up and was rewarded with a heel click and a hand kiss, followed by Herr Lau's heavily accented, 'Charmed, Mrs Mason.' Mamie blushed like a schoolgirl, even though Lau was just copying my suave patter. Last time I lift a line from a talking picture.

'And this gentleman is Matthias Huber, of Wien, in the Fatherland,' Dane introduced. 'Mr Bert Mason and Mrs Mamie Mason of the United States.'

'Wien, Osterreichs. You Americans say Vienna, Austria. Involuntarily of the Fatherland. I am pleased to meet you, Mrs Mason, Mr Mason.' Herr Huber bowed deeply from the waist.

'The *Anschluss* has been greeted with enthusiasm by the great majority, although not all, of the citizens of the former Austria,' Herr Lau said. 'Fortunately, Herr Huber's knowledge of wine and his passion for viniculture make up for his archaic political ways. Come now, Herr Huber, we are all Germans now, as we have been all along. Let us toast the Fatherland with this fine Riesling and put all unpleasantness aside.'

The wine waiter appeared with two tall bottles and no prompting, filling glasses for the entire company. Herr Huber, whatever his differences with the regime, was more than happy to put them aside to concentrate on the wine.

'Mr Mason, you have here an example of the finest of our Wachau Rieslings. When compared to an Alsace Riesling, you will find it to be less alcoholic, crisper, and with a more forthright fruit. And because of our *Urgestein*, our principal type of stone in the soil, the mineral elements cause the wine to be more aromatic and fuller-bodied than a German Riesling.' Huber emphasized the 'German'. 'Swirl and sniff, Mrs Mason.'

Mamie swirled, and dutifully sniffed.

'The nose is our vineyard peach, a variety that grows alongside our grapes. Now taste, *bitte.*'

Mamie took a tentative sip and brightened. 'That's damned, er, darn good, Herr Huber.'

The group laughed. Huber and Lau went on to engage in a good-humored parry and riposte over Austrian and German Rieslings.

'They are all German Rieslings now,' a high-pitched voice declared with as much authority as a high-pitched voice can have. Which is to say, not much. We all turned toward the sound, almost directly behind Mamie and me, to see two men. The one who had spoken was comically short, not a dwarf or a midget, but no more than four feet ten inches tall. He wore a black uniform ridiculously tricked out in all sorts of badges, insignia and medals, like a plain-featured woman trying to compensate by wearing scads of flashy jewelry. You could see in the man's eye that he carried a chip on his shoulder.

A step behind the smaller man, his companion was a model of the Teutonic ideal – tall, blond, fair-skinned, with a flush from days and weeks spent in the outdoors climbing mountains or swimming across roaring cataracts, ramrod straight, with bored blue eyes and a reserved demeanor. Unlike his associate, the tall man was in a nicely cut brown civilian suit. The only adornment on it was a lapel pin swastika, as unobtrusive as the smaller man's insignia were gaudy.

'*German* Rieslings,' the smaller man repeated. 'You would be wise to remember this, Herr . . .?' He drew himself up to his full four feet ten and leaned pugnaciously toward Herr Huber. The jolly tone of the impromptu wine tasting evaporated.

Herr Huber ignored the request for his name but apparently could not let go of his country's loss of sovereignty in the recent annexation. 'The soil in which my vines grow has been Austrian soil for a thousand years and it didn't cease to be so by a single act of . . . piracy.' The Austrian's nostrils flared and he seemed primed to put up the physical defense to his homeland's sovereignty that his country had not.

Captain Dane intervened. 'Gentlemen, gentlemen, let us enjoy this fine wine, good music and the company of these beautiful ladies and put aside petty differences. We are all far from our homelands and I always say that at sea all men are brothers. And I am not being a proper host. Let me introduce Sturmbannführer Jürgen Heissemeyer of the Schutzstaffel.' The captain gestured toward the man in the black uniform. 'And his aide-de-camp, Untersturmführer Kurt Haas.'

The captain proceeded with introductions all around. When he finally came to Herr Huber, Heissemeyer gave him a cold-eyed nod and whispered something over his shoulder to Haas. The aide-de-camp produced a pen and notepad from his suit pocket and ostentatiously scribbled on the pad for a few seconds before flipping it closed and returning it to its home. The taking of names again halted all conversation.

I could see that Captain Dane was casting about for something – anything – to remove the chill at the table, so I tried jumping in, figuring Mamie might be proud if I bailed the captain out. 'That sure is one Joe Brooks uniform you have there, Sturm . . . Sturmbannfannrer.'

'Sturmbannführer, Mr Mason.' At least Heissemeyer didn't sneer at me. 'If it is easier for you, the equivalent rank in the military of the United States for myself is major, and for Untersturmführer Haas here it is lieutenant. And who, or what, is this Joe Brooks?'

'Joe Brooks, you know? Snappy. Snazzy.' When the major still looked puzzled, I said, 'Good looking.'

The diminutive major raised his chin and smiled a sour smile befitting his attitude. I could see he liked his uniform a lot, so I kept on. 'What branch of the service are you in, Major? The army?'

Heissemeyer scoffed. 'The Wehrmacht? Those weak sisters? No, Mr Mason. The uniform is of the Schutzstaffel, the SS. You Americans have no equivalent branch in your armed forces. Think of our work as detection, sir, detection of the enemies of the Reich.'

'It wouldn't seem that there are too many enemies of the Reich out here in the middle of the Atlantic, Major. Are you and the lieutenant on holiday, like the rest of us?'

'You Americans are so charmingly naive, Mr Mason. The enemies of the Reich, I have learned since my days as one of the party's original Saar-Schutz in 1925, are anywhere and everywhere.' Major Heissemeyer cast his gaze slowly around the group when he said this, and everyone there who was German or resided in Germany's sphere of influence dropped their eyes to the table rather than meet his. Even Herr Huber seemed to lose his nerve. 'No, Lieutenant Haas and I are not on holiday. We are here to provide for the security of the *Columbus* while she journeys so far from the Fatherland in these uncertain times. While you Americans have remained reasonably and appropriately uninvolved in the tribulations of European politics, the same cannot be said of other nations. Our duty here, mine and the lieutenant's and that of every member of this ship's crew' – he looked significantly at Captain Dane and Herr Lau – 'is to see to the safe return of the *Columbus* to Germany if hostile nations on the continent persist in their aggressions against the Reich to the point of involving the German *Volk* in another war.'

'Surely you don't think there's a danger of war now, during this cruise,' Mamie said. 'I thought that England's Mr Chamberlain said there would be peace for our time.'

Señora de Ribera, who had been silent to this point, looked evenly across her glass at Major Heissemeyer and said,

'Just as the Germans and their lapdogs, Franco and his Nationalists, are the bringers of peace to my home country.'

'As you can see, Mrs Mason, while the German race desires nothing more than peace and *Lebensraum*, Bolshevism is an infection which has gained or seeks to gain a foothold among our European neighbors and must be safeguarded against at all costs. America would be wise to safeguard its shores, as well, from the Communist menace.'

Captain Dane looked uncomfortable and was about to speak when Mamie chimed in. 'You men with all your talk of politics. Can't you save it for the smoking room? Isn't that what the place is for, for all of you men to get together and plot the fate of the world without us females and our delicate sensibilities getting in the way? Can't we just talk about music, or art, or Africa, or . . . or food?'

'Of course, Mrs Mason,' Captain Dane smoothly said. 'And we can not only have a conversation about food, we can engage in its pleasurable consumption, which will set us all on a better course.' To the waiter standing nearby, 'Fritz, what do we have for the hors d'oeuvre this evening?'

Fritz came to almost military attention, his waxed mustache twitching, as he responded, 'Live boiled lobster, sir.'

'Why am I not surprised?' Mamie said.

FIVE

Seven days after leaving New York, and two days after passing close to the garden-like Azores, the *Columbus* will come to Casablanca, the western gateway to Morocco and the first port of call on this Cruise.

– *Round Africa Cruise brochure*

Mamie – February 11, 1939 – Casablanca, French Morocco

The captain's table dinner was not at all like what I thought it would be. Oh, it was glamorous, with the captain, First Officer Lau, and even that stick-in-the-mud Major Heissemeyer in their fancy uniforms, Señora de Ribera all darkly exotic, and even Bert cutting a pretty dashing figure in his dinner jacket and white tie. And the food was good; I may never get Bert off of roulade Saarlandaise and crêpes Valentine and back on to beef and spuds. But once those Nazi officers arrived, you could have cut the tension with a knife. Major Heissemeyer was just a threatening baby tyrant and Lieutenant Haas was too creepy for my tastes, with his white-blond hair and his cold blue stare. He didn't say anything during the entire meal.

It was a relief to get back to some normal folks, Americans like Bunky Olsen, at dinner the next evening. Even Bert seemed relieved to be away from our more exotic passengers for a night. True, Bunky's mind, and her conversation, flitted around like a fly in a stable full of draft horses, but at least we could talk to her about something without it being written down and reported back to Gestapo headquarters. Bert was certainly less tense when we returned to our cabin last night, while the night before he had tossed and turned and finally had to ask Steward Grap to bring him some warm milk to help him settle down.

Not that he'd stayed settled down. Not today with our first landfall on the African continent, at Casablanca. Which is

French but named by the Spanish, who translated the name from the Portuguese, all the while with the same Mohammedans living there while the country got swapped back and forth like an ugly pup at a dog show with a cash prize. Today Bert was up before dawn and standing at the deck rail when the crew tossed lines and hauled hawsers aboard from a bunch of cutthroat-looking Arab ruffians on the quay.

If you cast your vision beyond the ruffians on the dock, Casablanca is a pretty, if disorienting, town. The crates, cranes and confusion of the port give way very quickly to broad avenues and modern buildings, whitewashed and almost blinding in the morning sun. I expected mud and stick huts, and black natives, but there's nary a one of either to be seen. There are all manner of people other than Negroes – pasty whites in suits and ties; brown Arabs whose clothing seems to be made of nothing but folds and wraps of once-white cloth, now dirty gray with age and lack of laundering; portly men in embroidered vests, balloon-legged pantaloons and puttees, wearing pillbox hats and four-day beards.

The hats are the feature that really stands out. Imagine any type of hat and you can see it in Casablanca – pith helmets, turbans, tasseled fezzes, straw boaters, kaffiyeh, Panamas, flat kufis, Fulani hats that look like something a coolie would wear and, of course, veils on the non-Western ladies, something called a niqab. Not that you see many non-Western ladies around the port, other than the cheap quiffs standing in every dirty doorway and stair landing, wearing gaudy print dresses, or skirts with no top on, or sometimes nothing at all, not a stitch. And the gendarmes standing right there, with their stubby white batons, looking the other way because, Bert says, they are paid bribes to do so.

The first thing that happened this morning when the gangway went down was the arrival of several new passengers. Steward Grap says that they are more Europeans, flown in to join the cruise at the first port of call on this side of the Atlantic. By the time the dozen newcomers had boarded, Bert was champing at the bit to go ashore. I was ready for some dry land, too, after seven days at sea, although the weather and the seas during the crossing were pretty calm.

'Watch for pickpockets and cutpurses if you get in a crowd,' Steward Grap warned as we left our cabin after putting on our shore footwear. 'You should have no problem, Mr Mason, from footpads, not a man of your size.' Sometimes it's good that Bert is such a big galoot.

We no more than hit the bottom of the gangway than Bert grabbed my arm and stopped, sniffing the air like a crazed basset hound. 'You smell that, Mamie? That's the smell of Africa. I've been waiting to smell that smell my whole life.'

'All's I smell is rotting fish, tar, and I think maybe a tannery that's going to be a real doozy when the sun gets higher,' I said.

'That's all part of it, the exotic perfume of untamed Africa. Breathe deep, Mamie, take it all in, savor the experience.'

I don't know why I humor the man, but I dragged in another lungful, expecting eau-de-slaughterhouse to be layered on top of the dead fish and the putrid hides. Instead, I got the sumptuous scent of jasmine. And there wasn't a jasmine bush in sight.

'Ah, smell that, Mamie?' Bert had that perfume face men sometimes get, all wistful and soft-eyed.

'Excuse me,' said a voice behind us. Bert turned his wistful, soft eyes to the gangway behind us. Mine followed his. 'I see you are going ashore and my room steward recommended that I not go ashore alone – there have been instances of white slavery in the port area. I wonder if I might join you?'

It was then that I realized the jasmine was emanating from a dame, not a plant. Too late to steer Bert away. He already had the scent in his nose, like a compliant bloodhound.

'Sure, miss . . .' Bert said in his best protective-hero-in-Africa voice.

'Damgaard. Gitte Damgaard.' She held out a kid-gloved hand and flashed a perfect set of white teeth inside a shy smile. Reminded me of that new Scandinavian starlet that has just come to Hollywood, Ingrid Bergman. Except I instantly liked Miss Damgaard. I don't like Bergman; Bert likes her too much.

'Bert Mason.' Bert gave her the one-pump shake now that he'd sworn off hand kissing. 'My wife, Mamie.'

'Pleased to meet you,' Gitte Damgaard said. She had the Bergman accent, too, good English with a vaguely Nordic lilt.

'I haven't noticed you around the ship,' I said, not thinking that she may have been in one of the lower traveling classes. The design of the *Columbus* made certain that the various classes of passengers did not often mix.

'Oh, I just boarded this morning. I arrived at Anfa Airport from the continent yesterday evening. I will be joining the cruise from this point forward, all the way to New York City.'

'Well, you're more than welcome to come ashore with us,' I said. 'We are just headed into town for a look around and I thought maybe we could do some shopping.'

'That would be perfect, Mrs Mason. I need to pick up some clothing for the voyage.'

Bert didn't realize he had traveled all the way to Africa to spend his first hours on the continent traipsing from one ladies' boutique to the next. That really hadn't been my plan either, but it was how we spent most of that morning with Gitte Damgaard. Sure, we were able to stop at a leather shop – near the stinking tannery – to buy Bert a new passport wallet, and we all three got snared by a sidewalk tout to visit a rug seller's shop that we practically had to fight our way out of. But the bulk of our excursion was devoted to Miss Damgaard buying dresses, skirts, blouses, pants, shoes, even underwear, in shop after shop. Bert staggered for a while under a mountain of bags and boxes of her purchases, but finally slipped a couple of twenty-five centimes coins into the hands of a grubby one-eyed fellow who kept following us asking, 'Carry packages, missus? Carry packages?' No sooner had the coins passed from Bert's palm to his than a gang of ragamuffin children appeared. One-Eye gave one coin to the oldest of the gang, no more than eight, and pocketed the other. A stream of soft-spoken instructions in a language Bert said he thought was Berber followed, and One-Eye melted into the mid-morning crowd. Each of the ragamuffins picked up a box or package, and looked expectantly to us for direction.

'You lead, Mamie, with Miss Damgaard. I'll bring up the rear so none of the packages drift away like old One-Eye did.'

So Gitte Damgaard and I marched away, with the kid bearers

trailing behind us and the great Bwana Bert hindmost. After Bert snagged thc first one or two who broke out of line to make off with our goods down a side alley, the kids caught on and our miniature expedition made quite a sight as we entered the last three or four shops needed to finish kitting out Miss Damgaard.

It was ten thirty by the time we returned to the ship. We were to go on a shore excursion to Rabat and Salé at eleven. The crewman at the gangway forbade our child porters from coming aboard, so Bert shouldered the bags and boxes and flipped another twenty-five centimes to the kids' leader. His fellows converged on him and the wrestling match was still underway when we finished climbing the gangway and stepped aboard.

SIX

> There will be a motor-coach sightseeing drive in Casablanca, the Spanish-named gateway to French Morocco, and an all-day trip – one way by motor-coach and the other way by special train – from there to Rabat and the neighboring seaport of Salé, with sightseeing in both cities.
>
> – *Round Africa Cruise brochure*

Bert – February 11,1939 – Casablanca, French Morocco

It was more than a small surprise when I entered Gitte Damgaard's cabin loaded down with her purchases. Hers was just down the passageway from our stateroom, so assisting her was the only gentlemanly thing to do. Her cabin was a single, much tighter than ours, and when I entered the cramped space what did I find but *two* steamer trunks already inside. It beats me what she needed more clothing for, but I guess the mystery of women is just a part of their attraction. At least that's what Mamie tells me.

Steward Grap met Mamie and me at our door with warm towels and two iced bottles of Vichy water. We only had time to wash the street dust down and we were out again, for the day's sightseeing excursion.

I got to play the gallant once more, as our tour companions were Señora de Ribera and another passenger who had just embarked, Fräulein Beatta Schon. Joining the three ladies and me was our driver for the day, a nervous man named Mamoun, a chain smoker who put out his Gauloises by pinching it with his fingers and putting it in his coat pocket as we approached. He needn't have; he smelled so strongly of the Syrian tobacco that, in the confines of the car, it seemed like he was still smoking.

Mamoun's automobile was an immaculately polished

beige-over-black Renault Celtaquatre. Mamoun held the front passengcr suicide door first for me and then directed the ladies to crowd into the rear seat.

'*Mesdames et monsieur, regardez à droite la Place de la Victoire*,' Mamoun began, gesturing vaguely to the right as soon as he had slammed the door and cranked the engine. For the next half-hour, he tooled through the broad boulevards and narrow streets of Casablanca, always at the same pace, which was slightly faster than a brisk walk and well less than even I, at fifty-two, could keep on a steady run. After exhausting his repertoire of '*Regardez là, la Place de France*' and '*Regardez ici, le Boulevard du Quatrième Zouaves*,' Mamoun floored the accelerator, taking us all the way up to thirty-five miles per hour for the trip to Rabat.

We arrived in Rabat for a late lunch at a hash-house called Tout Va Bien. I was hoping for something adventurous. Maybe sitting on rush mats on the floor, and eating unidentifiable cuts of goat meat out of a communal dish with our hands, while veiled dancing girls gyrated in the background. Instead, we got an art deco brasserie with a stuffy maître d' that served food that looked, smelled and tasted like the food we had just spent the last week eating on the *Columbus*. I tried to head the whole thing off before we went in the front door, but Mamoun would have none of it, steering me and the ladies toward the door with a lot of '*Regardez ici, le dejeuner*', and then a stream of something, I'm guessing Berber, when he handed us off to the restaurant's sidewalk touts. With much cooing and gesticulation from them, we found ourselves spirited inside, where a troupe of French *garçons*, circling the table with wine glasses, mineral water, menus and officiousness, concluded our fate.

Mamie had dutifully swiveled her head left and right as Mamoun directed our attention '*ici*' and '*là*' during the morning drive but now, confronted by a lackadaisical French lunch and with no other distractions, she focused all of her wiles of female inquisition on the very young, very pretty, new passenger.

'Fräulein Schon, it is a great pleasure to have someone on the sunny side of thirty to talk with. I was beginning to think the *Columbus* was a floating old-age home,' Mamie said. She always fancied herself as one who belonged with a younger crowd. Her remark didn't win her any points with Señora de Ribera, who surely wasn't on the sunny side of thirty but didn't want anyone to overtly state it.

'Thank you, Mrs Mason.' The fräulein blushed nicely, apparently just from being directly addressed. She seemed painfully reserved.

Mamie, recognizing a soft target, continued to probe. 'You missed an entertaining crossing, joining the cruise so late.' It didn't sound like a question but it sure as shootin' was and the fräulein took it as such.

'I live in Danzig, so this was the earliest point to join the trip from there.'

'Danzig, where's that?' Shy, retiring Mamie.

'It is since the Great War a free city, administered by the League of Nations. Before the War, it was part of the German Empire.'

'So you're German.'

'Now we are in a customs union with Poland. And our foreign relations are, how you say, handled by Poland. While the majority of people are of German *Abstammung*, heritage, there are also many who are Poles. And Jews. I am of Polish heritage.'

'It sounds like a mixed-up place,' Mamie said.

Fräulein Schon smiled sadly. 'Mixed-up is a mild description for these days, Mrs Mason. Since 1933, the National Socialist party has controlled our legislative body. In recent years, the Nazis have voted themselves plenary powers. Unions are outlawed. Other political parties are outlawed. There is now a law for the Protection of German Blood and German Honor, prohibiting marriages between Jews and Germans. Jews are also ineligible to be civil servants, teachers, professors or judges. Only persons of Aryan descent are permitted to be citizens; all others are state subjects without citizen rights. So, yes, we are, as you say, mixed up.'

'If you think that is mixed up,' Señora de Ribera chimed in, 'wait until the shooting starts. And it will. Those damned Nazis made sure it happened in my Spain and they will make it happen to those undesirable "state subjects" in your free city, if it can still be called that.'

Mamie suddenly realized what her question-and-answer session had ignited and scouted about for help. Rescue came in the form of the wine waiter, and the arrival of the entrée, *Lapin à la cocotte.* Not bad for rabbit. At least they said it was rabbit, although I noticed a distinct absence of cats in the neighborhood of Brasserie Tout Va Bien.

SEVEN

> At Rabat the sightseeing will include the Sultan's Palace, the French Residency and Hasan's Tower with its magnificent panoramic view. At Salé there will be a conducted tour on foot through the Souks.
>
> – *Round Africa Cruise brochure*

Mamie – February 11, 1939 – Rabat, French Morocco

I was beginning to wonder what Señora de Ribera and Fräulein Schon were doing on a German boat, as much as they seemed to dislike Germans. Or, at least, Nazis. I really have nothing against Germans. After all, America is full of Germans, even if we weren't so ready to admit it when we got feet first into the Great War. I remember Mrs Schmitz down the road changing her name to Smith, and how all the German-language newspapers stopped publishing in 1917. But now it's different. Now we know we're all Americans, not Germans, or Irish, or Poles. Our parents or grandparents may have come from those places, but we Americans want to stay out of Europe's politics and controversies. And wars, if it ever comes to that again. Our side of the Atlantic is just fine for us, and if we need to cross it to see some of the Old World, we'll do it on a German boat, or an English boat, or otherwise. *Macht nichts aus*, as Steward Grap says. It matters not.

After our fabulous lunch in Rabat, old twitchy Mamoun, our driver, reappeared as soon as we emerged from the front door of the restaurant. The restaurant's touts, having hooked us in, were no longer interested in keeping us as their exclusive prey, and abandoned us to an army of hawkers and costermongers who harangued us for the thirty feet from the restaurant to the car with offers of oranges, eggs, leather goods, small bottles of elixir 'good for the tourist belly', and dolls made from scraps. Mamoun led us back to the car but did nothing to dissuade the hawkers. It fell to Bert to elbow his way through the crowd in advance of us ladies. Bert is a big man and none of the noisy salesmen were over five feet two and a hundred twenty pounds, so it was easy for him to plow a path. We all arrived at the Renault with our jewelry and purses intact, no thanks to Mamoun, who immediately began our afternoon of '*regardez là*' and '*regardez ici*' as soon as the last door slammed.

The Sultan's Palace was pretty nifty, with its ornate blue inlay gate. The French Residence was sharp, too, and it had the usual quota of snooty Frenchmen hanging around and stamping the papers that Mamoun had to present before we could enter. But the real sight was Hasan's Tower. Mamoun called it a church, but it wasn't like any church I'd ever seen – a rectangular tower of reddish stone, at one time intricately carved but now worn with time, standing in the middle of a vast field of columns. Mamoun said it had never been completed and that we could climb the tower.

It became evident that Mamoun had no intention of scrambling up the tower with us. Bert, however, had no hesitation, and we three ladies followed, since after the hawkers outside Tout Va Bien, none of us felt comfortable without male protection and Mamoun certainly didn't fit into that category. The climb proved easier than I thought it would be, since there was a wide ramp to walk up instead of stairs. We arrived at the top and Bert was the only one winded. Magnificent Rabat spread before us, a low-rise city of streets and alleys that twisted and curved, and unpainted buildings blending with the brown color of the surrounding countryside.

We had been at the top for maybe five minutes when who should show up but the obnoxious Major Heissemeyer, his notebook man, Lieutenant Haas, and Herr Huber. Both the military men were in civilian clothes, with the major wearing a pith helmet that made him look like a really short man in a pith helmet, and the lieutenant in a khaki suit that made him look like a very blond Gary Cooper from that movie *Morocco* with Marlene Dietrich. Poor Herr Huber was disheveled and worn, either from the tower climb or from spending most of the day in the company of the two humorless Nazis, with the prospect of still more to come.

'I see, Mr Mason, that your driver was as keen to climb the ramp as ours was,' Major Heissemeyer said by way of recognition.

'That might be sensible once you've seen this sight a time or ten,' Bert said.

'It is more likely a reflection of the inferior race of the North African,' the Nazi opined. I had the sense that he spent most of his time making sure those around him knew who was inferior and superior.

While the major was busy putting his best racist foot forward, Lieutenant Haas's eyes fell on Fräulein Schon, and hers on him. He was not wearing his little swastika badge. I doubt that Beatta Schon would have seen it even if he had been. She was too busy being locked in his adoring gaze, and he in hers. Honestly, I have never seen a shy flower like Fräulein Schon move to full bloom so quickly. Her cheeks blushed, her eyes shined brightly under fluttering lids, and her once-demure smile now said 'come hither'.

For his part, Lieutenant Haas was receiving the message and acknowledging it with every handsome Aryan bone in his body. He reached for her hand and, in a most un-German gesture, kissed it formally and lightly, after introducing himself.

'Have you seen the view of the Oued Bou Regreg, Fräulein Schon?' Haas said. He laid the suave on pretty thick and she lapped it up.

'Why, no. What is that?' She lowered her forehead and gazed up at the tall Haas through her long lashes. The move had the desired effect – he was as smitten as if she had delivered a left hook to his square jaw.

'The river,' he stammered. 'And beyond, you can see the charming village of Salé. Come see.' He seemed ready to compete with Mamoun as tour guide, with a touch more energy in his delivery.

She extended her hand and the two waltzed over to the east parapet, where they made goo-goo eyes at each other instead of looking at the river. Ah, young love. I remember when Bert and I were like that. Even now, sometimes, I see that same handsome young man I married thirty years ago when I look in his eyes.

After a few more minutes of doing the tourist google at the sights from on high, we all descended to find Mamoun and the second car's driver, a cherubic French expat named Marcel, pitching centimes against the wall of the tower. They walked us to the riverbank a short distance away, where a bright turquoise rowing boat, large enough to hold all of us plus the two boatmen, waited at a stone quay. It was drowsily sunny and warm, and the boatmen chanted in time as they rowed us across to Salé on the north bank.

'*Ici le Souk de Salé*,' intoned Mamoun, sweeping his hand with a flourish toward a jumble of rickety stalls that started at the river's edge with fish sellers and moved up the labyrinth of streets away from the water.

'Look here, Mamie!' Bert shouted above the general hubbub of people haggling, and the brays, honks, bleats and calls of donkeys, goats, sheep, birds and even monkeys. 'A real live snake charmer.' Bert moved in close for a good look, apparently too close, as the next thing I knew Marcel had grabbed him by the coat sleeve to draw him away. Bert watched for another minute or two from a safer distance and then tossed a coin into the charmer's tip basket. This betrayed Bert to the crowds of vendors as a foreigner who was loose with his money, prompting calls of 'Hey, English mister, fine rugs here, you come in, see', and 'Tall sir, best leather goods in Morocco, belt wallet, jacket, we make your size', or my favorite 'Handsome mister, pure gold, best prices, come buy here for pretty wife, or concubine . . . or both.'

Bert was in his glory, moving through from stall to stall, sniffing proffered spices and joshing hucksters as they tried to sell him myna birds and fake antique swords. I must say it was all interesting in its own way, but after an hour, I was ready to move on.

The same could not be said for the two youngest of our companions, who had moved well beyond becoming fast friends. Lieutenant Haas and Fräulein Schon navigated through the throng hand in hand, eyes on each other, chatting, oblivious to the cacophony of sound around them which must have obscured their words. Nothing, however, could mask their adoration for each other. He stopped their progress at a flower vendor and bought her a riot of blooms. She bargained for a bottle of myrrh and bergamot cologne and presented it to him. Just when I was sure their next stop would be at the justice of the peace – which I'm certain the souk had somewhere; it had everything else – I heard Mamoun's '*Ici le chemin-de-fer*,' and he and Marcel herded us all, including the smitten couple, on to the train for a return to Casablanca.

Marcel distributed box suppers to us, procured from a vendor beside the tracks, just before he and Mamoun stepped off the car and the train departed. Herr Huber produced a bottle of Blaufränkisch he had been carrying in a leather messenger bag, together with tiny paper cups, and we made a railroad picnic. Bert got his wish for exotic food at last. The box suppers consisted of cold, greasy meat that I hoped was lamb or goat, on top of a salad of peas, apricots and something the conductor called *couscous*. Bert wolfed his all down, smacked his lips, and seemed satisfied at last. I passed mine over to a veil-shrouded mother and two kids. You would have thought I had given them a million bucks. I contented myself with a couple snorts of Herr Huber's hearty red wine. The last thing I remember before falling asleep on Bert's shoulder was glancing across the aisle and seeing Beatta Schon napping against the arm of Kurt Haas. He was still awake, and smiling. It was the first time I remembered seeing him smile.

EIGHT

> With a length of 775 feet and a width of 83 feet, the *Columbus* is able to provide her passengers with comfort and beauty in generous measure.
>
> – *Round Africa Cruise brochure*

Bert – February 12, 1939 – At sea

We returned from the shore excursion to Casablanca and Rabat last night at about eleven thirty. The train ride back from Rabat was just that, a train ride. We could have experienced the same thing whisking through the countryside between Chicago and Des Moines. Except that our Pullman car companions on a trip through the night in the American Midwest probably would not have included men in djellabas, women completely covered except for their eyes, a cage of guinea fowl, a goat, and two Nazis. So maybe it was a touch different.

The excursion itself was both exciting and disappointing. Some of it involved things I'd heard about and hoped to see – the cobra charmer, the bustling souk, the ancient Hasan's Tower. But it was disappointing that there was so much chaperoning going on. We could have gotten a better feel for the place without it. As it was, it seemed like we spent most of our time traveling, shopping and eating, all of which had the thinly veiled purpose of relieving us of a few francs along the way. I guess that being separated from their cash is the traveler's lot in life. I'll bet even the ancient vagabonds, the Carthaginians, Romans and Vandals, felt the same way. On second thought, maybe not the Vandals.

When we arrived at the ship, I almost had to carry Mamie up the gangway like a sleeping child. As late as it was, Steward Grap met us at our stateroom door with two mugs of hot milk. Mamie downed hers and was out for the count by midnight.

I was restless and went out to the rail to watch the crew cast off and move the ship out of the harbor.

There was a nip in the night air. The milk had warmed my insides but I shivered once or twice, until a figure came out of the shadows and placed a steamer blanket around my shoulders.

'You don't miss a trick, do you, Grap?' I said, as he took my empty cup after placing the blanket.

'It is my duty, sir, to see to your and Mrs Mason's comfort,' the young steward said.

'Do you ever sleep, son?'

Grap laughed softly. 'Some days it doesn't seem like I do, but I always manage to get a few winks in. I can sleep sitting up or leaning against a bulkhead wall to get a few minutes in here and there.'

'Do they give you a regular bunk or do you spend the whole voyage catnapping against walls?'

'Oh, yes, sir. All of us stewards have a lovely place we share below, on the deck below D Deck. I have a hammock and a space below it for my footlocker. The other stewards keep quiet when they are there, so it's easy to sleep, even though the light stays on day and night.'

'Is your father a seafaring man, too?'

'No, sir. My father was a farmer, a Brit. He was without land of his own and went to Belgium in 1914 to work as a farm laborer. He was there when the Germans invaded. Since he wasn't a soldier, he wasn't put in a POW camp, but he was sent to a labor camp as a part of a Zivilarbeiter Bataillon, a civilian workers' battalion. My mum was a cook in the camp and, despite all, they fell in love. After the war, he took her to England and I was born there in 1919. He died when I was fifteen and I signed on to a ship at Southampton to support myself and my mum. I have been on ships, White Star line and Norddeutscher Lloyd line, ever since.'

'Do you ever get back home to England?'

'It's been a few years now, since I was hired by NDL. I hope to return for the Christmas holidays this year though.'

The young fellow appeared downright pleased to chat, but he reverted to steward form, fading away when the figure of another person moved toward us along the railing. When the man got closer, I saw it was Herr Huber. He joined me, leaning against the rail and staring back at the lights of Casablanca.

'I see you are not yet able to retire, Mr Mason,' Huber sighed.

'Too wound up from today, I guess.'

'As am I. I am not certain I can survive another shore excursion like today's.'

'You'll miss a big part of the trip if you skip the shore excursions, Herr Huber. You can't see the Pyramids from the A Deck, you know.' I thought a touch of humor might lighten his mood.

'If I could be guaranteed freedom from the contemptible presence of Sturmbannführer Heissemeyer, I would find the excursions more pleasant.'

'He seems like a decent enough sort, once you get past the fancy uniform,' I said. 'Maybe he is a little overzealous.' Ma Mason always taught me to speak well of every person, even if they were a sawed-off officious jackass like Major Heissemeyer.

'You did not have the pleasure – and I use the word in its most facetious sense – of his Nazi company for the entire day at Rabat and Salé, Mr Mason.' Huber stopped and looked me straight in the eye, appraising, I thought. 'Between us?'

'Of course.'

'Between us, the sight of the disgusting little tyrant turns my stomach. He and his kind, they are fools and buffoons, I once thought. Now I have learned they are fools of the most dangerous sort – fools handed power. Germany is governed by a mob, Mr Mason, a mob who believes everyone and everything is inferior to them and must be exterminated. A mob does not think, Mr Mason; does not have decency, civility, tolerance or a heart. It thrives on all that is base and degrading. It tramples the innocent underfoot, flouts justice, and destroys all who would disagree with it.

'I know that sounds harsh and judgmental but I speak from experience. My own family has suffered at the hands of men like Sturmbannführer Heissemeyer. My younger brother, a man of the cloth, an upright Lutheran clergyman, has been sent to one of their "camps" for "re-education". A camp – ha! It is a prison. As if my brother, my dear Klaus, who loves poetry and would not harm a fly, is some kind of despicable criminal. What was his crime, Mr Mason? He performed his work as a clergyman, conducted a funeral service for one of his congregation who happened to be a Communist. Do you see the heartless brutality of the like of these Nazis, Mr Mason, that even the dead, and one who gives comfort to those who mourn the dead, are vilified and imprisoned and worse?

'Do you see now why I do not sleep tonight? I took this cruise to leave those people and their ilk behind, to leave them in their *Vaterland*, even as they have expanded it, and be out among people who are untouched by their darkness. And yet they seem to follow me, out of Austria, out of Europe, to the very edge of civilization in Africa. Bah, to hell with those bastards. I am very sorry I burden you with this, Mr Mason.'

'That's terrible about your brother,' I said.

'What is worse is that they torment me with it. That's right, that Heissemeyer knows my brother is imprisoned. He made sure to mention it to me. No, no, he didn't mention it, he lorded it over me, threatened that Klaus's entire family, myself included, should be held responsible for his conduct. I do not know what to do. I fear he will arrest me, here in the middle of the Atlantic Ocean, for something with which I had nothing to do. For something that any human being with an ounce of decency would consider to be the very opposite of a crime.'

Herr Huber let out an audible sob and suddenly fled into the shadows, leaving me alone at the rail. The ship had cleared the harbor headlands. The lights of Casablanca faded to a faint glow on the horizon. *Columbus* turned southwest on a course parallel to the coast, the land visible only as an indistinct mass at the boundary of the sea.

I returned to our cabin, where Mamie snored softly. I must confess, I did not sleep much during the rest of the night.

NINE

> The Canaries are a group of islands of volcanic origin that lie some sixty miles off the west coast of Africa. They are generally supposed to have been Plato's 'Islands of the Blessed' and the 'Fortunate Isles' of the Romans, and in the second century Ptolemy regarded them as the western edge of the world.
>
> – *Round Africa Cruise brochure*

Mamie – February 13, 1939 – Teneriffe, Canary Islands

Bert and I can't seem to get our schedules in sync, as the fellas who make the talking pictures say. I drifted off to sleep on the train back from Rabat last night and don't remember much other than Steward Grap with a nice warm cup of milk after that. I woke up early this morning and Bert, who I think was out strolling the deck till all hours, was still dead to the world when I toddled out for some deck time of my own.

The air felt different when I came on deck. In the North Atlantic, it was crisp, bracing, clean. In Casablanca, it was still cool but there was something stale about it, like it had been breathed too many times and needed a rest. This morning, though, I stepped from the cabin and inhaled warmth, gentle humidity, and the scent of flowers. A bask in the sun was in order, I decided, so I ambled around the front of the boat, the bow the sailors call it, to the left side, the port side the sailors call it, and a comfy deck chair.

'Coffee, tea or cocoa, Mrs Mason?' That Steward Grap shows up just when you need him.

'A cuppa joe would be great, thanks,' I said.

'Joe?'

'Coffee, Grap.'

'Ah, yes. Right away, Mrs Mason.'

The deck chaise didn't require a blanket today. I settled in to let the sun warm me like a self-satisfied cat. Africa had disappeared sometime during the night. The only land in sight was some islands to the east, the largest of which was dominated by a volcanic cone, with snow – snow, this far south – on its high slopes.

'That is Teneriffe,' a voice I recognized as Señora de Ribera's said behind me. 'May I join you?'

'Sure, Señora. Park it anywhere. So those are the Canary Islands?'

'Yes. I visited here once before, when Spain was still Spain.' The señora's face matched the melancholy of her voice.

I tried to lighten the mood. 'I can't wait to see the birds there. I always loved the way canaries sing.'

The señora smiled a wistful smile. 'You do realize the islands are not named after the birds?'

'No. Are there no birds?'

'Oh, there are a few, far off in the forests. If you are lucky you may see one or two. But the birds are named for the islands, not the islands for the birds. The Romans named the islands Canaria, the land of wild dogs.'

'I don't like dogs.' We had a pug once, but she was really Bert's dog. Trailed along after him all day. Worshipped the ground he walked on. I'm a cat person myself. Cats don't give a damn. I like that in a pet. 'Are there many wild dogs there?'

'No, no.' The señora chuckled. 'Ah, Mrs Mason, you make me laugh.'

'We can all use some laughter now and then.'

'You are right, Mrs Mason, but it is hard for me to laugh here, in this place, where so much that is bad began.'

'What bad began here?'

'The coup, Mrs Mason, that started our Spanish Civil War. Franco was commandant of the Canaries, and he and his minions hatched their plot here.'

'To save the Spanish people from the specter of Bolshevism,' Major Heissemeyer, striding toward us, said. Apparently listening in on private conversations was a Nazi specialty. 'And with generous assistance in strategy and materials from the

German people, Generalissimo Franco is on the verge of completely exorcising the Communist demon.'

'With the blood of thousands of Spaniards who love their country on his hands,' Señora de Ribera spat out.

'There are occasions where blood must be spilled to save country and race. I submit to you, Señora, that there are also occasions where it must be spilled to allow countries to rise to greatness. It is in such spilling of blood that the true patriot demonstrates his love of country.'

Major Heissemeyer enjoyed this talk of spilling blood a tad much for my taste. And for the señora's. 'The spilling of blood for the sake of obtaining naked power is never a patriotic act, whether the blood is Spanish or German,' she said.

'Or Jewish, Señora? I understand your husband darkens your children's otherwise pure Aryan blood by having a Jewish mother,' Heissemeyer said with a self-satisfied smile.

A look of panic flashed across Señora de Ribera's face, and then she composed herself and shot back 'How can you claim to know such a thing? That is nonsense.'

'To quote Shakespeare, the famous Aryan playwright, the lady doth protest too much, methinks. How can I claim to know? It is the business of the SS to know. Do you disagree that your husband elected in 1933 to reside in Spain, despite his significant business interests in Germany and despite your German citizenship, while he, as an Argentine, had no connection to Spain? Do you disagree that his mother was the daughter of French Jews with the surname Halevy who settled in Buenos Aires in the 1850s?' Major Heissemeyer jutted his chin. It reminded me of that Italian character, Mussolini. 'Have I struck a chord?'

'You are a vile man. Your kind is vile,' Señora de Ribera said.

'Not so vile as those citizens of the Reich who violate its laws against racial infamy. You are reminded, Señora, that this is a German ship. Those aboard are subject to German law and arrest for the violation thereof. You cannot hide behind the Spanish passport you carry by virtue of your dual citizenship. And even if you could, I seriously doubt the regime soon to complete its consolidation of power in your adopted country would stand in the way if your arrest became necessary.'

Señora de Ribera, who had appeared to be so strong, dissolved into tears. I could no longer be a bystander. 'Please, Major, this cruise is for all our pleasure, for which we have all paid good money to the NDL with the expectation that it would be peaceful and relaxing.'

'Señora de Ribera's lack of peace and inability to relax are of her own doing, Mrs Mason, and, unfortunately for her, I have a sworn duty to the Führer and the *Vaterland* which requires me to ferret out violators of our laws. Nonetheless, Mrs Mason, I will speak of this no more now, in deference to your wishes.' Major Heissemeyer pulled his best bored policeman mug as he said this and ended with a nod to the señora. 'Until later, Señora de Ribera.'

The shrimp-tyrant marched off along the deck like he was leading a parade. His short-legged goose-step would have been comic if he hadn't terrified Señora de Ribera so. She continued to cry, sniffling, 'What am I to do? He is going to have me arrested. If not today, sometime before I return to New York, and my husband. What am I to do?'

'There, there, sis,' I said, patting her shoulder. 'It can't be as bad as all that, can it? He's just a tin-pot soldier trying to scare you.'

'He has scared me. I will not go ashore today, where they can claim to arrest me on Spanish soil and extradite me to Germany. From here on, we are not visiting any German or Spanish territories until Gibraltar, which Spain disputes. Oh, dear God, I feel so threatened.'

I can't say I disagreed with her.

TEN

> Long before the *Columbus* nears Santa Cruz (its port and the capital of the Canaries) the white summit of the Peak of Teyde, often called the 'Peak of Teneriffe,' will be seen, a true volcanic cone but now happily dormant.
>
> – *Round Africa Cruise brochure*

Bert – February 13, 1939 – Teneriffe, Canary Islands

Mamie started the day in a huff, at least the part after I woke up. She was already gone when I rolled out of bed at eight, and was muttering about Major Heissemeyer and a confrontation he had with Señora de Ribera when I chased her down to have breakfast at eight fifteen.

Today we were off to see the island of Teneriffe. From the harbor at Santa Cruz, it's a different world when compared to Casablanca. Casablanca's harbor was low to the dirty water, decaying and seedy. Santa Cruz has a backdrop of verdant mountains, a tumble of well-kept whitewashed houses spilling down to a bay filled with colorful fishing boats, and a wide tan beach, all bordered by an air-clear emerald sea. From the ship you can make out flowers in the window boxes of the houses and men passing with burros in the cobbled streets. If I had been dropped in blindfolded, I would have assumed I was in southern Spain or the French Riviera rather than off the coast of Africa. I guess that is what travel is all about, learning how misplaced your expectations about a place can be.

We were paired for the excursion with Fräulein Schon and the two German officers, Lieutenant Haas and Major Heissemeyer. Ever since we were invited to the captain's table after my fake shoot-em-up with Purser Blanck, we have been paired with our companions from that evening for shore trips. That suits me just fine. I figure traveling with those European types is part of the adventure. Mamie doesn't feel the same way, whether because of the dust-up between Major Heissemeyer and Señora de Ribera she witnessed this morning, or because she misses the company of American friends like Jack and Bunky Olsen we made during the first days of the voyage, I can't say.

Anyway, we had no choice in the matter as the purser assigns who rides with who on these shore trips. I suspect he thought he was doing us a favor. If the car we got was any indication, he was. It was something called a Hispano-Suiza, and it was one long drink of water. There was plenty of room for the five of us plus the driver. The convertible top was down to take in the fine weather with the sights. It was painted a snazzy butter yellow and had a V-8 under the hood which our driver, a local fellow named Hidalgo, was more than pleased to show me while we waited for the major and lieutenant to join us quayside. Hidalgo loved that car. He even wiped his fingerprints off the hood when he closed it after showing me the engine.

The only thing Hidalgo may have had more of an eye for than his Hispano-Suiza was Fräulein Schon. One gander at the fräulein's doe eyes and the young guide turned on the charm, swinging open the car door and dusting the oxblood leather seat before taking the young woman's hand to assist her in entering. Mamie, on the other hand, had to find her way into the seat beside the fräulein on her own. I joined the two ladies in the rear seat, just in time for the appearance of Lieutenant Haas and Major Heissemeyer. Haas clicked his heels and bowed slightly in the direction of the ladies. Fräulein Schon colored nicely at the attention shown by the Aryan knight, a fact not lost on Hidalgo, who placed the lieutenant in the position in the front seat where it would be most difficult to speak to and see the young woman. Major Heissemeyer was installed in the front between Hidalgo and Haas, where he appeared affronted by his poor positioning.

As we moved sedately from the dock to the low road through town and along the seashore, Heissemeyer turned to the three of us in the rear seat. 'You are most fortunate to be riding with Lieutenant Haas and me today.' He puffed up with importance despite his middle-seat ignominy. 'In addition to the tourist itinerary set out in your excursion brochures, we will be paying a visit to the headquarters of the expedition of the Ahnenerbe, the Reich Academy of Science, here in the Canary Islands. Reichsführer Himmler has personally approved the expedition to locate the Lost City of Atlantis and the pure Nordic race of those islands. I believe it will be most edifying for you.' The major indulged in a self-satisfied smile and turned to face forward.

'Asshole,' Mamie muttered under her breath. Mamie doesn't have much of a tolerance for assholes.

'Please, Mrs Mason.' Beatta Schon spoke in a hushed tone, placing a pale hand on Mamie's arm. 'You do not want to offend a long-standing member of the SS like Major Heissemeyer. Trust me, I speak from experience.'

Mamie nodded and we settled back into the plush seats as Hidalgo guided the great boat of a car through the sun-drenched streets of Santa Cruz and out into the countryside.

'The Orotava Valley,' he said, waving an arm at the picturesque fields of lavender dotted with scruffy cattle. We were destined for La Laguna, which Hidalgo described as 'the former capital'. There we were to visit the cathedral to carry out the important task of gazing upon the tomb of Alonso de Lugo, conqueror of the islands. I'd have just as soon kept up the cow viewing.

After dutifully trooping into La Laguna's palm-shaded cathedral to stare at the dusty stones atop the long-dead de Lugo, we were mercifully released back into the countryside. Hidalgo halted the Hispano-Suiza at – as he described it – 'the most best vantage in all the African continent and its islands, two thousand meters above the level of the seas.'

We all stretched and slapped the road dust off our arms and chests, and appropriately oohed and aahed at the view. The Orotava Valley spread below, an undulation of purple, green and brown fields punctuated by whitewashed tile-roofed hamlets, stretching to the Atlantic. To the left, the snow-capped cone of Teyde towered above all. It wasn't Tarzan and the jungle, or the plains of the Serengeti, but Africa still provided the dramatic and unexpected.

Major Heissemeyer and Lieutenant Haas separated

themselves by a few yards and stood overlooking the valley, the major gesticulating seaward, lecturing the younger man who stood silent and attentive. Fräulein Schon looked on nervously while this occurred, more concerned with the two men than the splendid panorama before us. After three minutes, the major concluded his lecture and folded his hands behind his back, still staring out to sea. The blond Haas brought his movie-star looks over and took Fräulein Schon away by the hand, strolling along the cliff edge.

'This sight-seeing tour seems to be about much other than the seeing of sights,' a miffed Hidalgo, coming up behind Mamie and me, said. You could tell he was just a local boy with a fancy car, not a pro like Mamoun. He had none of the oily polish that our man in Casablanca had. 'The señorita, she and the yellow-haired man, they are, how you say . . . an idem?'

'An item,' Mamie said. 'And yes, Hidalgo, they are.'

'She is very beautiful,' he said.

I looked at the couple and realized that she was indeed beautiful, when she was with Kurt Haas. She bloomed in his presence, like one of the rare orchids I keep in the flower house of the greenhouse back home. I noticed then that someone else was looking at the pair as they walked. Major Heissemeyer gazed at the two with what I could swear was a look of jealousy on his face.

Hidalgo started us down a switchback course to the sea. Partway, we stopped under what he said was a dragon tree. 'Its red sap is like the red blood of a dragon.' It reminded me of a stalk of broccoli in shape. Its shade was welcome as we made a picnic of the box lunches that the ship had supplied – ham sandwiches and dark bottled beer – before continuing on to Puerto Orotava.

Puerto Orotava was a pretty hamlet, milk-colored houses with the disorderly beauty of bougainvilleas tumbling over their walls and roofs. Our destination was a black-sand bathing beach, which was also the shore-side headquarters of the Ahnenerbe expedition that Major Heissemeyer wanted to inspect.

Our party was met on the road above the strand by a

contingent of Germans fitted out in khaki shorts and shirts, and pith helmets like they were about to go out searching for Dr Livingstone. The day had turned blisteringly hot; the blue froth of the waves against the black sand of the beach was most inviting.

'Mr and Mrs Mason, would you care to join Lieutenant Haas and me for our inspection of the Ahnenerbe facilities? This is a unique opportunity to see the uncovering of the true origins of the Aryan race and the lost city from which they arose,' preened Major Heissemeyer before the gaggle of obsequious archeologists and assorted other functionaries. He pointedly left Fräulein Schon out of the invitation.

Mamie nudged me in the ribs hard enough to kickstart a recalcitrant mule and hissed 'No.' It was a subtle hint for her but one I picked up on from years of experience. 'Sorry, Major, but with the heat and all I was hankering for a swim and that water's an inviting blue. The missus and I were kind of counting on it.'

Major Heissemeyer harrumphed 'Very well. Come Haas.' The lieutenant glanced over his shoulder at Fräulein Schon as he trailed away after the tiny strutting major and his entourage of grave robbers.

The beach was a nice set-up, with a row of changing booths at the upper edge of the tideline. Mamie, Fräulein Schon and I changed into our swimming costumes, I guess they call them bathing suits now, and splashed into the surf. It was good and clean and exhilarating, and after half an hour we laid out on the volcanic sand on towels rented from an attendant for two pesetas.

The fräulein was somber for one so young on a sunny beach. Mamie asked if she was feeling all right. The question generated tears and a sniffled, 'Kurt says Major Heissemeyer told him I'm not worthy of him because I am Polish.'

'Who cares what the little twerp thinks?' Mamie said. 'What does being Polish have to do with anything?'

'Kurt says he doesn't care,' Fräulein Schon said. 'But the major can make trouble for him, believe me.'

'Just because you're Polish?'

'Yes. But I'm not. But if the major thinks I'm an

unsatisfactory match – not Aryan – he can have Kurt dismissed from the SS if Kurt doesn't drop me. And, being from Danzig, we are all so mixed together there, I'm certain that if the major makes up his mind and digs deeply enough he will find some . . . undesirable blood in my background.'

More tears flowed. Mamie took the young woman into her arms, where she had a long, sobbing cry while I sat wondering why I had to come all the way to Africa for this.

By the time Major Heissemeyer and Lieutenant Haas returned, striding in jackboots on the hot sand, their uniforms mottled with sweat, Fräulein Schon had composed herself and remade her face. She even managed to laugh gaily on the way back to the ship, after I said I was becoming motion-sick in the rear seat and asked Lieutenant Haas to switch places with me. It was a lengthy ride back to Santa Cruz with Major Heissemeyer sitting silent and stone-faced beside me but I enjoyed it. A farmer always enjoys a ride in the country.

ELEVEN

> The steward service on the *Columbus* is noted for its unremitting but unobtrusive attentiveness and its deft expertness.
>
> – *Round Africa Cruise brochure*

Mamie – February 14, 1939 – At sea

It's Valentine's Day. I had forgotten, being at sea and on this trip away from the usual flowers and boxed candy that Bert always turns up with. Oh, he is a sly dog. Just when I think we are an old married couple, satisfied and stodgy, Bert comes along with something sweet and romantic. At least for a farmer.

Today, though, the reminder that it is Valentine's Day came not from Bert but from the ever-present Steward Grap. The conscientious young man has caught on that my day doesn't really begin until I've had that first steaming cup of coffee and he has taken to making sure that I have it soon after I rise. That is no mean task, since Bert and I are usually up at 6.00 a.m. Today at a quarter past six there was a soft rap on the stateroom door, not enough to awaken anyone who was still sleeping. I had just dressed.

My 'Come in' resulted in Grap entering with cups and a silver pot with a stick handle on the side for pouring. The sea air, saline and humid, entered with him, mingling with the rich black bouquet of the coffee.

'Your cup of joe, Mrs Mason,' Grap grinned. 'And Happy St Valentine's Day to you, and to you, Mr Mason.'

'Thanks, Grap,' Bert said. Bert's a man of few words early in the day.

'Captain Dane sends his compliments and requests that you join him at his table this evening to celebrate the lovers' holiday.' Steward Grap then unboxed a boutonniere for Bert and a knock-out corsage made from Canary Island bell-flowers and bird-of-paradise for me. 'These were picked just before departure and held in the galley coolers. They should last until this evening if you put them in water, ma'am.'

'You and the captain sure know how to make a lady welcome,' I said and meant it. All I could think about was if the ladies at the Soroptimist Club in Hills Corners could see me tonight.

Bert and I spent the day lolling in deck chairs and swimming in the pool on the Beach Club Deck. It seemed silly, or maybe frivolous is a better word, to go swimming in water that's in a pool on a ship that's itself on the water. But I got over the frivolous feeling quickly because it was so gosh darned pleasant there in the sun, all warm in February, instead of the cold and the gray and the slush of the Ohio winter. I actually got a good bit of sunburn – can you imagine, in February? – but I think it will be just enough to give me a peach glow when I put on my finery for the evening. With luck, maybe Bert and that handsome Captain Dane will have a wee tug-of-war over my affections. Of course, I'll make sure Bert wins.

The main dining room of the *Columbus* was decorated in a Valentine's Day theme when we entered. All the white tablecloths and napkins had been switched out for red and pink ones, and cut-outs of hearts and Cupids were scattered on the tabletops and hung from the wall sconces to give a festive air. Speaking of Cupid, Herr Blanck, the purser, went over the top and appeared as the cherub, carrying a bow and a quiver of red arrows, and dressing neck to toe in a red and white leotard and what looked like a diaper. He had a garland of green leaves in his hair, too. He went from group to group, spouting love sonnets and pretending to notch and fire his love-arrows at unsuspecting couples. Those Germans have such a dour reputation but they're proving themselves to be a ton of fun on this trip. At least some of them are.

Bert was a pip in his monkey suit with its gardenia boutonniere. He is one smooth joe when you dress him up and get the dirt out from under his fingernails. Not that I was any slouch myself, in my beaded House of Worth evening gown adorned with Steward Grap's spray of bellflowers and bird-of-paradise. Bert and I made one flash couple.

'Oh, aren't you as pretty as a spotted horse in a daisy field,' said Bunky Olsen from our left as we stepped through the polished mahogany dining-room doors.

'Well, the same to you, Bunky,' I said, though she was about as elegant as a mud fence in a dowdy left-over-from-the-Twenties dress that had been washed so many times it had faded to the gray of the wash water itself. Jack Olsen wasn't doing much better. He was in a suit, and a brown one at that, the only man in sight who wasn't in a tuxedo or dress uniform, save for one sport who was wearing a kilt, I guess for ventilation.

'We've an invitation to the captain's table tonight,' Bunky trilled. 'Steward Grap told us you did, too, so I guess we'll be joining you.' She stuck out her chicken-wing arm to Bert, so she could be escorted in on the arm of a handsome man, and he had to oblige. I followed, stuck with lumpy Jack Olsen in his brown tweed packaging.

The captain's table had been extended to almost double its regular size for the lovers' holiday. Fräulein Schon and Gitte Damgaard together with the usual suspects from our first meal with Captain Dane filled the space. Captain Dane was momentarily delayed with ship's business, according to First Officer Lau, but would join us shortly. As Bert and I were the only ones present who knew everyone at the table, we made introductions all around.

The company was only through the vichyssoise and the first glass of Weissburgunder when Captain Dane bustled in, making no excuses for his late appearance because he was, after all, the captain of the ship. Bunky took in his dress uniform and dreamy eyes and I thought she was going to swoon like a teenager. She made her way through Dane's greeting to her by fanning herself vigorously as beads of perspiration appeared on the tiny hairs above her upper lip.

'Why, Captain Dane, it must be a tremendous responsibility running such an important ship as the *Columbus*,' Bunky finally managed to stammer out.

'Indeed, Mrs Olsen, but with a fine crew of German sailors such as we have, not an overwhelming one,' Captain Dane said, the lids of those eyes at half-staff. I thought for a moment that *I* might be the one to swoon like a teenager.

'Our merchant fleet is the finest civilian fleet in the world,' crowed Major Heissemeyer, too long silent for his own sense of self-importance. He wore a dress SS uniform instead of a tuxedo. The black fabric and the numerous emblems and gewgaws made him look like a cross between an undertaker and a trolly motorman. 'Second fleet in the world only to our Kriegsmarine, our glorious navy.'

I thought I saw Captain Dane's face contort in disgust, but it was only for a beat or two before he recomposed into his usual placid facade. It seemed like it might be the start of another unpleasant session with Major Heissemeyer and his ego, but Herr Blanck appeared in his Cupid outfit, setting all the ladies to giggling and the men, other than Heissemeyer, to rolling their eyes in embarrassment for the purser.

'Good evening, *Damen und Herren*, and welcome to love's holiday here on the SS *Columbus*. As the god of desire, erotic love, attraction, and affection, it is my pleasure, and soon to be yours, to introduce you to a fine old German game called in English 'Who will be the binder?' Now, mere mortals, arise and bow before the god of love.' Herr Blanck cast a deferential eye toward Captain Dane. 'Of course, as the Zeus of our majestic floating world, Herr Captain is exempt.'

Dane remained seated while the rest of us rose and were arranged by the Cupid-purser, boy-girl-boy-girl, in a circle, all holding hands. This caused a halt to the dinner service for our table, much to my disappointment. It felt like a long while since lunch, and the shipboard routine had developed in me a liking for having my meals at a prompt and regular time. The smoked trout, ox tongue and Saratoga chips would have to wait while Cupid played his game. It wouldn't hurt; I could tell I was putting on a few pounds. Not that I minded much. Bert always likes a little jiggle in my wiggle, he says.

While some of the other diners looked on, getting a peek at their future fate at the hands of Herr Blanck's alter ego as he made his way from table to table, the band struck up a brief flourish. The purser, sensing that Herr Huber knew the game, placed the Austrian in the middle of our circle and recited, first in German and then in English:

It snows and blows, and it's cold frosty weather,
Here comes the farmer drinking all his cider:
I'll be the reaper, who'll be the binder?
I've lost my true love, where shall I find her?

At the conclusion of the verse, Herr Huber split the circle to Bert's right, breaking Bert's grip on Señora de Ribera's hand. Much to the señora's surprise, Huber planted a big smacker right on her lips, taking her hand and mine in his and shoving Bert into the center of the re-formed circle.

The purser recited again, this time in German only, with some of the diners at the nearest tables boisterously joining in to shout the rhyme. Bert catches on to some things quickly, unfortunately for him, and when the couplet ended, he broke the circle, laying a big theatrical kiss on Bunky Olsen. Bert has always been a touch clumsy in the romance department and people got jostled around when he moved to break the circle. Somehow, I accidentally stepped, hard, on Bunky's foot in the confusion.

'Ow!' she said and glared at me. How was I supposed to miss those great flapjacks attached to her ankles? They were easily size twelves. And I don't mean ladies' twelves, either.

Bert's collision with the circle dislodged Lieutenant Haas, who up to that moment had been holding Bunky's hand on one side and Major Heissemeyer's, through some odd twist in the ordering of the circle, on the other. The virile Aryan man jumped to the center and waited for most of the rhyme before tearing over to petite Beatta Schon, and tilting her into a passionate embrace and a long slow kiss.

The entire dining room hooted and whistled with approval as the young couple remained in thrall, the kiss and embrace extending from good-natured, to steamy, to downright lustful. One thing was certain, Cupid Blanck was getting results with that game of his.

'Lieutenant Haas!' The shrill voice of Major Heissemeyer

cut through the whistles and laughter for all except Kurt Haas and Beatta Schon.

'Lieutenant Haas!' The major was now red in the face, upset far beyond what I thought an officer should be by a subordinate's minor breach of decorum.

'Kurt!' The room became silent. Lieutenant Haas and Fräulein Schon fell a step back from each other, bewildered by the volume of Major Heissemeyer's shout, which had finally filtered through the magic barrier of their mutual desire. The major stepped forward and slapped Lieutenant Haas. The slap was not a manly gesture or a challenge, but much like an angry or hurt girl. '*Hure!*' he cried, spittle at the corners of his mouth. He said it looking at Haas, not Fräulein Schon, as I might have expected. Then, turning to her, said, '*Unreine Jüdin.*'

After this last remark, all three remained in the center of our circle, each one staring at the other two, eyes welling with tears. Yes, tears, even Major Heissemeyer. This frozen tableau lasted for ten seconds until the spell was broken by Heissemeyer cutting through the boundary of the circle and running from the room. Fräulein Schon was next, fleeing through a door on to the deck on the opposite side of the ship from the exit taken by the major. Lieutenant Haas, left alone, looked in the direction taken by Heissemeyer and then pivoted and fled after Fräulein Schon.

The voice of Captain Dane calmly interrupted the silence left by the trio's departure. 'Even on the lovers' holiday, it seems, the course of love does not run smooth, to paraphrase one more sage than I. Herr Blanck, perhaps we should exclude "Who'll be the binder?" from the festivities for the rest of the evening.'

'Of course, Herr Kapitän,' the baffled Cupid-purser answered.

'Let us have some dinner music,' Dane ordered. The band struck up a Strauss waltz.

We resumed our seats and spent a quiet meal talking about the weather. And wondering just who the lovers in the circle of three were.

TWELVE

Dakar, the capital of French Senegal, is the greatest peanut port in the world and one of its 'sights' is the mountain of peanuts alongside its dock awaiting shipment.

– *Round Africa Cruise brochure*

Bert – February 15, 1939 – Dakar, French Senegal

It will be good to get off the ship in some different company today. That scene between the two German officers over Fräulein Schon last night told me that we were all keeping too close company, and maybe we needed a break from each other. I think – I'm not quite sure what was going on. Mamie said she had her speculations, something about Major Heissemeyer being unnaturally concerned over Lieutenant Haas, and not just because Heissemeyer believed Fräulein Schon was a bad match for the younger officer. She thinks there is something going on between the two men. I've heard of such stuff, don't get me wrong, but I got no nose for it. Still, it doesn't strike me that Haas is any kind of a nancy boy. Or Heissemeyer, for that matter, just excessively high-strung. Probably his size.

Whatever's going on there, it will be good to get away from the whole crew today and see some of the real Africa. I figure the real Africa, of Dr Livingstone, tribesmen, white hunters, native kings, and cannibals, starts here in Dakar.

We made port sometime during the night. I heard the crew going through the docking process but I was only half awake and didn't bother to get up. This morning, when I finally went out on deck, I was greeted by the sight of a modern port that didn't look like it belonged in 'wildest' Africa. The French, whose territory we had returned to after our sojourn in Spanish land in the Canaries, had poured their best efforts into the port and it showed. The *Columbus* was tied up to a concrete dock, with cranes busy at work unloading two freighters opposite us and landing stores on to our deck. Rows of warehouses lined the shore. Every manner of ship or boat within the imagination could be seen crisscrossing the teeming harbor. French officials on the quay marched about in crisp tropic-weight suits with clipboards in hand and an air of authority in their step. Thinking back to the down-at-the-heels shabbiness of Casablanca, I wondered if the France in charge of that African colony was the same France running this clean, efficient place.

'Good morning, sir. Cuppa joe?' Steward Grap loved exercising his new vocabulary.

'No, thanks, Grap. I think I'll wander ashore to see if there's anything wild about this place.'

'I doubt that, sir. This is the one place in the world where the French act more like the Swiss.' Grap made a joke. I like the boy.

'Well, I want to see for myself,' I said.

My passport was quickly examined at the foot of the gangway, then I stepped on to the soil of the real Africa. Other than a smattering of French who were giving orders to everyone else, there were no white faces to be seen. I expected the natives to be lethargic and half-naked but everyone I saw moved along rapidly to some urgent destination, and both men and women were clothed in large flowing robes, which I later learned were called *boubou.*

At the end of the quay, I made my way around a massive mountain of peanuts, to which a string of trucks coming from town were adding and from which a steady line of long-shoremen, like an endless troupe of ants, were subtracting, bagging the legumes with shovels and shouldering them into the holds of several waiting steamers.

Off the docks on the land side, I picked a direction and was soon making my way along a palm-lined boulevard, peopled with more dark faces and colorful robes, until I was the only white man in sight.

'*Ça va, patron?*' a voice to my left said as I gawked at a donkey laden with enough straw baskets to completely shade the animal and its master from the waxing heat of the sun. I turned to face a tall, skinny kid in a flowing *boubou* that looked like it hadn't been washed since . . . ever. The boy was dark, so dark that the whites of his eyes shocked by their whiteness in comparison.

'No parley, son,' I said.

'Englishman!' the kid exclaimed. I had never seen anyone quite so excited at the prospect of meeting an Englishman. I could only figure that the kid collected encounters with tourists like kids in the States collected baseball cards. Getting an Englishman in these parts must be like getting a Tattoo Orbit Dizzy Dean back home.

'Not English. American.'

'Joe Louis. Brown Bomber.'

'That's right, kid. Do you speak English?'

'Yes, much. The sisters teach me. *Français et Anglais.* You need guide?'

'No, son. I have a guide for the day, from the ship.' I pointed toward the harbor.

'No good. Ship guides charge much, only show French buildings, French monuments, French restaurants, even French post office. I can show you *l'Afrique Sénégalaise.*' The kid eyed me expectantly, hoping his pitch had worked.

I've got to admit, it struck a chord. If I had wanted to see France, Mamie and I would have been in Paris right then, staring down one of those café *garçons* trying to get a cup of American coffee instead of that whitewash they call *café au lait.* I had dragged Mamie across the Atlantic to see Africa, and so far we'd seen Africa made to look like France and, if you count the Canary Islands, Africa made to look like Spain.

'What's your name, son?' I asked.

'Amadou.' The kid stood quiet, sensing I was weighing his proposition.

'How much for the day, Amadou, and what will you show me?'

A broad smile crossed the boy's face, knowing he had one on the hook, if he could just reel him in. 'Fifty centimes and I show you best place to eat, the market, and my house.'

I had already forked out nine dollars for me and Mamie to

take the ship's guided car tour, and there wasn't much question that we would be walking if we went with this kid. Still, I knew if I didn't see some real Africa soon I'd just explode. I couldn't take another day of '*ici la cathédrale.*'

'And you aren't snookering me, are you, kid?'

'What is this snooking?' Amadou looked puzzled.

'You are a guide, right? And you're not just setting me up to be robbed?'

'I am the most best guide for Dakar and the nuns teach me thou shalt not steal.'

I hoped the nuns' teachings had taken hold. I decided the kid looked honest enough. 'OK, Amadou, you're hired. Twenty-five centimes now and twenty-five at the end of the day.' I dropped three coins into his outstretched hand. He had the same expression on his face as if he had won the Spanish lottery.

'Now, son, here's your first task – take me back to the harbor.'

'I don't know why we have to go with this guide you hired when we have already paid for a car guide and a shore excursion,' Mamie said. We were in our cabin, Amadou having flawlessly returned me to the ship. He was waiting now, I suspected, at the end of the ship's gangway where I had left him. I noticed that he kept twenty feet or so between him and the ship's personnel and customs officers clustered at the foot of the gangway. My guess is that neither would give him a very civil reception.

'And I'm to put on my walking shoes, you say? This guide doesn't have a car?' Mamie scoffed but I knew she was game. She'd tramped plenty of miles in the greenhouse. She was no delicate flower.

'What we'll be seeing can't be seen by automobile.' It was probably true but it just drew an additional gibe not worth writing down here.

It was nigh on ten o'clock in the morning when we finally headed off the ship. Amadou was there but not alone, being engaged in a smiling patter with another victim who had her back turned to us.

'See, mister go with us,' Amadou said, my status as his first mark lending apparent credibility to his attempt to snag a second. The new mark turned our way.

'Ah, Mr and Mrs Mason. You are going out with this boy guide?' Gitte Damgaard asked. She was attired for a day of wandering the city streets or trekking the African *veldt*, in sturdy shoes, a broad-brimmed hat, cotton shirt and wide-legged pantaloons. On her shoulder was a canvas messenger bag in lieu of a lady's purse.

'Yes, Miss Damgaard.'

'Would you mind terribly if I joined you? I did not sign up for a shore excursion, thinking I would explore on my own. But now Prince Amadou here says he will make me a discounted price if you allow me to join you and Mrs Mason. Only one franc, for all day.'

I twitched a brow at Amadou, who cut his eyes sideways and gave the almost imperceptible negative head-shake of those caught in the act and hoping for mercy. Then he turned his eyes up, puppy-dog pleading brimming in them. It worked.

'We'd be pleased to have you join us,' I said. Amadou's countenance quaked with visible relief. 'And I'll just bet Amadou can do a little better on his guide fee, Miss Damgaard, since we're starting late in the morning and three of us are pooling our payment to him.'

Amadou opened his mouth to protest but stopped short when I gave him the same eye I give the men in the greenhouse crew when they try to get something over on me. He said, 'If mademoiselle is a friend of mister, there is, of course, a discount. Fifty centimes.' The two words of the price were bitten off like a bitter pill.

'How delightful,' said Miss Damgaard.

We trooped toward the broad Boulevard Corniche behind Amadou, passing a string of automobiles there boarding our shipmates for their shore excursion. Mamie mumbled under her breath as we followed our urchin guide into the warren of streets that grew narrower and less European as we moved away from the port.

Amadou knew where his bread was buttered and steered us to a row of stalls which supplied ladies' clothing. He stopped before one and introduced us to the proprietress, 'my auntie', who greeted Mamie with a stream of French like she was a long-lost sister. A connection was made and after a half-hour of clucking and conferring, Mamie emerged with a smile on her face and an orange, yellow and black *boubou* which she swore she would wear to her first Soroptimist meeting when we got home.

Thereafter, Amadou could do no wrong. At a beach away from the harbor, he showed us the day's catch, garishly colored boats, and the dried and smoked final product of the seaside neighborhood.

As the midday mealtime neared, he made certain we traversed an alleyway redolent with the smell of roast meat. At one butcher stall, he brought us to a jolly man, 'my uncle', who shooed three tea-drinking lingerers from a low table and brought us skewer after skewer of the savory meat.

'What is this, Amadou?' Mamie asked.

'*Vonti*. The best bits,' he replied.

'The best bits of what?' I asked.

'The *best* bits,' the boy said in a 'don't-ask' tone.

At the meal's end, there was no bill; the jolly owner simply counted the fourteen empty skewers. '*Soixante centimes*,' he smiled.

The afternoon was a flurry of leather sellers' shops, wood-carvers, blacksmiths' forges, and even meeting with an animist shaman in a dusty square in the shade of a mango tree. 'Now this is Africa, Mamie,' I said, as the old man chanted and scratched figures with a stick in the dust.

Amadou knew he had hit a home run and probably harbored hopes of a twenty-centimes tip as we turned toward the setting sun and began the long march back to the ship. By then, Mamie and I had firmly established ourselves as non-French speakers. Gitte Damgaard had proven the opposite during the course of the day, and now she whispered a stream of rapid French to Amadou, who responded '*Oui, oui, oui*' as she went on.

Until that point we had avoided places that felt less than safe to me. True, we had been in areas that were run-down, crowded and odiferous, but there was never any sense that we were in danger.

Now, at the behest of Miss Damgaard, Amadou led us into an alley where there were no shops. The sun only penetrated the narrow passage at midday, a time long since passed. A man with a club leaning against the mud wall beside him stood at the entrance to the alley. Amadou spoke to him in some native dialect before we were permitted to pass.

'You may wait here if you wish, while I take the lady where she asked to go,' Amadou said to Mamie and me.

'I think we'll stick with you, son,' I said. There was no way Mamie and I were staying alone with the man and his club in the deserted alley. I began to seriously question my conclusion that Amadou was honest.

'Then you may come with us this way,' the boy said.

I noticed that Gitte Damgaard was fazed by none of this, as if she did this in her hometown in Denmark once a week, just to keep in practice.

Amadou steered us to the very end of the narrow pathway, where there was a blank wall with only a door in it. The door was of thick planking, with heavy iron hinges and strapping. It probably couldn't have been battered in by an army that had a week to accomplish the task. Amadou spoke to the door loudly in the native tongue, though I could see no one there to hear him. After a moment, what can only be described as a giant swung the door open. The giant wore an honest-to-God scimitar at his belt. His hands looked like they could crush a coconut, or a man's skull, with minimal effort. He motioned for us to enter with a grunt.

I thought about grabbing Mamie's hand and making a dash down the alley to take our chances with the man and his club, but both ladies had already bustled inside. There was nothing gallant to do but follow.

The room we entered had a low table in the center. Grimy rugs had been laid on the bare dirt floor as seating. Amadou motioned to sit, placing himself beside Gitte Damgaard at the center of the table, with Mamie and I behind the two of them. The giant loomed behind us all, a hand on the hilt of his blade.

I was beginning to think this was more adventure than I had bargained for, when a bespectacled man in a flowing white *boubou* embroidered with gold thread came into the room through a low portal on the opposite side of the table. On closer inspection, I saw that his round eyeglasses were of clear glass. He had a warm demeanor, modestly smiling and nodding to all of us, and greeting us, '*Bonjour, madame et monsieur. Bonjour, mademoiselle.*'

Mamie and I, unsure of why we were there, responded with our own '*Bonjour*' and fell silent. Miss Damgaard, not in the least unsure why she was there, launched into a breakneck torrent of French. The only thing I could make out was her greeting '*bonjour*', which was curt and perfunctory.

Our host responded with a languid dissertation, ending by reaching into his robes and coming out with a fistful of paper packets. He laid them on the table in front of Amadou and Miss Damgaard, spilling out dozens of uncut gemstones, primarily in shades of deep blue but also a few with the yellow cast of a cat's eye.

Mamie let out a quiet 'Oh' on seeing the tumble of stones. Gitte Damgaard was not fazed. She reached for the gems but the man covered them with his hands and calmly said something to her, smiling all the time. Miss Damgaard did not respond in kind but her next act had a salutary effect on our host well beyond that which, I suspect, would have been produced by a dozen welcoming smiles. She reached into her messenger bag and emerged with a wad of French banknotes that dwarfed the delicate hand in which she held them. Placing the cash on the table, she reached for the stones. Our host withdrew his hands from them, clapping loudly and calling out in a language that certainly was not French.

Miss Damgaard pored over the stones, examining each with a jeweler's loupe drawn from her bag. The reason for the man's shout materialized in the form of a boy, no more than six years old, carrying a silver tray with *demitasses* of coffee for all. The brew was bitter and strong, despite an attempt to cut its potency with a whopping dose of sugar. The grounds formed a sandy pile in the bottom of each cup.

Our host raised his cup to us and drank with relish. Mamie and I did the same, sipping with polite fakery. Gitte Damgaard ignored her cup and, after completing her examination of the last stone, stated a figure in French that had a lot of syllables to it. It must not have been as large as it sounded, as our host exploded in a rage of ragged French, scooped up the stones, stood, and retreated toward the portal where he had entered.

Miss Damgaard spoke in a conciliatory tone and the man stopped at the frame of the portal. After a moment, he countered with another long number in French, returning to his seat at the table as he spoke.

Now it was Miss Damgaard's turn. She put on a show equal to that of the gem seller, snatching up the wad of cash and pushing past the scimitar-wielding giant at the door. Amadou, Mamie and I scrambled to our feet to follow.

The flow of conciliation now came from our host. Gitte Damgaard said a sharp word or two and returned with her bankroll to the table. The back and forth between the two continued until a handshake sealed the deal. Miss Damgaard counted out most of the francs from her wad on to the table, and took possession of the gems, putting them and the remaining cash in her messenger bag. When she did this, I caught a glimpse of what appeared to be a Colt 1911 in the bag. Accurately applied, a .45 slug from that cannon would have probably stopped even the monster doorman. And after seeing Gitte Damgaard in action, I had no doubt she would be capable of doing just that, if necessary.

We all rose and parted, the gem seller and Miss Damgaard smiling genially at each other now. But I noticed she kept a hand in her bag as we departed, and all the way during our uneventful walk back to the *Columbus.*

The sun was low in the west when we reached the ship. Amadou grinned and held out his hand. I poured twenty-five centimes into it and made a little show of dropping in an extra twenty. Miss Damgaard was next at the boy's open palm.

She slipped a thousand-franc note into it before marching resolutely up the gangway.

THIRTEEN

> A varied program of entertainments and festivities, including concerts, costume balls, moving pictures, lectures, bridge and sport tournaments, will take full advantage of the splendid decks and public rooms of the *Columbus.*
>
> – *Round Africa Cruise brochure*

Mamie – February 16, 1939 – At sea

Maybe I was as scared at some point in my life as I was yesterday afternoon, with that great big brute and his sword between us and the door, but if I was I can't remember when. It didn't help that Bert told me afterward that Miss Damgaard was carrying a gun. Why does she need a gun, anyway? I guess if you're putting yourself in the position of haggling over jewels in back alleys with people who have hulking bodyguards, maybe you do need a gun, but myself, I'd find another hobby. All I know is I'm ready for a nice, safe, civilized day aboard ship, far away from the mean back alleys of Dakar.

Bert, on the other hand, is ready to go back and do it all again today. He filled young Steward Grap's ears with it when he brought our coffee, as a warm-up to an enhanced version recounted to Jack and Bunky Olsen by the pool on the Beach Club Deck. I swear, if he goes to tell it again, he'll have Gitte Damgaard shooting her way out of that dingy lane while riding him piggy-back, with that Goliath and his sword right on our heels.

Fortunately, there will be other diversions at sea today. Herr Blanck has been on deck all morning telling anyone who will listen that we will be crossing the equator at mid-afternoon, and Neptune and his court will appear at that time to consider the worthiness of all landlubbers aboard for admission into the Fellowship of the High Seas. Bunky Olsen, who once cruised to Rio de Janeiro and crossed the great line in the process, told me about her experience on that trip and I am looking forward to some fun. Nice, tame fun.

Bert seems to be ready for something less dangerous today as well. Not that he hasn't jumped in with both feet, viewing the upcoming meeting with the King of the Deep as another phase of the African adventure. He asked Steward Grap about appropriate attire for the occasion and was told that Neptune's sergeants would consider anything more than sackcloth or its equivalent as not being sufficiently humble and unpretentious before their mighty god. That sent Bert on a quest for sackcloth. By his transmitted enthusiasm and urgency, he soon had almost all the passengers on the hunt for material from which to fashion suitably simple garments for their audience with the Great One. Sackcloth proved to be absent from the ship's stores but soon Grap and a committee of his fellow stewards, appointed to the task by Third Officer Kletz, produced sufficient numbers of old sheets and tablecloths to allow for the clothing of us penitents.

Bert is seeing to the manufacture of our outfits as I write this at a writing table outside the ship's library. When I left our cabin, he was hacking at two old sheets with the aplomb and finesse of Cleveland's Torso Murderer, gleefully laughing as he labored. Sometimes I wonder about that man.

Bunky Olsen says we'll be dunked in sea water, made to perform tricks and recite oaths, and generally be the objects of mockery by those who have crossed the line before. That tells me that, no matter what unholy togs Bert sews together, I'll be wearing my bathing costume underneath. A lady must maintain a certain dignity, even when placed in undignified circumstances.

FOURTEEN

> Built primarily for the highest class of Transatlantic service, the *Columbus* has more than met its exacting requirements and from her very first cruise has been extremely popular.
>
> – *Round Africa Cruise brochure*

Bert – February 18, 1939 – At sea

Mamie can color up pretty good when she gets ticked off. 'You expect me to parade around on deck, in public, in this?' she squawked. She was the color of one of those juicy, vine-ripe tomatoes we raise, a color I love to see in the greenhouse but not in my home. Or, in our current situation on vacation.

'Look here, you pull it over your head, like so' – I showed her on myself – 'and then belt it up with this length of cordage I got from one of the deckhands' – I tied and knotted – 'and you're all set.'

'Set to embarrass myself, all that skin showing like . . . like Sally Rand,' Mamie sputtered.

'She always manages to put the fans in the right places, at the right times . . . I hear.' No sense in letting Mamie know about that trip Joe Hargis, Ed Baines and I took to the Canton Burlesque a few years back when we supposedly were going to a meeting at the Masonic Temple in New Philadelphia.

'You hear? Ha. Don't you mean you saw, that time you went to the burlies in Canton a few years back?' That woman doesn't miss a trick. She wiggled into her costume, her bathing gear underneath. 'I guess this will have to do.'

'You look fine for a woman your age.' Oh, man, did I stick my foot in my mouth with that one. I knew the second I said it. Mamie was just about to unload on me when a voice from on deck called: 'All passengers immediately to the Beach Club

Deck. All passengers proceed without delay to the Beach Club Deck.'

Mamie and I stepped out of our stateroom into another world. The man calling for all passengers was right outside the door, covered in strands of seaweed and rope, using a large conch shell as a megaphone. Crew members ran back and forth, knocking on cabin doors and urging passengers to move to the assembly. None of the crew were in uniform or their regular working attire. They all looked as if they had been dredged from the bottom of the sea, clad in shells, garlands of sargassum weed, and fish fins and tails. There were men dressed as mermaids with flowing locks, and women as bearded old seamen with hooks for hands and patches over an eye. The decks of the *Columbus* were one giant, salty phantasmagoria.

We passengers were a sad lot in our rag-tag get-ups of sheets and rope, though I must admit Mamie and I outshone most of the others, thanks to my handiwork. I noticed she didn't complain anymore when she saw the outfits some of the others were wearing.

The crew herded us aft with good-natured taunts and gibes, calling us landlubbers and pollywogs. I noticed others from our gang carried along with the flood – Herr Huber wrapped in what seemed like yards of bed sheeting; Gitte Damgaard done up mousy and unobtrusive, obviously not packing her .45; Señora de Ribera appearing the Grecian statue with her stylish folds of tablecloth and perfect olive skin. But the real show-stoppers were Lieutenant Haas and Fräulein Schon. The less they wore, the better they looked – he, the manly Teutonic Donar, she, the dark-eyed beauty of luscious curve and virginal flesh, barely concealed beneath the sheer cloth drifting loosely from her shoulders. The uncrowned royalty of the ship, they walked hand in hand, both crew and passengers parting before them.

'What is this charade?' a voice indignantly demanded from the crowded deck ahead. The throng was growing denser now, tight-packed as we funneled to the staircase leading to the Beach Club Deck, all of us pushed along by the force of the bodies around us. I seized Mamie's hand and hung on tight as we climbed the treads. I couldn't see the speaker of the irate words ahead of us. It sounded as though he was being carried along with the crowd.

The sight which greeted us at the top might have depicted the ocean's depths after the sinking of our liner, or the passage of souls into purgatory in a medieval painting. We passengers, clad in our rags and roping, milled disorganized about the deck. At the fringes of the horde were fantastic creatures and beings, part-man and part-fish, whales and seals, robed and bearded, clad in scale, shell and all manner of flotsam and jetsam. On close inspection I recognized some of the myriad creatures as members of the crew – a troupe of wine waiters arranged as piscine attendants around a throne at the edge of the swimming pool; Herr Pfennig, the second officer, wearing a half-mask shaped like a dolphin's head and carrying a trident; Herr Doktor Ehring, the ship's surgeon, feathered and tailed as an albatross.

The only one who appeared in his regular attire was Major Heissemeyer, who was now trying unsuccessfully to bull his way down the stairs from the Beach Club Deck against the tide of costumed passengers and crew. He shouted, 'Make way! Make way!' to no avail. I recognized his as the voice I had heard earlier shouting about a charade on the lower deck. Apparently word of the day's festivities had not filtered through to him. He finally gave up his fight against the human tide and sidled off to a corner, his black uniform rumpled, his medals and insignia askew.

When all passengers were finally assembled on the Beach Club Deck, the ship's horn blew loud and long, immediately followed by the toot and bleat of tin horns and whistles as a procession approached from the port side of the ship.

'Bow, pollywogs, before the great and powerful Neptune, lord of the deep; the beauteous Salacia, his queen; handsome Triton, their child and prince; and their court of nobles of the watery kingdom,' I heard the voice of Steward Grap intone from beside me. I turned to find him attired, head to toe, as a hippocampus. He gave me a broad wink of his seahorse eye and pushed me gently from the shoulder until I bowed. Mamie, laughing, and soon the other passengers, followed suit.

Except one, the now-incensed Major Heissemeyer who, for the first time in his life, stood head and shoulders above the genuflecting crowd.

'The SS bows before none, other than the Führer,' he proclaimed to all who would hear.

It was at this precise time that King Neptune made his appearance. Drawn by a score of burly engine-room stokers outfitting as manatees and sea elephants, the God of the Deep rode in a cart made to resemble a triton shell. Beside him sat Queen Salacia, played by the alluring Stewardess Ella Althane, who I recognized from her earlier role as a corpse in the vignette in which I played a modest part. She had let her long blonde tresses down to meet a green-scale body that terminated in a broad tail where her feet should have been. At her side was a great, flabby man with a beer gut, wearing only a massive diaper. I guessed this fellow was supposed to be the infant Prince Triton.

'Who dares not bow before the almighty Neptune?' the sea god thundered, his gaze focused on the little Gestapo man who had just spoken. Despite his words, Neptune was smiling with good humor as he spoke.

Grap, standing over me as I bowed, whispered, 'That's Heinrich Becker, the chief fireman. He was in the Kaiserliche Marine, fought at Jutland on the SMS *Lützow* as a stoker. I wouldn't mess about with him.'

'The SS does not bow to fake gods and fat men,' Heissemeyer said. The tolerant smile evaporated from the chief fireman's lips.

'Davey Jones, bring that impudent polliwog before me,' Chief Becker said.

What had been fun was turning quickly into something else, but neither of the participants were prepared to back down. Davey Jones, portrayed by the largest and strongest of the engine-room gang, moved with two of his brawny fellows to each side of the major, while Neptune assumed his throne and his courtiers arrayed themselves around him.

Heissemeyer spoke to the crowd in a general way. 'The captain, bring Captain Dane here this minute.' No one moved except Davey Jones, who placed a firm hand on the major's arm just above the elbow. Jones's companion on the other side did the same. In one swift movement Major Heissemeyer was lifted off his feet and carried forward to be deposited before Neptune as if he had flown there on the wings of a school of flying fish.

'Ach, I thought this was a polliwog,' said Neptune. 'But it turns out it is a shrimp.' The gathering, both polliwogs and shellbacks, roared with laughter.

The joke by the chief fireman, maybe intended as rough humor or, more likely, as a taunt by the old navy man against the tin-pot soldier, didn't help the situation.

'In the name of the SS, I order you to unhand me and stop this nonsense.' Heissemeyer's face turned an ugly shade of purple as he said this.

No one moved to the major's aid, not even his own aide-de-camp who was, I noticed, watching impassively from the back of the crowd.

'Neptune takes orders from no man, not shellback, nor polliwog, nor shrimp. Nor the SS,' Neptune thundered. 'If you will not bow before me, you shall at least acknowledge the rightful heir to my watery throne. You, shrimp, shall kiss my beautiful baby's belly.'

The beer-gutted baby Triton wobbled forward from beside Neptune's throne and protruded his white hairy belly in the major's direction. Davey Jones placed a hand on Major Heissemeyer's neck and shoved forward. The major went pale white and, with an adrenaline-fueled burst of strength, twisted away from his captors and sprinted from the deck and down the stairs.

Both crew and passengers again burst out laughing, willing to enjoy themselves at the expense of the threatening prig, I suspect, because of the way we had all seen him treat others since the beginning of the voyage.

Neptune himself was greatly amused by Major Heissemeyer's humiliation and swept his arm expansively to the crowd. 'Lowly polliwogs who remain, I am pleased by your fortitude and your attitude. You shall be my guests now, at a banquet featuring the finest delicacies of my ocean realm. No more shall you pollute your bodies with bully beef and fatted lamb.

Enjoy now the urchin, the eel, the salty stingray. Taste the nectar of the anemone. Savor thc squid. Bring thc first course, my dolphin chefs.'

With the clacking of shells, the tooting of horns and whistles, and the dull thump of shagreen drums, a line of cooks from the galley, all done up as mermen, set up a buffet table with soup bowls and stockpots. Grap and the other stewards formed us into a serving line.

'Spoons are an abomination,' Neptune bellowed. 'Knives are a lubber's tool. The only true fork is a trident and its purpose is too noble for the feeding of polliwogs. Serve them, sea-cooks, and let them fend.'

We passed one by one before the mermen-cooks and were ladled a bowl of turbid broth, with no spoon to consume it. When all had been served, Neptune shouted, 'Raise your bowls, polliwogs, and taste of the sea's finest.'

Almost everyone drank simultaneously and deeply. The taste of the concoction could best be described as fusty salt fish boiled in salt water. Grimacing passengers spat the vile chowder back into their bowls or on to the deck.

'I am not pleased that you rabble so ill-treat our best sea fare,' Neptune said. 'But I should expect no less from worthless polliwogs and lubbers. I shall permit you all the same chance at redemption as I did the shrimp – you shall kiss my beautiful baby Triton's belly and be cleansed by a plunge in the sea.'

What ensued was a long queue of passengers quickly dipping to kiss the sloppy baby's hirsute tummy and then plunging into the salt water of the pool. We emerged on the far side of the pool, helped out by a host of shellbacks, soaking wet in the tropical sun. The wine waiter-fishes poured flutes of champagne for all.

When the last polliwog on deck had bussed Triton's belly and taken the plunge, Neptune intoned, 'You mortals, former polliwogs, now appear favorable in our sight. I declare you all to be shellbacks and welcome you to our domain and to the most noble fellowship of the high seas.'

A cheer went up and the wine flowed freely for the rest of the afternoon and into the early evening. As the sun was growing lower, Captain Dane made his appearance, bringing with him a stack of elaborate proclamations of our initiation as citizens of Neptune's kingdom, which he signed and presented to each passenger with a flourish.

The crowd grew quite tipsy, Mamie included. Captain Dane was about halfway through signing everyone's proclamations when Major Heissemeyer appeared. He marched directly up to the captain. 'Captain Dane, I want that man taken under arrest and imprisoned immediately,' Heissemeyer said, pointing directly at the now-inebriated King Neptune.

'But why, Major?'

'He has affronted the dignity of the SS and the Reich.'

'How has he done that, Major?'

'He tried to force me to . . . kiss a baby's belly. I mean, the belly of a man dressed as a baby.' The Nazi flustered at the ridiculous sound of the charge as he stated it.

Captain Dane called the chief fireman over to him and solemnly asked, 'Chief Becker, did you try to force Sturmbannführer Heissemeyer to kiss a baby's belly?'

'A man dressed as a baby,' the major corrected, his neck bright red.

'Oh, no, Herr Kapitän. I would never do that,' Becker answered with bluff sobriety.

Captain Dane turned to Major Heissemeyer. 'Chief Becker denies the charge. Do you have any witnesses, Sturmbannführer?'

'Of course. All these people saw it.'

Dane considered for a moment and said, 'Would anyone who saw the affront to the dignity of the SS in the form of Chief Becker forcing Major Heissemeyer to kiss the belly of a man dressed as a baby please come forward.'

A titter of wine-fueled laughter rippled through the crowd but no one stepped forward.

'I am sorry, Sturmbannführer, but there are no witnesses to the affront which you contend happened before all these good people.'

Heissemeyer scanned the crowd, seething with anger. His eye settled on Lieutenant Haas, whose head was visible at the rear of the group, Fräulein Schon's shorter form beside the younger officer hidden from view. 'Untersturmführer Haas saw everything, I am certain. Step forward, Untersturmführer.'

The lieutenant stepped up and came to attention. For anyone else, doing so in a bedsheet would have been a comic action, but when Lieutenant Haas did it, it appeared to be the epitome of German martial dignity.

Before Major Heissemeyer could interject, Captain Dane asked 'Untersturmführer, did you see the incident Sturmbannführer Heissemeyer has described?'

Haas's face remained stolid. 'No, Herr Kapitän.'

'Thank you,' Captain Dane said, turning to the major before the smaller man could address Haas. 'Unfortunately, Sturmbannführer, I can find no basis to arrest Chief Becker.'

'What? How dare you?' Heissemeyer sputtered. He scanned the faces of the crowd as if looking for support and, finding none, rushed from the Beach Club Deck for the second time in as many hours.

As he was wont to do in almost all uncomfortable situations, Captain Dane waved his hand to the band to begin playing. They were all dressed as fishes but they sounded just fine.

Mamie and I danced most of the evening away, retiring to our cabin at about ten. The party was still going strong when we left.

I fell into bed immediately, not bothering to change out of my equator-crossing outfit, and I was out. I'll admit that maybe I had more than my share of the champagne.

I awakened when I heard Mamie scream.

FIFTEEN

> The feature of the *Columbus* that is especially attractive on cruises, such as this, in warm waters, is her abundance of deck space, with room for hundreds of steamer chairs in a single row, for deck tennis, shuffle-board and other sports, and for sunbathing and outdoor dancing.
>
> – *Round Africa Cruise brochure*

Mamie – February 19, 1939 – At sea

I wish Bert had been there when it happened. Maybe he could have done something to stop it. At least he would have seen what I saw, so there would be some corroboration for what I said. Maybe the ship wouldn't have kept on moving and the poor man might have had a chance.

Bert, of course, was not there when it happened because he was in bed, sleeping off the champagne and an evening of dancing like a crazy man. I have never seen the man dance more than one or two dances anytime we had been dancing. Until last night, and then he's a regular Fred Astaire. He started with me and we tripped the light fantastic until my dogs ached and I cried uncle. He had some more of that sparkling juice, which acted like gasoline on a forest fire for him, and moved on to other victims, first Bunky Olsen, then pretty Beatta Schon, and finished with Señora de Ribera and a butchery of a tango, or a flamingo, or whatever the dance is where you snap your fingers and stamp your feet. At home in the Grange Hall, Bert is a stick in the mud with two left feet, but put him under a carpet of stars off the mysterious coast of Africa, mix in a few exotic women, and he's the life of the party.

After that flamingo dance, Bert faded fast, and it took both me and the ever-present Steward Grap to drag-carry him back to our A Deck stateroom.

'He should be all right now, Mrs Mason,' Grap said, after

gently laying Bert on to his bunk. 'I'll be heading back to the festivities, as I suspect I'll have others among my charges who will need assistance tonight.' He tipped the nose of his seahorse mask like a hat and was gone.

I got Bert's shoes off and decided the rest of his get-up could stay where it was until morning. I was still all keyed-up from the day and hadn't gone to the champagne well as often as Bert had, so I wasn't ready for bed.

I stepped from our room on to the deck and leaned against the rail. Laughter filtered down from the Beach Club Deck above, blended with the mellow modulations of a clarinet and the thrum of a bass. The stars, so prominent minutes before, had disappeared. We had cruised into a fog bank, the tendrils of humid air enveloping the angles and lines of the *Columbus*'s superstructure, softening its edges. A Deck was empty except for me, and as I leaned on the rail and looked below, B Deck was also deserted. At least it was until two figures moved like ghosts to the rail at the ship's stern.

At first I could make out nothing about them, but then the wisps of fog parted enough for me to see that one of them was Major Heissemeyer, still in his black uniform. He waved his hands in animated conversation with the other person, the words lost among the music and the distance and the churn of the ship's propellers. The person the major spoke to was in some kind of costume, a vestige of this day where almost everyone wore something different than their regular attire.

The two figures moved closer to each other, the major still waving his arms. I could not tell if the other figure was a man or woman or a seahorse or merman risen from the South Atlantic. The second figure seemed taller than the major, but the perspective looking down at the two, with the major further from me, could have skewed my perception of their relative sizes. Then again, the major was smaller than almost everyone I had seen aboard ship.

Heissemeyer gave an emphatic shake of his head and pounded his fist into the palm of his other hand. In response, his companion moved closer. The two suddenly grappled, and Major Heissemeyer went over the rail and fell without a sound into the black water.

I think I screamed then, because the person who had pushed Major Heissemeyer overboard looked up briefly toward me and then turned and vanished from sight. In the split second he or she looked up, I could not see an identifiable face.

I know I screamed after that, and then Bert was at the rail beside me.

He took my shoulders and turned me to face him. 'Mamie, what is it? Are you all right?'

'They threw him off the ship, Bert. Someone threw Major Heissemeyer off the ship.' Tears came to my eyes. I was upset. I had never seen anything like that.

'What do you mean? Who is "they"?' Bert became Mr Twenty Questions and that only upset me more. Maybe I became a little hysterical because the next thing I remember is being back inside our cabin, sitting on the bed, cheeks wet with tears.

'Take a deep breath and tell me what happened,' Bert said.

'There was a man, or a woman – I don't know which, they were in costume – with Major Heissemeyer down on B Deck, near the stern. I could see them as I leaned on the rail. They seemed to be arguing about something, or at least Major Heissemeyer was very agitated. He was waving his arms and pounding his fist. All of a sudden, they kind of wrestled with each other and the person in costume shoved Major Heissemeyer over the rail. I saw him fall into the water.'

'Mamie, are you sure? Maybe this was another part of the hijinks going on tonight.' Bert can be dense sometimes.

I'd recovered my composure now. 'I tell you, Bert, I know what I saw and I saw Major Heissemeyer go over the side.' I used that tone of voice I sometimes use to let Bert know I mean business.

'OK, OK, Mamie. We better go tell someone. Grap doesn't seem to be around. We'd better find another crew member.'

We did a quick traverse of our half of A Deck and found no crew members. A couple of passengers necking in a corner were the only people on deck. They were no help; they were completely blotto and had to lean on each other just to stay standing.

We decided to go to the ship's bridge and, after climbing

two flights, came to the base of the bridge stairs. A light chain across the stairs held a sign that said '*Passagiere Verboten*' in German and 'No passengers beyond this point' in English.

Bert unsnapped the chain, dropped it, and bounded up the bridge stairwell. I haven't seen him move like that since he was twenty-five and he went to break up a fight between Dennis Magyar and Dave Hink at the church picnic. I followed him and came in off the bridge wing just in time to see First Officer Lau's surprised look at a passenger busting into the wheelhouse.

'Major Heissemeyer has gone overboard.' Bert didn't mince words.

Herr Lau's beard bristled like a scared cat's tail. He asked, 'What? What do you mean, sir?' and stepped close to Bert, putting himself in between Bert and the helmsman.

'I tell you, Mamie saw someone push Major Heissemeyer over the deck rail and off the ship just now,' Bert said.

Herr Lau's eyes narrowed. He was close enough to Bert to smell the champagne that oozed out of Bert's every pore and see its effect in Bert's bloodshot eyes. You could tell Lau was assessing, and considering whether this was just another passenger done in by the day's, and night's, merrymaking.

'That's right,' I said. 'You have to turn this ship around now. You may be able to save him yet.' I hadn't been in the bubble water as much as Bert and I hoped it showed. Maybe the first officer would believe me.

'Mrs . . . Mason,' Herr Lau said, searching his memory for my name. 'I cannot just turn the ship around without more information. Please tell me what occurred.'

I may have been just a touch unreasonable then, upset by the shock of it all, the long day and the late hour. I raised my voice. 'My god, man, he could be drowning back there while we . . .'

'Who could be drowning back where?'

I turned to face the unruffled scrutiny of Captain Dane's ice-blue eyes.

'Mr and Mrs Mason say that someone has pushed Sturmbannführer Heissemeyer over the stern deck rail and into the water.' Herr Lau spoke quietly in English. I'm guessing the helmsman was a German speaker, and the first officer didn't feel the need to have him included in the conversation, even as a listener.

'Did you both see this?' Captain Dane asked Bert.

'No, only me,' I said. 'You've got to do something.'

'Dead slow ahead,' Dane ordered. Herr Lau immediately racked the engine order telegraph to the setting marked DEAD SLOW. Bells clanged but the ship continued on. Its pace gradually lessened but its course remained unaltered.

'You've got to go back,' I said.

'Indeed,' Captain Dane said. 'But the *Columbus,* Mrs Mason, does not, as you Americans say, turn on a dime. We are only continuing forward at a slow speed to maintain steerageway so that we may turn the vessel to the correct course when I have more information. Now, when did this happen?'

I thought for a short time, realizing a man's life might depend on my answer. I hadn't seen a clock or watch and there was that space of time when I was 'out'. 'I'm not sure,' I said.

'Mamie was . . . upset for a short time,' Bert chimed in.

'I see,' Captain Dane said, like a voice from the grave. 'Was it more than ten minutes ago? Half an hour? More?'

'A half-hour, I guess.'

'Herr Lau, were there any course changes made in the last hour?' Dane asked.

'No, Herr Kapitän.'

'What was your speed until I ordered the reduction just now?'

'Full ahead.'

'Wind direction and speed?'

'South-southeast at four knots, Herr Kapitän.'

'Come about, Herr Lau, to a course north by east, thirty degrees, full ahead. When you are on the course heading, run full ahead for twenty minutes and then go to dead slow ahead. Sound man overboard.'

Three blasts of the ship's whistle were sounded, and seconds later the *Columbus* was bathed in the brilliant light of a flare shot overhead. Crew members appeared from everywhere, positioning themselves along the rails of the decks and in the bow and stern. Fixed searchlights and hand lights criss-crossed the night waters as the *Columbus* executed a shuddering turn at its maximum speed.

Twenty minutes later, Herr Lau rang up dead slow ahead and two blasts of the whistle sounded. Everyone on the bridge and at the rails strained to find the floating form of Major Heissemeyer or, at the very least, pick up traces of the ship's wake, which might provide a path to the major's location.

The search went on all night and into the following morning. By noon, though, it seemed clear that Sturmbannführer Jürgen Heissemeyer had found his way into that place he had so resisted going, the domain of Neptune, never to return.

SIXTEEN

The entire trip will be of extraordinary interest.
– *Round Africa Cruise brochure*

Bert – February 19, 1939 – At sea

It had been a long night and a longer morning since Mamie's screams awakened me at 1.00 a.m. Mamie and I had been on the bridge of the *Columbus* since we had ignored the stairwell sign and gone where passengers were forbidden to go, now almost twelve hours ago.

Captain Dane remained impassive beside the helmsman during all of those dark hours, assigning course corrections, receiving reports, and generally directing the search for Major Heissemeyer. At one o'clock in the afternoon, he glanced at his wristwatch and spoke to Herr Lau, who had also been at his post throughout the night.

'Herr Lau, terminate the man-overboard rescue procedures. Resume your course for St Helena.'

'Yes, Captain,' Lau said, and gave a staccato string of orders to the helmsman, to Herr Pfennig to set the regular watch, and to the radioman to broadcast the abandonment of the search by the *Columbus* and the estimated location where the major went overboard so that any passing ships might keep an eye out for him.

'Are there any other ships nearby?' I asked.

'No,' said Herr Lau, all emotion absent from his voice. The word hung in the air on the bridge, a dark shadow on a sunny equatorial afternoon.

'Herr Lau, please summon Untersturmführer Haas to meet with me in my cabin in half an hour,' Captain Dane said. 'Mr and Mrs Mason, if you will come this way with me, please.' Dane exited the bridge through an unmarked door located behind the helmsman. A crewman held the door for Mamie and me.

The door communicated directly with the captain's cabin. As we stepped in, I could have sworn we had entered a Bavarian hunting lodge. The sitting area immediately inside the door featured a rectangular black walnut table and leather wing chairs. Wood paneling covered all the walls. A baize-topped writing desk, covered with orderly stacks of what appeared to be log books, stood in a corner with its companion high-backed chesterfield. There was even a rack of roebuck horns above the enormous bedstead. The only thing missing was a stuffed Russian boar. It was difficult to envision these items as belonging to Captain Dane. It was difficult to envision him having any life so far removed from the sea.

'Please sit,' he said, waving toward the chairs surrounding the table. When we were seated, he offered Mamie and me cigarettes from an onyx casket on the table, and when we refused, selected one for himself.

'May I?' he said to Mamie, lighting the coffin nail as she nodded affirmatively. He drew in a deep lungful of smoke and seemed relaxed by it.

'It has been a number of hours now, Mrs Mason, but I must ask you to again describe the circumstances leading to Major Heissemeyer's loss overboard.'

'Loss overboard' was a curious way of describing being pushed into the drink. I wondered if Captain Dane was giving Mamie a chance to change her story. If he was, she didn't take it, describing the incident in almost exactly the same words as she had in the excitement twelve hours before.

'Very well,' Dane said at the end of Mamie's description. 'This is a possible criminal matter. I must ask that you both not speak to others about what you saw and heard until we place this in the hands of the proper authorities.'

'Who might those proper authorities be, Captain?' I asked.

'The SS *Columbus* operates under the flag of the Deutsches Reich and, of course, Major Heissemeyer was a citizen of the Reich. Germany has jurisdiction over the investigation and prosecution of this crime, but as seamen we are neither equipped nor trained for such matters and we are far from German territory and proper German authorities. If this incident had taken place within the territorial waters of another nation, I would hazard a guess that the other nation would also have jurisdiction. But as we were well within international waters, no nation has that as a basis for jurisdiction.

'There is, of course, the more practical approach that mariners have taken throughout the ages, placing the matter in the hands of the police authorities at the next port of call. For us, those authorities will be the British police on St Helena. That is what I plan to do. It will, regrettably, involve you and Mrs Mason traveling to the police station on St Helena with Herr Lau when we arrive there tomorrow.'

'Anything we can do to help, of course,' I said. Mamie nodded her assent.

'Very well, then. I am sorry your trip has been disrupted in this manner.' A sharp rap sounded on the bridge room door and Herr Lau entered, followed by a bewildered Lieutenant Haas.

Kurt Haas appeared much the worse for wear. Maybe he was like most of the other passengers, recovering from an afternoon and evening of drink and hijinks followed by the long night of searchlights, whistles and crew noise disrupting his sleep. But there seemed to be more, a sadness, not just fatigue, about him, and I wondered if he had already learned of his superior's demise.

Captain Dane put that question quickly to rest. 'Untersturmführer Haas, I have the sad task of informing you that Sturmbannführer Heissemeyer was lost overboard early this morning and we have been unable to locate him despite our extensive search. We must presume that he is deceased.'

Lieutenant Haas was not visibly moved by the news. Maybe he was trying to put on a soldier's face, stoic in the presence of death, but no man should be so completely and utterly dispassionate in receiving such information.

I glanced at Mamie. She twitched an eyebrow; she had seen what I had seen.

'Sit, please, Untersturmführer,' Captain Dane continued.

Haas dropped into a chair. 'How did this happen?' he asked.

Captain Dane paused briefly and then said, 'We are uncertain as to the exact circumstances.'

'Really,' Haas said, his voice eerily calm. He turned his

eyes on Mamie and me. 'I take it Mr and Mrs Mason are here because they saw or heard something.'

I did not like the way the young officer said that. I did not like the way his eyes tracked languidly from Mamie to me, and back. I did not like it that now another person knew or at least suspected of our involvement. We had come to Africa for adventure but not this kind of adventure. This kind of adventure you could get on the streets of Chicago or New York City, and was made no more pleasant or exotic by the African setting.

'What do you mean by that?' Feisty Mamie piped up. I give the old girl credit. She's no shrinking violet.

'Why, nothing, Mrs Mason,' the lieutenant said, behind a slight, cold smile. 'I was merely trying to ascertain who might have information on how this . . . this incident had occurred.'

'That task, Untersturmführer, is within my purview as captain of this vessel,' Captain Dane intervened. 'I can assure you, Untersturmführer' – Dane emphasized the 'Unter' – 'that I take the matter very seriously and will deal with it appropriately. I can assure you as well that I will brook no interference in the handling of the matter.'

'Of course, Herr Kapitän,' Haas said. 'I am certain the matter is in good hands and did not mean to imply otherwise.'

These Germans sure are touchy about their turf. From what I'd seen so far on this voyage, the SS thinks their turf is everywhere. I also gathered that Captain Dane did not think 'everywhere' included his ship.

'We have no information with which to notify Sturmbannführer Heissemeyer's next of kin. Do you know who we might notify?'

'No, Herr Kapitän, I do not,' Lieutenant Haas said. 'I do know he was unmarried, and I never heard him speak of any family. Like so many loyal Germans, the Nationalsozialistische Deutsche Arbeiterpartei was his family.'

'Admirable dedication,' Captain Dane said, with a tone of voice that sounded like 'more's the pity'. I wondered how much, if at all, anyone would miss the minuscule tyrant.

'Perhaps it would be best to notify his commanding officer,

Standartenführer Kumm, in Berlin. I will provide your radio operator with address information for the Standartenführer.'

'Very well, then, Lieutenant. My condolences.' Captain Dane rose. And with that, all the picayune formalities over the life and demise of Sturmbannführer Heissemeyer were concluded.

SEVENTEEN

St. Helena is charming, with flowery valleys, sightly hills and a rich flora of a dozen lands.

– *Round Africa Cruise brochure*

Mamie – February 20, 1939 – Territory of St Helena

We were late getting to St Helena but it didn't matter much, as there is really nothing to see there. From the Promenade Deck, the village of Jamestown looks like someone wedged an English country town in a crease between two humped peaks, with the Anglican church steeple being the most prominent feature of the puny burg. The place doesn't even have a wharf; if you want to disembark, you get taken down a gangway to a lifeboat and motor in to the beach.

I thought about skipping the island altogether. I'm not the best in little boats and I was just tuckered and more than a little rattled from the night before last. I've never seen a man . . . well, murdered, before and I think I'm all right but I'm not quite sure. Things like this take a while to sink in, I guess. But, sunk in or not, Steward Grap brought an invitation to go ashore that was more like a summons with my morning cup of joe. Bert and I were to accompany Herr Lau to visit the police, the note said. It was signed 'Dane, Commanding Officer', like we were in the navy.

After a sloppy ride to the beach, Herr Lau, Bert and I trudged up a dusty street with houses and a few shops layered up a valley. They call this their capital but I can't even call it a town, and I'm a country girl. There were few people to be seen and even fewer birds, just a skinny-legged bird here and there that Herr Lau said were wirebirds. The whole place looked abandoned, or forgotten is actually a better word, a place the rest of the world had passed by. The last big thing that had happened to the island was Napoleon's exile, and that was over a century ago. It seemed now that donkeys had taken over; they wandered the street and flicked tails aimlessly in the black shade of the buildings.

There was a dearth of signage. Herr Lau finally asked one of the locals, who call themselves 'saints', where we might find the police constabulary.

'Rate ova yawndor' the young woman replied, awed to converse with three vagabond strangers and exceedingly pregnant. She pointed further up the valley along the single road. Of course. Where else would it be?

Two minutes' walk put us in front of a large official-looking building. Herr Lau stepped to its open front door, peered inside and motioned for us to come in with him.

Once inside, it was evident that the place served as His Royal Majesty's Prison as well as the headquarters of the police. Unoccupied cells could be seen from the lobby. Two men, one in a threadbare blue police uniform, conversed near a central desk.

'The plot had bite, then nice drop stubs an' nice bitter swing round later in the evening,' the uniformed man said to the other as we entered. The local lingo sounded like English but it was definitely not like any English that had ever reached my ears before.

The second man's clothing matched the tattered condition of that of the policeman, except for a bright red bow tie loosely attached to an old-fashioned celluloid collar topping his once-white, now-yellowish, shirt. He spotted us, and seeing Herr Lau's uniform, said, 'Hello, officer. Have you got one complaint?'

'What, sir?' Herr Lau's English was very good but not good enough to work through the gibberish spoken here. Neither was mine.

'Werry sorry, mate. I had up late today. I'll begin splittin' the dick, speak proper English. I'm Inspector Basil Moyce, St Helena Police Service. How can I help you?'

Herr Lau introduced us and said, 'We had a death at sea which appears to be a murder and Mrs Mason here was a witness to it.'

'Murder, ya say?' Inspector Moyce rubbed his stubbled chin. 'Us ain' had one murder in years. Last here was a bar fight, fifteen year ago, tween one saint and a visitin' sailor. Dozen witnesses. Saint were acquit. Self-defense. Who died?'

'A German citizen, a military officer, Major Jürgen Heissemeyer,' Lau said, giving the inspector the more understandable rank-equivalent instead of Sturmbannführer. I suspected the first officer had already sized Moyce up as not too bright or ambitious, a plodding breaker-up-of-bar-brawls.

'Who done it?' the inspector asked, as if seeking to disprove Herr Lau's barely concealed skepticism by showing he could jump directly to the meat of the matter.

'We do not know, Inspector. Mrs Mason was the only witness when Major Heissemeyer was pushed overboard, and could not identify his assailant in the darkness.'

Inspector Moyce perked up appreciably. 'Darkness, ya say?'

'Yes. The incident took place yesterday at approximately one in the morning.'

'You wasn't here then? I had no' see you ship 'til today.'

'No, we were at sea.'

Moyce's eyes narrowed. 'In saint waters?'

'About two hundred fifty nautical miles north of here,' Herr Lau said. The first officer was oblivious, but I could see the wheels turning behind Inspector Moyce's blue saint eyes.

'What you last port o' call?' Moyce honed in.

'Dakar.'

'What the port of origin for you cruise?'

'New York City, in the United States.'

'Herr Lau, I has no jurisdiction over you case, see? The crime, if there were even a crime, were not in saint waters, were on a German-flag ship, with a German citizen killed, with no English port of origin, an' no English port as last port o' call.' Moyce smiled slightly and moved his eyes from Lau's, flicking a crumb from his most recent meal which had lingered, unbidden, on his ragged coat sleeve.

'But, sir, this crime cannot go uninvestigated.' Lau's beard puffed up like the hair on an angry kitten.

'On this we are agreed, Mister Lau,' the policeman said,

levelly. 'It's jus' who will do the investigatin'. And that shall not be the St Helena Police Service, see?'

Thwarted, Herr Lau stood and shepherded Bert and me from St Helena's font of justice. As we left, we could hear Inspector Basil Moyce and his uniformed companion chuckling inside.

Minutes later we were back in the lifeboat, plunging through the green surf to where the *Columbus* waited at anchor. Waited with a murderer on board, a murderer who I had seen but could not identify. A murderer who might have seen me and might want to get rid of the only witness to his or her heinous crime. It all finally sunk in.

And I was terrified.

EIGHTEEN

> The *Columbus* has made an enviable record and there are few steamships of any size and probably none as large as she that have as many special cruises on their log books.
>
> – *Round Africa Cruise brochure*

Mamie – February 22, 1939 – Swakopmund, South-West Africa

'Bit of fog today, Mrs Mason. Just like my days as a boy in Southampton,' Steward Grap, cheerful as always, said as he entered with Bert's and my morning 'cuppa joe'. 'It happens most of the time when we pass by here. There's a cold current, the Benguela current, that flows up from the south and collides with the warm air flowing off the Namib desert. Makes a devilish fog all along the coast.'

'Along what coast, Grap?' Bert asked. Bert still had a rumpled look from the last several days, even with a good night's sleep. I, on the other hand, had made a full recovery to my previous state of radiant allure. I know because it had taken me almost an hour in front of the make-up mirror this morning before Steward Grap brought coffee.

'The coast of South-West Africa, sir,' Grap said. 'A wild place. Most of the area is more primitive than any of our ports of call on this voyage. Today's stop is unscheduled.'

'Unscheduled? Is there a problem?' I asked.

'I believe the stop relates to Major Heissemeyer's untoward demise and the unwillingness of the authorities on St Helena to investigate,' the steward said. Bert had filled him in on our shore trip to St Helena at afternoon tea yesterday, while Grap wrangled the teapot, cookies and bullion.

'In fact,' the young man continued, 'Captain Dane sends his regards and requests that you both prepare to accompany *him* ashore after breakfast. It's a rare thing that the captain goes ashore during a cruise. I believe he intends to meet with the German consul in Swakopmund.'

'Here's hoping that German consul fellow can get to the bottom of Major Heissemeyer's "untoward demise" as you call it, Grap,' I said. And, by the way, save my skin and let me sleep with less than one eye open. This was turning out to be one hell of a vacation, emphasis on the h-e-double hockey sticks.

'Swakopmund. That even sounds savage and exotic,' Bert said, grinning with relish and somehow oblivious to the danger I felt I was in. Do I have to tell the man everything I feel so he gets it?

Primitive, savage and wild don't light my fire quite the way they do Bert's. And Grap certainly didn't do anything to stoke my enthusiasm with his next remark.

'I suggest that you wear clothing suitable to a rather rugged beach landing. Swakopmund has no docks and it is well known for its considerable surf.'

An hour later found Bert and me in a small boat, much smaller than the one used to land us at St Helena, powered by six rowing sailors. The third officer, Herr Kletz, manned the rudder and Captain Dane, like us, sat on a narrow seat wedged between the oarsmen. A long, rolling swell had lifted and dropped the boat alongside the *Columbus* as we disembarked through the lowest gangway port, the gray waves slapping the boat against the towering hulk of the ship, despite the oarsmen's best efforts to stave off contact until the very moment when one of us dropped on to the thwarts. Bert had entered the boat first, bruising a shin, followed by Captain Dane, who landed on his feet like a seagoing cat. I was last, manhandled out the port like a particularly delicate piece of cargo, to be dropped three feet into the arms of Bert and Captain Dane. I brushed my cheek against the captain's neck and shoulder in the process, and caught a whiff of pipe tobacco and musky cologne before he deposited me into the safety of my seat. Don't tell Bert, but that moment in Captain Dane's arms was almost worth the risk of jumping down into an open boat in the frigid waters. Wait till Bunky Olsen hears.

I couldn't see the shore through the fog when we started

out, but I sure could hear the smash of the surf against the beach somewhere out in the grayness. In between the thump and rush of the surf, the fog muffled all sound save for the coordinated splash of the oars and the grunts of the sailors heaving against them. It was cold, so cold and damp, the first time I had felt that way since leaving New York.

'How are you going to land this boat in that surf?' Bert sounded doubtful and I didn't blame him. I was doubtful, too, no matter how handsome the captain and skilled the sailors. I didn't come all the way to Africa to drown on some desolate beach.

'We are not going to land on the beach, Mr Mason,' Captain Dane said. 'The locals have built a mole that extends just beyond the surf line, and they have a clever device to unload passengers there.'

'You mean we'll dock?'

'Not exactly.'

I learned what 'not exactly' meant a couple minutes later as we approached this mole thing, which was nothing more than an elongated pile of rocks running from the shore into the water. The mole was so primitive that turbid waves washed over its seaward end, soaking the handful of men standing on it to their knees. The men had a pile of rope netting tied to a round wooden seat with them. The other end of the netting was tied to a rope which was attached to a long pole. The pole was fitted into a slot in a head-high wooden post set into the rocks at the end of the mole. The pole was, in essence, a lever used to lift and swing the netting and its board seat over the water. As we approached in the boat, the men on the mole swung the net and seat above the churning waves toward the boat.

'Watch what I do, and do the same when your turn comes,' Captain Dane called above the roar of the sea. The oarsmen pulled back and forth to hold the boat somewhat steady in the swell and the pole-men levered the net over us. Without a second's hesitation, Captain Dane tumbled headfirst into the net and rolled to plant himself on the board seat. With a shout, the men on the pole heaved and swung the seat on to the mole. Captain Dane alighted as if stepping from a standing car on to smooth pavement.

The pole swung back and Captain Dane called for Bert. My man gamely tumbled into the net and soon rolled himself, less gracefully, on to the mole on his hands and knees. He scrambled to his feet and yelled above the smash of the waves 'Whoooo, what a ride! C'mon, Mamie!'

The pole swung back and, against my better judgment, I dipped my head and rolled into the net. I noticed midway to the mole that my feet were pointed at the sky, and my slip, to say the least, was showing. The boys on the pole were momentarily dumbfounded by the free show they were receiving and allowed the lower half of the net, and my lower half, to dip into the frigid water. I was not amused when Bert and Captain Dane hustled me on to the rocks from the soggy net.

'You lugs never seen a woman before?' I spat at the sheepish cluster of farm boys operating the pole-net. They all turned their eyes down and hung back on the mole while Bert, Captain Dane and I jumped and picked our way along the rocky pier to shore.

My shoes, sensible flats for the rugged conditions, squelched water as I stepped. I took them off when we hit the sand of the beach. We were met there by a barrel-chested customs official who conversed with Captain Dane in German, gave our passports a cursory reading and directed us along the strand to a point where a cobblestone street led out of the sand.

My waterlogged shoes went back on and we walked into Germany. Or at least a place that someone from Germany would build in an African desert. The few public buildings could easily have been transplanted to Munich or Bremen without a flicker of concern from the residents of those towns. The private houses, many half-timbered, would have looked fine in the Bavarian Alps. Lord knows where they got the timber for their half-timbered houses; there was not a tree or stick of wood in sight. Beyond the edge of town, a gravel desert void of any plant or animal life stretched to the horizon.

The fog ended a few hundred feet from shore and so did Swakopmund. 'It's almost like they want to be in the fog,' I remarked, looking out between the gray wisps to the clear air, dazzling sun and blue sky beyond.

'They do,' Captain Dane said. 'The sun inland, in the Namib, is relentless, and the air is devoid of humidity. The local folks, mostly Afrikaans and German farmers, vacation here for relief from the heat and the dryness.'

True enough, the sunburned farmers in broad hats and short breeches on the streets seemed to be in a holiday mood, chatting and wandering, taking the air. Their spavined wives, ill-used by the hard desert, trailed along behind, looking like a two-week vacation in the cloudy humidity beside the chill ocean couldn't possibly be long enough to rehydrate them.

Captain Dane stopped at a building more German-looking than all the other German-looking buildings in town. A slender native soldier in a ragged uniform, and barefoot, guarded the front door with a rifle and bayonet so large that it threatened to tip him over. The captain conversed in German with the guard and we were admitted.

A German flag, black swastika on a red background, stood on a stand in the dusty foyer. The soldier called, loudly and unintelligibly, into the building and a man, in genuine *leder-hosen*, displaying meaty mottled legs, appeared. He stiffened to quasi-attention on seeing Captain Dane's uniform and said something in German which I assume was a greeting. There was a further exchange between them which ended with the man saying '*Ja, ja*, I can English speak.'

Captain Dane turned to Bert and me. 'This is Herr Zoeller, the German consul for South-West Africa. Herr Zoeller, may I present Mr and Mrs Mason of the United States of America, two of the passengers on the *Columbus*.'

'A pleasure, Mr and Mrs Mason,' Herr Zoeller said, after which he immediately fixed his attention on Captain Dane. 'What brings you to Swakopmund and the Reich's consul? Has the war begun? Has the Kriegsmarine taken Walvis Bay?' I noticed that Herr Zoeller had tiny eyes that tried to bulge when he was excited but couldn't quite make it. He was excited now.

'War? What war?' Captain Dane asked.

'Why, the war where the Reich finally asserts its rightful

claims for *Lebensraum* in Europe and regains control of its colonies lost in the last war. Including Deutsch-Südwestafrika, of course. Has it not begun? Are you not here carrying the news of the Reich's victories?' Consul Zoeller stiffened to attention and gave a Nazi salute. It could have been a parody but I'm sure it was not. Were all these Nazi types assholes? Every one I met seemed to be.

'No, Herr Zoeller, there is no state of war,' Captain Dane said.

'I thought perhaps . . . well, we are out of the mainstream here and sometimes news reaches us slowly. Even official news.' The tiny eyes turned baleful, the man behind them acknowledging to himself that his Nazi Party loyalty had only served to reward him with this inconsequential posting in a foggy African backwater.

'No, Herr Zoeller. We come to you because of a crime which has taken place aboard the *Columbus,* the murder of a German citizen, an SS Sturmbannführer named Jürgen Heissemeyer. We tried to enlist the help of the police authorities on St Helena, the nearest port of call, but they claimed to be without jurisdiction. I was hoping the relationship with the local police you have here as German consul would persuade them to investigate the matter.'

'The SWAPOL? Those South African *Hunde* don't care a kudu's ass for a German life. They don't keep the *Schwarzen* properly in their place. That black one at the door, you think he is there to protect me? No, he is a policeman, posted here to keep an eye on me. Bad enough that they watch my comings and goings, but assigning a *dreckigen Schwarzen* to do it . . . that's an insult to the Reich.'

'Am I to take it, Herr Zoeller, that you do not have a working relationship with the local police, this SWAPOL?' Captain Dane asked.

'My working relationship is to work for their overthrow, Captain, and to rightly restore these lands and their valuable resources to the Reich.' Herr Zoeller injected another spontaneous stiff-armed salute, an action made all the more ridiculous by his leather shorts and sausage legs. His voice dropped to a conspiratorial tone. 'No, I do not work with them, I work against them. They are few in number here, less than fifty men spread over thousands of hectares. A force of one hundred well-equipped men, led resolutely, could take the whole territory. Tell me, Kapitän Dane, do you have arms aboard the *Columbus*?'

'I . . . we are a passenger ship, Herr Zoeller.'

Zoeller's tiny eyes narrowed to impossibly small slits. Beads of sweat popped out along the brow above them as he said, conspiratorially, 'So you are armed – I knew it. Your crew is trained, no doubt. Bring them ashore. Let the spark ignite here!'

Genuine alarm passed across Captain Dane's face for the first time since we had begun the cruise. 'Eh, thank you, Herr Zoeller, for your assistance,' he said, as he gently took my elbow and steered me to the door. Bert, not wanting to be left alone with the crazy, puny-eyed, leather-shorted Nazi, followed closely.

'We can do this for the *Vaterland*, Kapitän,' Zoeller shouted as we hustled out the door. 'We will be heroes. The Führer will award us the Iron Cross!'

Captain Dane marched Bert and me double-quick through town, to the beach, and out on to the rocky mole. He fidgeted impatiently while the boat from the *Columbus*, standing off outside the surf break, made it within range of the pole-net.

The boys on the pole-net dipped my backside into the icy water again as they swung me out to the boat. I was in such a hurry to leave I didn't even mind.

NINETEEN

> The seamanship of the Lloyd officers and sailors is of the highest type and has been a tradition for generations.
>
> – *Round Africa Cruise brochure*

Bert – February 23, 1939 – At sea

I had no idea what Captain Dane wanted when he summoned us to his cabin today. Oh, I knew it had to be about the murder, but I figured after yesterday's meeting with that crazy man in Swakopmund we would hear nothing more about police or investigations. That didn't exactly sit right with me. Even though Major Heissemeyer was an obnoxious little cuss, he didn't deserve to be killed for it, and whoever knocked him off needed to be brought to justice somehow. And there was the matter of Mamie being the only witness. No police involvement and no investigation didn't make her any safer. Only finding the major's killer would make her safe. But the possibility of that seemed remote, as remote as the empty stretch of ocean where the major had met his maker.

At the hour designated, Mamie and I were met at the 'No passengers beyond this point' chain on the steps leading to the bridge by Herr Blanck. He was looking pretty spry for a man who I had shot and killed two weeks ago, I thought. Maybe it was the sea air.

The purser took us through the bridge to the anonymous door to the captain's cabin, knocked twice on the mahogany door, bowed, and disappeared. The door was opened by the bewhiskered Herr Lau, his bearish countenance all business and formality as he clicked heels in greeting and waved Mamie and me in. Captain Dane was seated at his walnut chart table, swept clean of papers and instruments. He rose as we entered.

'Good morning, Mr and Mrs Mason. I trust you slept well?'

Captain Dane was cordial and I was a bit surprised. He usually didn't waste time with this kind of chit-chat. He was more than a tad circumspect about our meeting.

'Well enough, Captain, after our boat ride yesterday and our stroll through little Bavaria in Africa. And Mamie's dip in the sea,' I said. I winked at Mamie and she flushed and tapped me on the arm.

'Yes, I know,' Dane said. 'Our shore excursion yesterday was uncomfortable on sea and on land. My apologies for putting you both through that, something I would never have done had I known it would be so fruitless.'

'No apologies needed, Captain Dane,' Mamie said. She felt more generous now that she had dried off from her involuntary sea bath. 'You were just trying to do what you could to get an investigation of Major Heissemeyer's death.'

'It is that very topic which caused me to ask you here this morning.' Dane looked me in the eye with those peepers that Mamie calls soulful and I could see what she means. 'After the police in St Helena rejected jurisdiction, and the failure yesterday in Swakopmund, I am left with few options for the proper investigation into the major's death. I fear that if it waits until our return to New York City, or longer still, to Germany, the perpetrator and the witnesses to events leading up to the crime and the crime itself will disperse and become unavailable to the eventual investigator. I hold no hope that the police authorities on the future legs of our voyage will have any interest in investigating as we will visit no other territories with close associations to Germany. I have concluded that an investigation of Major Heissemeyer's murder will need to be conducted by a person or persons on this ship, if there is to be any chance of bringing his killer to justice.'

'I can't say that I disagree with you, Captain, but what does that have to do with Mamie and me?' I asked.

'Precisely this, Mr Mason. There are no officers or crew on the *Columbus* who have any experience at criminal investigation. And, so far as I can determine, there is only one passenger with such experience. That passenger is you.'

'So?' I said. I thought I could see where this was headed but I was still hoping I was wrong. I'm sure Mamie thought

I was dense. I think I caught an eye roll from her as she sat at my side.

'So we, meaning myself and the officers of the ship, would like you to undertake the investigation of the murder of Jürgen Heissemeyer. You will have free rein to conduct it as you please, full access to all areas of the ship, and, of course, the complete cooperation of the officers and crew, myself included.'

'Now hold on a minute, Captain,' I said. 'I was only a sheriff's deputy for a year and that was almost twenty years ago. I was hired because the county sheriff lost his only deputy to the draft in the Great War and the sheriff needed another body around so he could take a day off once in a while. I fed a couple prisoners during that year, wrote a few traffic tickets, gave a drunk or two a ride home, and never drew my gun. I never made a felony arrest. Hell, I never made a misdemeanor arrest. The only investigations I was involved in were two burglaries, where I trailed along after the sheriff when he went to look at the windows busted to enter the houses that had been robbed. Then he went right to the man who did the breaking and entering, because he knew he was a second story man, and arrested him. Brought the man back to jail and, I'm not proud to say, slapped the suspect around while I watched. True, the sheriff got a confession and the man had probably even done the crime, but I had no stomach for that kind of mistreatment, even of a crook, and I quit. If you call that investigative experience, then I guess I have it, but I wouldn't want to be relying on my crime-solving capabilities if I was you.'

'On the contrary, Mr Mason, your integrity in the situation you describe is precisely what I am looking for in this matter. And there are two other logical reasons for you to take on the job, one important to me and the other, I hope, important to you.

'It is important to me that the investigation of the death of an SS officer on my ship be conducted in the most unbiased manner, without a hint of impropriety or prejudice. You, I believe, have no ax to grind, as you Americans say. Indeed, you and Mrs Mason, as the reporters of the crime, may be the only two persons aboard the *Columbus* who are above suspicion.

'The second reason is, I can only assume, most important to you. Think about it. There is only one witness to this crime and you, Mrs Mason' – Captain Dane turned to Mamie – 'are she. If I were the person who had pushed Major Heissemeyer overboard and I learned there was a witness to the crime, I would seriously consider whether it might be in my interest to do to the witness what I had done to Major Heissemeyer.'

Captain Dane turned back to me. 'So, Mr Mason, if I were you, I would want to do everything in my power to remove that potential threat to Mrs Mason. The best way to remove the threat is to investigate Major Heissemeyer's murder, identify the killer, and have that man or woman placed in chains until we reach a port with authorities willing to prosecute.'

After a moment's consideration, I had to agree.

TWENTY

> Cape Town, even though it had nothing else to show, would draw discerning travelers by the sheer beauty of the location.
>
> – *Round Africa Cruise brochure*

Mamie – February 24, 1939 – Cape Town, Union of South Africa

'Just how am I supposed to find this killer?' Bert said. He tossed down his napkin on to his half-eaten meal of mutton with red-currant jelly. Bert loves mutton and he loves to eat. For him to be off his feed means that something is really eating at him.

This trip is turning into something very different from what we had expected. I gazed across the fine china and glittering crystal set out for our lunch in the paneled dining room of the *Columbus* to the deep blue waters of Cape Town's magnificent harbor and the flat black visage of Table Mountain beyond. By now, Bert should be filled with excited anticipation of seeing lions and zebras and the dances of Zulu princesses. He should be donning his silly pith helmet and sturdy shoes, champing at the bit to conquer the Dark Continent. He should be being Bert-in-Africa, not Bert the Reluctant Detective. And me? Well, maybe I wouldn't be playing Jane to Bert's Tarzan exactly, but I should be enjoying floating in the deck pool by day and dancing under the stars by night. Instead, a chill runs down my spine when I hear a footstep behind me. What Captain Dane said is right. It would make sense for the killer to get rid of the only witness – me. I don't want to be in fear like this, on vacation or otherwise. My Bert has always been my knight in shining, if somewhat tarnished, armor. I guess now he really has to step up and save his gruff little damsel. No wonder he feels the pressure.

'I should never have told Herr Blanck that I had been a deputy when he asked me to pull that gun act at the beginning of the trip,' he said, glum eyes on the cooling remains of the sacrificed lamb.

'I should never have gone out on deck after we came back to the cabin that night,' I said.

'Well, neither of us can undo what we did, so I guess we need to go ahead and solve this. Are you game for it, old girl?' Bert, you are so romantic. I've heard him call Molly, the draft horse they use to work up the ground in the greenhouse, 'old girl' for years now. It's nice to know I fall into the same category.

'Sure, Bert,' I said. 'Maybe we can still enjoy part of the trip if we solve the murder quickly enough. How hard can it be?'

'True.' Bert pondered. 'We just look for clues and they will point us to someone. Find someone with a motive. Talk to the witnesses.'

'The witnesses?'

'Yeah, the people who saw something.'

'Bert, you're talking to her. I'm it and I didn't see much.'

'Maybe you saw more than you think. Let's take a rerun at some of this. Now, was the person you saw push Major Heissemeyer overboard a man or a woman?'

'I don't know. I couldn't tell from what they were wearing, just a shapeless toga-thing like we all were wearing that night. All the passengers, anyway.'

'Or someone who wanted to appear to be one of the passengers,' Bert said. 'Could you see a face? Don't try to describe it; just think whether you could see one at all.'

'Yes, I could see something of a face but not much. I could see there was no facial hair, no beard or mustache.'

'There, see,' Bert said. 'We've eliminated Herr Lau as a suspect already. What about hair on the head? What about eyes, nose, chin, anything memorable?'

'Sorry, Bert, any hair was concealed by the floppy hood attached to the toga. And it was too foggy and the glimpse I got was too brief to make out eyes, chin, nose or any facial features.'

‘Footwear. Did you see shoes?’

‘Not that I remember.’

‘Legs? Man’s or woman’s?’

‘I don’t think I saw any legs at all.’

‘What about height? Was the person tall?’

‘Taller than Major Heissemeyer, but that includes most of the Western world over age nine. And I was looking down from above at kind of an odd angle, so it was really difficult to judge height.’

‘Did you hear anything? Did the pusher speak?’

‘No. I saw Major Heissemeyer speaking and gesturing, and he was very forceful, but I couldn’t even hear him over the sound of the propellers and the ship’s movement.’

Bert pursed his lips. He does that when he’s irritated, like he was expecting something sweet and got a lemon instead. It’s cute. ‘So much for talking to the witness.’

‘Hey, bud, I saw what I saw, OK?’

‘I know, Mamie. I’m just frustrated. What about motives?’

‘What about we see some of Cape Town and work on motives later?’

‘Sounds good to me. Me Tarzan, you Jane?’

‘Not in your wildest dreams, Bert.’

‘Uncivilized’ Africa was at its most tame and civilized the moment we strolled off the *Columbus* gangway in the early afternoon. Cape Town is hardly the jungle; dramatic folds of mountain overshadow a homely town of neat houses with picket fences that called to mind the better neighborhoods of an American small city. Negro gardeners snipped languidly at well-groomed hedges. Negro servants minded Afrikaans children and Negro laborers hauled goods and materials through the streets. The Afrikaans planters and businessmen sauntered along the streets like princes, usually attended by a black man to carry their bags. White women in pairs and threes strolled too, all of childbearing age but with no children in tow because, I suspected, they were being cared for by the Negroes. I swear if there weren’t automobiles on the broad boulevard called Orange Street, and modern clothing on the white folks, I would have believed I was in the antebellum South.

I observed all this seated in the gardens at the Mount Nelson Hotel, a great pink pile of a place that was, at the moment, trying to out-English the English. Bert and I had stumbled on it in our wanderings, just in time for tea.

Tea had become an afternoon ritual for us aboard the *Columbus*, thanks to Steward Grap, who always produced a hot pot of tea and small sandwiches and tidbits promptly at four each afternoon. It didn't seem like a very Teutonic habit to me and Grap agreed, saying it was his English father's side coming out in him. He laid out the tea, he said, in return for us teaching him the invigorating qualities of a morning cup of joe.

Tea in the garden at the Mount Nelson Hotel was more fancy ritual than modest snack, and not just the tea and food. The gardens were as lush as any I had seen, as if the jungle had been tamed and made orderly and restrained, but still struggled and rebelled against the restraint by producing massive leaves, riotous blooms and towering royal palms. Waiters hovered, took orders, and answered inquiries but never touched the food or plates. The fetching and removal of food and tea was handled by a cadre of velvet-skinned black girls who did not speak to or make eye contact with the customers, moving with ghostly grace from kitchen to garden and back. The food was hearty, a mix of local and pseudo-British treats. The tea, just so-so.

Bert chewed vigorously. 'This meat is tasty,' then to the lingering waiter, 'What is this, son?'

'Biltong, sir,' the waiter sniffed.

'What's that?'

'Game, sir. Probably gemsbok. Dried, sir. In the sun.'

'Oh.' Bert seemed to lose some of his enthusiasm. He changed the subject so as to divert his stomach's attention from the leathery uncooked meat he had just ingested. 'So, Mamie, who had a motive to kill Major Heissemeyer?'

I saw the waiter's expression shift and Bert, following my eyes, saw the same. 'I think we are good for a while, waiter,' he said.

'Yes, sir.' The waiter sidled away to eavesdrop on another conversation I'm sure he found much less entertaining.

'Who didn't, Bert?' I said, back on the topic of motive. 'He offended everyone he came in contact with. He threatened Señora de Ribera. Herr Huber thinks all Nazis are the bane of the world, the oppressors of Austria, and responsible for imprisoning his brother. Heck, they did imprison his brother. Lieutenant Haas and Beatta Schon are in love and he wanted to break them up because she might not be Aryan enough for him. And he was probably under the skin of half the crew on the ship, if not for his general treatment of them, then certainly for his performance at the equator-crossing shindig. The only two I can think of that he hasn't gotten in a lather are Captain Dane and that Damgaard dame.'

'Dane is one cool customer and he knows his onions. There's no way he would even think of doing anything like that and, if he had, he sure wouldn't ask us to investigate when he could simply let it all pass,' Bert said. 'As for Miss Damgaard, well, that jane doesn't seem on the up and up, with the way she did things back in Dakar.'

'But that doesn't mean she tossed the major overboard, Bert. She's a hard case, all right, but nothing points to her having a beef with him.'

'Maybe he threatened her, too,' Bert said.

'About what?'

'To turn her in for smuggling gems.'

'Far as I know, she hasn't done anything illegal yet,' I said. 'Wouldn't she have to try to get through customs in New York before it would be smuggling?'

'I guess you're right,' Bert said. 'Maybe he was going to turn her in and he let her know. He did like to throw his weight around, puny as it was.'

'I'm beginning to think we shouldn't underestimate the Nazis, Bert, crazy as they may be.'

'What's that supposed to mean?' Bert tore off another rope of biltong with his teeth and swallowed it with a chaser of cucumber sandwich.

I took a long sip of tea and wished I had a shot of bourbon to fortify it.

'It means that almost everyone on the damn boat had a motive, dear.'

TWENTY-ONE

> History and romance meet in the sunny streets of Cape Town.
>
> – *Round Africa Cruise brochure*

Bert – February 26, 1939 – Cape Town, Union of South Africa

Old Sheriff Bill Marley, who I had served as a deputy until he slapped around that suspect, used to say that any crime committed by mortal man could be solved by just keeping your eyes and ears open.

True, that was a county sheriff in a place where you knew everyone. And you knew everything about everyone. You could figure who'd stuck his hand in the till at the New Philadelphia Drugstore by seeing who turned up with a new suit in town the following Saturday night. But I still thought the eyes-and-ears method would work in the situation of Major Heissemeyer's death, even if we were on a ship making its way around an uncivilized continent with over two thousand passengers and crew, some of whom I already suspected were more sophisticated criminals, in one way or another, than anyone Sheriff Marley had ever come up against in his thirty years of winning elections – always – and enforcing the law – sometimes – in Tuscarawas County, Ohio. So, after Mamie's and my discussion at high tea in Cape Town a couple days ago, I started watching and listening.

It didn't take but a day to learn the first thing about some underground workings on the *Columbus*, though not of a criminal nature. You see, soon after Mamie and I had been in Cape Town that day and returned to the ship, I noticed Steward Grap was acting strange. He was hovering like a daddy watching his sixteen-year-old daughter on the porch swing with a handsome date who couldn't be trusted.

I finally confronted him. 'Grap, is something wrong?'

'Why, no, sir. What would be wrong?' The steward was all innocence. 'I was just wondering, sir, if you would like to have your trousers pressed before dinner this evening?'

'No, son, they're fine.'

'Yes, sir,' Grap said, and didn't leave the open cabin door. 'Can I do anything else for you or Mrs Mason?'

Mamie, feet up after a difficult tourist day of tramping around the sedate avenues of Cape Town, said, 'We're fine, Mr Grap. We'll just be taking it easy today.'

'Ah, yes, madam, I see,' he said, tipped his cap, and closed the door.

An hour later I went out for air. Grap was a few feet from our door, loitering in the passageway. And loitering was something I had not seen Steward Grap do all the way across the Atlantic Ocean and down the west coast of Africa.

'What's going on, Grap?'

'Sir?'

'Why are you hanging around like a tom cat waiting for the sun to go down?'

'Sir?' There was true puzzlement on the steward's face now.

'Don't you have someone else to attend to?' I let a touch of frustration creep into my tone of voice.

'I, er . . .' Grap hemmed, then straightened his shoulders. 'No, sir, I do not.'

'What do you mean, Grap? I thought you had half a dozen cabins under your loving care.'

'I have been relieved of all duties – beyond the care of yourself and Mrs Mason.'

'By who?'

'By direct order of Captain Dane, sir.'

'But, why?'

'For your safety, sir,' Grap said, relaxing his stance with relief that his secret was out. 'You see, sir, Captain Dane has a concern about Mrs Mason's and your safety, given what Mrs Mason has recently witnessed. The Kapitän had no other crewman with the necessary experience to protect you.'

'And you do?'

'Yes, sir. In between jobs on merchant ships, I did a stint in the Royal Marines. Portsmouth Division.'

'So our German captain has assigned a former British Royal Marine to watch over an American couple, one of whom witnessed the death of a Nazi SS officer.'

'Yes, sir.'

I suppose it made sense. 'Does everyone on the crew know about this?'

'They know I have been reassigned and my duties reduced, sir. They assume, I suspect, that it was for disciplinary reasons.'

'Disciplinary reasons? Having your work reduced?'

'Yes, sir. Having fewer cabins under my charge will mean fewer tips at the end of the voyage. That is the way most ships discipline a . . . problematic steward.'

'Well, Grap, it looks like I better be prepared to leave you a pretty substantial tip at the end of the trip, especially if you end up saving Mrs Mason's and my skins.'

'Yes, sir.' Steward Grap smiled broadly.

'Well, just keep an eye out here, Grap. I'm headed to the smoking room. I think I'll be safe there in broad daylight.'

'I rather think so, sir.'

TWENTY-TWO

Table Bay, brilliantly blue, spreads out to curving white beaches, while behind the sturdy buildings of the city towers Table Mountain, square, upright, and flat as a hewn stone.

– *Round Africa Cruise brochure*

Bert – February 28, 1939 – Cape Town, Union of South Africa

Cape Town is sizable but not a truly big city like Cleveland. The fact is, Bert and I have been toddling around this burg for the last three days and have seen everything worth seeing and most of what isn't. I can't believe Bert has converted me to a vagabond but right now I feel the need to get out of Dodge, or, in this case, Cape Town.

'I see what you're writing, old girl,' I said, leaning over Mamie's shoulder at the writing desk in the corridor outside the *Columbus*'s library. 'I'm not keen on tromping Cape Town's streets again today either. How would you like to go up that Table Mountain, instead?'

'Won't that be just as hard on the hooves, Bert?'

'No, I mean to hire a car and driver. Head for the top, maybe with a picnic. We'll see this place from above and get out into the country for a change. I didn't come to Africa to spend all my time in the city.'

'Nor did I, Mr Mason,' a passing voice said. I turned to see Herr Huber over my left shoulder. 'Perhaps you and Mrs Mason would care to join me. I have hired a car to take me to the summit of the mountain later this morning. Too much time on the flat sea for a boy like me, raised up in the mountains of Österreich. And it is a shame to make the trip alone.'

Mamie glanced at me and gave our secret high sign, which

I am not about to let you in on. It wouldn't be a secret then, would it?

'OK, Herr Huber, that sounds like the cat's pajamas . . .' I began.

'The cat's pajamas?' Herr Huber must not be up on colorful modern American expressions.

'It means "that's great",' I said. 'How's about we bring along a picnic lunch. I'll bet Steward Grap can put a dandy one together for us.'

'That would be excellent, Mr Mason,' Huber said. 'Shall we meet at the gangway at eleven of the clock?' He gave an abbreviated bow and departed.

My eyes followed the man's formal gait.

'Don't even know the cat's pajamas. Odd guy.'

'I tried to get some of the quality local foods for you,' Steward Grap said, handing me a wicker picnic basket so crammed that it felt like it was loaded with bricks. 'Herr Huber said he would take care of the drinks.'

Sure enough, when Mamie and I met the portly Austrian at the foot of the gangway, he carried a wicker basket himself, taller than ours. Despite its height, it still exposed the green necks of four bottles of wine and sounded with the musical clink of crystal stemware when he loaded it into our hired car.

Willy, who pronounced it Vil-ee, our Afrikaans driver, took enormous pride in his 1931 Crossley Golden. He presented it to us with a sweeping wave of the hand like he was unveiling a great work of art. Turns out hand gestures were his primary means of communication. I don't think he said more than ten words during the entire drive up and down the mountain. At least it was better than '*ici la*' this and '*ici le*' that. And he opened the door for Mamie first.

I thought we would be driving to the top of the mountain but, after leaving the abbreviated Cape Town suburbs and climbing a winding dirt road along its lower slope, we halted at a stone building on the roadside. Vil-ee popped out, threw open the doors, and expended two words – 'cable tram' – while pointing upslope.

I looked up and loved what I saw, two pairs of cables to

the top of Table Mountain, each with a single car in motion, one moving up and one down.

Mamie had different thoughts. 'I'm not climbing in that thing, Bert. Not for all the tea in China.'

'But, Mrs Mason, I am told the views are glorious. And we will also possibly encounter the dassie there. It is the closest living relative of the elephant, you know,' Herr Huber cajoled. 'Perhaps you would feel more relaxed if we had a sip of wine before we began our ride.'

Huber was doing his level best and it worked. That, and a generous glass of still-chilled Rotgipfler soon had Mamie calmed to the point that she hummed an off-key version of 'She'll be Comin' Round the Mountain' to herself as we swung and jolted upward in the tram. Near the top it appeared we would drift right into the straight gray walls of stone, but the tram slipped nimbly over the cliff edge and we were deposited in a second stone hut, a twin to the one from which we had embarked.

'There, Mrs Mason, that was not so difficult, was it?' Huber said, pronouncing 'was' as 'vas'.

'Not too bad, Herr Huber, but I may need another glass of that rotgutler before the ride down,' Mamie said.

'Rotgipfler, Mrs Mason. The type of grape, not the quality of the wine.' Herr Huber pointed. 'Ah, look there, by the rocks, the elusive dassie.'

A rodent-looking animal, the size of a woodchuck, scrambled away among the rocks outside the tram hut but it was the view that caught my eye. Cape Town was arrayed below like a babe in a bassinet, bounded by a thin golden strip of sand, the endless sea and a flawless sky. As the city suburbs petered out, a low brown and green landscape of scrub, punctuated by odd trees shaped like upturned shaving brushes, curved up to the sheer cliffs of the mountain.

'Nothing like this in Hills Corners, is there, Mamie?' I said.

'No Bert,' she replied through a bleary smile.

'It reminds me of the Alps in my home nation,' Herr Huber sighed. 'Though we have no sea, of course. Still, the place is paradise to me, a paradise lost now.'

I felt sorry for the man. 'Is it really so bad, Herr Huber?

The Germans on this trip don't seem to be bad types, just a little stiff and officious. Captain Dane, for example, and his officers. You'll never meet nicer guys.'

'Even the master race has its better angels, Mr Mason, though for every one of them these days there are ten like Sturmbannführer Heissemeyer, schoolyard louts who have graduated to bullying their own people and those of the nations on their borders.'

'But I thought that the Austrian people wanted – voted for – the combination with Germany,' Mamie said.

'It was made to appear that way but things are not always as they appear. The election which brought about the *Anschluss* was rigged, fixed, or whatever you Americans use these days as the term for crushing the will of the people. The Nazi bullies made certain that the right people voted and the wrong people not just stayed home but were imprisoned, or beaten outside the polls, or worse. It provided a lesson to me, an otherwise peaceful man, that these Nazi *Tyrannen* must be exterminated like rats, one by one if need be, and it is the duty of all who love freedom to carry the extermination out.'

As he spoke, Herr Huber's cherubic face took on a fevered appearance, a fact he must have realized when he shifted his eyes to Mamie and caught her expression of surprise. 'Please excuse me, Mrs Mason. I did not mean to allow my . . . passion over the loss of my homeland to ruin our outing today. Look, another dassie! He looks like the fat alpine marmot of Austria but I understand he is related not only to the elephant but also the manatee and dugong. How interesting! How charming!'

Mamie's fuzzy edge from the wine had worn away and she gave me a knowing look as Huber scrambled over the rocks after the dassie. 'I could use some food,' she said, and lifted the lid of the varnished wicker picnic basket. Soon she had the spread that Steward Grap had packed for us laid out on a blanket on the grassy slope. Grap had labeled the food-stuffs we might not recognize. We lazed beneath the cloudless African sky and lunched on figs, biltong, brie, spanspeck and mealie bread, a type of sweet corn bread. And, naturally, more of Herr Huber's 'rotgutler' wine, which was anything but rotgut.

The clement sun and the glow of the wine and food soon had Herr Huber drowsing, while his beloved dassies gamboled among the rocks surrounding our picnic ground. Mamie and I wandered off on one of the paths that circled the flat top of the mountain, and when we were out of earshot, she said, 'What do you think, Bert?'

'I think we have our first real suspect,' I said.

TWENTY-THREE

> Terraced Port Elizabeth lies along the shores of an azure lagoon known as Algoa Bay and climbs the hills behind amidst tropical shrubbery and gardens.
>
> – *Round Africa Cruise brochure*

Mamie – March 1, 1939 – Port Elizabeth, Union of South Africa

Bert has a bad belly today. He was up in the middle of the night, groaning and whining the way men do, or at least the way he does, when the tiniest thing is wrong with their health. I know if Bert had been pregnant three times, instead of me, I would not have survived the whining. I'm thoroughly convinced it was easier for me to suffer the morning sickness and the labor pains myself than it would have been to listen to Bert if he'd had to go through them.

By dawn, the ship had pulled into Port Elizabeth, Cape Town's little sister, a burg with broad green lawns, a fairy-tale lighthouse, and the small-town appeal of a Canton, or maybe an Akron; just big enough but not too big.

Steward Grap noticed Bert was still green around the gills when he brought the morning joe. 'Are you feeling all right, Mr Mason?' Grap asked as he poured my cup.

'I'm feeling pretty poorly, Grap,' Bert managed, in a voice whispering, you would think, from the very brink of death. 'I believe I may have had too much biltong. But I'll make it through. No coffee for me. And no shore excursion today.'

'I'll bring some rooibos tea for you, sir,' Grap said, disappearing on his urgent mission of mercy. No one is more sympathetic to a man nurturing a histrionic illness than another man.

Ever the dutiful wife, I said, 'I'll stay here with you today, Bert. There's nothing in Port Elizabeth I can't live without seeing.'

Truth be told, there were two things I wanted to see – the Snake Park and the Feather Market. Bunky Olsen had been talking about them for the last two days.

Grap reappeared and poured his red-black tea while making soothing, nursemaidly sounds. Bert lapped it up – both the tea and the nursemaiding. 'This is good, Grap.'

'An herb tea, sir. It is good for the digestion,' the steward cooed.

Bert, sensing he had in Steward Grap a more sympathetic ear for his complaints, said, 'Mamie, there's no reason for you to miss Port Elizabeth. Steward Grap can take care of anything I need, right Grap?'

'Yes, sir, I can, but what about Mrs Mason's safety?'

It rankled to hear these two cavemen making plans for me, like I was some doll they had knocked over the head and dragged in by the hair. 'I'll be just fine, Grap, and so will you, Bert, after Grap nursemaids you all day.'

Both men looked like I'd just given them a good smack in the kisser, and neither said a word. I, however, was committed now, so I pushed out the stateroom door, past the steward, and bumped right into Gitte Damgaard and Pia de Ribera as they walked by in their shore excursion clothes.

'Oh, excuse me, ladies,' I said.

'Mrs Mason, how are you? You appear to be . . . in a hurry,' Gitte Damgaard said.

'Oh, just headed ashore.'

'Without Mr Mason?' Señora de Ribera asked.

'He's not feeling well. Tijuana trots, you know.'

'No, I don't. What is this Tijuana trots?'

Miss Damgaard, all worldly wise, laughed and said, 'You don't want to know,' and then, to me, 'Would you care to join us? We are skipping the standard tour – too many municipal buildings and war memorials – and going to see what we really want to see, the Snake Farm and the Feather Market. And then we're going to the beach.'

I saw that they each carried a bag for their bathing costumes. I wondered if Gitte Damgaard was also packing heat in the form of her Colt that Bert had seen in that gem seller's place in Dakar. Well, more's the better if she was, not that I thought there was any danger, what with three of us out together in public places in broad daylight.

'Let me get my bathing costume and I'll join you.' I plunged back in the cabin door, disrupting a cozy domestic scene of Steward Grap pouring Bert a second cup of herbal tea, tossed my swimming gear in a bag, and was out before either of the men could speak.

'How're we traveling?' I asked.

'We have hired a car,' Miss Damgaard said and, sure enough, at the end of the gangway, there stood Ten-Word Willy and his Crossley Golden. He must have followed the ship overland from Cape Town. He had us in the automobile with a silent flourish and we were off.

'I am the Guardian of the Snakes,' the wizened Negro greeted us. He was standing in the deep shade of what Pia de Ribera said were milkweed trees, outside the entrance to the Snake Farm. The dense foliage of the tree where he stood was sprinkled with greenish flowers that smelled like a swamp and provided a meal to clouds of spotted mousey birds with high head crests and spike-feathered tails as long as their bodies.

'Those are speckled mousebirds,' the Guardian of the Snakes said, seeing me staring up into the noisy clot of birds. Speckled mousebirds – are all naturalists masters of the obvious?

'Are you ma'ams here to see the birds or the snakes?' the guardian continued. It was then I noticed a short brown snake levitating up from inside his ragged shirt. Another, larger specimen followed, curling along an arm, and I started to have misgivings.

'The snakes,' Gitte Damgaard said, without hesitation.

'Then you ladies have come to the right place,' the guardian said, nodding in the direction of two wooden doors which opened on to a half-walled arcade. The roof of the arcade was latticework, providing shade.

'Wait here.' The guardian disappeared around a corner and reappeared on the other side of the half-wall, in a stone courtyard. He chanted undecipherable words in a monotone and soon snakes, first one or two, and then dozens, slithered from hiding places toward him, the stuff of nightmares. He continued his call and the reptiles wrapped around his legs, curled up his chest, and draped from his arms. He altered his call, a sharper pitch now, and a trio of hooded cobras, each ten feet of muscle and danger, arrayed themselves around him, holding heads and hoods a yard above the dusty stones of the courtyard.

The Guardian of the Snakes swayed and the cobras followed his movement. Suddenly he cast three of the snakes coiled on his arms into the air, one toward each of the cobras. Hoods flared, the big snakes struck, and in seconds it was over, the carcasses of the victims simply a bulge in the larger cobras' bodies.

'Marvelous!' Gitte Damgaard cheered. Señora de Ribera watched in cold silence. It was evident that neither woman experienced fear of the spectacle, only fascination. I must tell you, it was the same for me.

Back at Willy's Crossley, Miss Damgaard was exhilarated. 'How did you like it, Pia?' she asked.

'Seeing those cold-eyed assassins reminded me of nothing so much as the Nazis in Germany before Rolando and I left,' de Ribera whispered. 'They, too, readily killed those of their own kind who were only slightly different from them. They are all like that bastard Heissemeyer was. So cold, so methodical, so at ease with dispensing death.'

No love lost between Pia de Ribera and the late Major Heissemeyer, but that was no news flash. I would have to speak to Bert about her as our second, but maybe not our last, suspect.

'Feather Market,' said the expansive Willy, coasting the Crossley to the edge of the road by an ornate pink palace of a building a few minutes after leaving the Snake Farm. I was surprised; I thought it would be like the markets in Casablanca and Dakar, with stalls and hawkers, smells and sounds. This place looked more like the fine French country home of someone with bad color sense.

We piled out of the car and entered into what can only be called a fan dancer's fantasy of feathers: large ones, small ones, sheafs, baskets, bundles of feathers. I wondered how many ostriches had given their lives for the fluffy plenitude we wandered through.

The Feather Market was no tourist trap. Dusty Afrikaans hunters moved about, haggling and talking, trailed by Negroes bearing bundles of feathers. Soon a dark-suited man with an aristocrat's bearing moved purposefully through the hall to the dais at one end. As he passed, conversation dropped off to silence, so that when he reached his post at the podium atop the dais no sound was heard other than the click of his heels on the wood.

'First lot,' the suited man said, his voice echoing through the hall. A squat frontiersman in a slouch hat and knee boots motioned with his hand and two servants with bundles of feathers moved to the floor in front of the podium. A lively auction ensued, with three or four bidders making offers by barely perceptible twitches of eyebrow or finger, and in no time the bundles of feathers were sold. The contract was settled immediately before everyone, with the man in the slouch hat walking away with a fistful of one hundred pound notes, trailed by his servants.

'The Jews are the feather merchants,' Pia de Ribera said as we watched. 'South Africa was a haven but now it is no longer safe. The Greyshirts, the local *fascista*, have brought the persecution here.'

Gitte Damgaard nodded with absent-minded sympathy, her eyes on the wads of cash being exchanged. I pretended not to hear. I was neutral on the issue, just as the United States would be neutral if the nations of Europe and their surrogates around the globe began another one of their squabbling wars. I didn't want to see my son Lee fighting to save France, or Belgium, or England, from Nazi Germany.

The excitement of the auction and the spectacle of rafts of graceful ostrich plumes began to fade and we stepped out into the heat of the austral summer afternoon.

I looked at my two flushed companions and said, 'To the beach, Vil-ee!' and we piled into the Crossley like giggly schoolgirls on holiday.

'The public beach?' Willy asked, the strain of stringing together three words evident on his furrowed brow.

'Is there any other?' I asked.

'Yes.'

'Well, what about it?' I said. Extracting a word from Willy was like pulling teeth from a tiger.

'There is a beach to the north. Pretty.' Boy, when that Willy gets going you can't shut him up.

'Are you game, girls?' I said. There were laughing nods all around. 'OK, Vil-ee, take us to your secret beach.'

That set us on an automobile ride through Port Elizabeth and its compact outskirts, out into the countryside. At first we were within sight of the coast, but the road then veered inland for a while. The traffic, light enough in town, thinned to nothing by the time Willy halted, pointed in the general direction of the water, and said, 'There.'

Dunes blocked the view of the sea but we took Willy at his word and set out. Halfway up the first dune I looked back to see him, head back, hat over his eyes, apparently asleep. Not surprising since he probably had to drive all night to get to Port Elizabeth from Cape Town in time to pick us up this morning.

Cresting the dune, we were greeted by the sight of a mile of ice-blue breakers marching evenly on to a tawny sand beach. And not another soul to be seen.

'There's no place to change,' Señora de Ribera said.

'Oh, yes there is. The back of that dune is my changing room,' I said. 'Gitte, yours is on the right. Pia, yours is on the left. See you back here in five minutes.'

And in five minutes we rejoined and charged down the dune slope and into the cool water, squealing when we dove in. An hour of splashing in the surf left us refreshed and the best kind of tired.

'I'm down for a nap, ladies,' I said, spreading my towel at the base of the dune closest to the water.

'I'm for a walk. I used to beachcomb in Torremolinos and I never could abide just sitting or lying on the sand,' Pia said. 'I'm just too restive to stay in one place for too long.'

'Fine,' Gitte said. 'We'll be here.'

I closed my eyes and allowed the late afternoon sun to warm and dry me, just as I had as a child after my brothers and I had gone skinny-dipping in the Tuscarawas River in the heat of the Ohio summer. I must have drifted off to sleep. When I awoke, the sun was low in the sky. Pia and Gitte were gone. After sitting up and clearing my frowsy head, I saw that footprints trailed off in both directions from where I sat.

One set of prints headed north, fragmented where the incoming surf had washed away parts of the trail. There was no one in sight in that direction, though there was an unobstructed view along the entire sweep of the beach.

The second set of footprints went in the opposite direction. A low point only a few hundred feet away marked their end, or at least the end of their visibility to me. I stood and marched off in that direction, thinking Gitte Damgaard had gone that way and hoping to find her just around the point.

After walking less than a quarter mile, I decided to cut across the dunes rather than following the shoreline around the point. The shortcut would allow me to catch up to Gitte quickly and, I must confess, I was suddenly concerned about being alone on a desolate beach on the empty coast of Africa. It wasn't like lions and leopards were going to carry me away, but I felt a sense of unease. It was nothing, I told myself as I walked toward the top of the first dune, but I still picked up my pace.

After walking over the dune and reaching its lower edge, I found myself in a sandy bowl, cut off from views of the beach or the water, and in shadow, with only indirect light from the setting sun.

Then there was the rank odor of sweat, sudden and pungent, followed instantly by my vision being cut off. The scratch of rough fiber told me a cloth bag had been put over my head. Strong hands already had a rope around my neck before I realized what was happening. No sound came when I tried to scream.

I struggled but my assailant had the advantage of surprise, putting me in a bear hug from behind. He, and it had to be a man because of the strength, seemed to be intent on squeezing the air out of my lungs, and the rope around my neck wouldn't let any back in. I was going out, I knew, and I also knew that the prospect of ever waking up again if I did go out was slim.

I kicked up and back as hard as I could with my right leg, and heard, felt and smelled a rush of fetid breath expelled from my attacker. He almost released his grasp but clamped down again after a moment. He was able, while all this was going on, to twist the rope more tightly around my throat. The hazy light inside the burlap bag began to narrow from my vision's periphery. Just before it went out completely, I heard a noise.

My last thought was how odd it was that Bert was here among the dunes with the little popgun he had used to shoot the purser.

TWENTY-FOUR

> Hellville is exactly the kind of port one associates with the tropics. The docks and jetties are washed by warm southern waters; the houses, half-hidden by the verdure, are close to the lush jungle; small avenues are shaded by dark mango trees while miniature parks are planted with palms and ylang-ylang.
>
> – *Round Africa Cruise brochure*

Bert – March 2, 1939 – Hellville, Nossi-Bé, Madagascar

They call this place Hellville but it seems like heaven after what happened in South Africa. I was a fool to let Mamie go off by herself like that. It won't ever happen again. It's just lucky she made it alive. If she hadn't, I don't know if I could have ever forgiven myself.

My belly was still grumbling from bad biltong when they brought Mamie to the cabin about an hour after sunset. She was still in and out of consciousness, with sand all over her and ugly black and blue bruising around her neck.

'My God, what's happened?' Steward Grap cried as he opened the door to two crewmen, half carrying and half supporting Mamie, followed by Señora de Ribera and Miss Damgaard. Señora de Ribera was flushed and worn. Gitte Damgaard also had a feverish appearance and was dirty, but she appeared excited, energized.

'I had to shoot a man,' Damgaard said, looking levelly into my eyes. 'He was assaulting Mamie. He would have killed her if I had not shot him.' In the closeness of the cabin, I could smell the gunpowder residue on her.

'Who? Why?' I started to question and then, more sensibly, 'Get the ship's doctor – fast.'

The crew had already acted on that need. Herr Doktor Ehring appeared as I finished the sentence. He pushed past everyone to where the crewmen had placed Mamie on the bed and began an examination, checking her breathing and feeling her head, neck, arms and legs for broken bones and other injuries.

The cabin air was hot and dank as we all watched Doctor Ehring work. Finally, he spoke. 'There are no apparent injuries other than some minor contusions on her arms and the very severe ones on her neck. She is breathing clearly and her pulse is rapid, but strong.'

The doctor drew a capsule from his medical bag, crushed it, and waved it beneath Mamie's nose. Her eyes fluttered for a moment and then flew open, wide and terrified. She struggled to rise but Doctor Ehring gently held her down, whispering, 'Mrs Mason, you are in safe hands. You are back aboard the *Columbus*. You have been injured but you will recover soon, and completely. Now you must rest.'

Mamie's eyes caught mine and I took her hand. That seemed to reassure her and she relaxed back into the bed.

Doctor Ehring went to his bag again and came out with a packet of two pills. 'Steward, water,' he said to Grap, and then to Mamie, 'You must take these pills. They will help you rest.'

Mamie's eyes searched over the doctor's shoulder for me. 'It's all right, Mamie. I'll be right here. I won't leave your side,' I said.

Mamie swallowed the pills with a sip of water and fell asleep after a restless minute or two.

'She should be fine,' Doctor Ehring said. 'She will have some discomfort swallowing from the neck injury for a few days. I can prescribe a painkiller for that if necessary. Otherwise, a day or two of rest is what is needed. Please send the steward for me if her condition changes abruptly or for any problem she may experience.' Doctor Ehring and the two crewmen then left. Steward Grap, looking concerned, hovered behind the two ladies.

'Now, tell me what happened,' I said.

'We did some sightseeing in town and then Willy, the driver, took us to the beach,' Gitte Damgaard began. 'Mamie said Willy had been your driver in Cape Town.'

I nodded.

'Willy waited with the car while we walked over the dunes

to the beach. We swam and then Pia went for a walk while Mamie and I lay out to dry off. Mamie fell asleep and after a half hour, I decided to walk, too. I was around a point on the beach when I thought I heard muffled screams. I ran back and saw a man with Mamie among the dunes. She was trying to get away from him and when I got closer I saw that he had a bag over her head and a rope around her neck and was trying to choke her.'

'Jesus,' I said.

'So I shot him,' Gitte Damgaard said.

'Jesus, Mary and Joseph,' I said.

'I had to. He would have killed her. It was Willy.'

'Willy the driver? Why would he do that?'

'I don't know.' Her voice was calm, almost cold. 'And we can't ask him now. He was dead before he hit the ground. I got Mamie sort of awake and helped her towards the road as best I could.'

'I heard the shots and came running to find them,' Señora de Ribera interjected. 'We got her to the car and Gitte drove us right back here.'

'What about Willy?' I asked.

'We left the bastard at the bottom of the dune where he fell,' Miss Damgaard said. She is a tough customer, I'll tell you. I wouldn't want to tangle with her. 'I suppose the police will need to be called.'

'The police have already been called,' said a voice from the doorway. In all the excitement, the cabin door had been left ajar when Doctor Ehring departed. Now it swung wide open and a silver-haired figure in a khaki uniform filled most of the doorframe. 'Lieutenant Frederick Coetzee, South African Police.'

No sooner had Lieutenant Coetzee made his presence known than Captain Dane appeared behind him, and introduced himself.

While niceties were exchanged between the captain and Lieutenant Coetzee, it was evident that both men were all business. As soon as introductions were concluded, the lieutenant asked, 'Who did the shooting?'

'I did.' Miss Damgaard stepped forward, chin up, shoulders back.

'Do you still have the weapon with you, miss?' Coetzee was courtly but firm.

'I do.'

'Then I must ask you to surrender it, please.'

Gitte Damgaard rummaged in her bag for a moment and eased out the Colt 1911 automatic I had first seen back in Dakar. She handed it, butt first, to the big policeman, who took it with an abbreviated bow, released the clip, and racked the slide. An unfired .45 shell that had been in the chamber clattered to the floor. Coetzee picked up the bullet and then smelled the open chamber of the gun.

'How many times did you fire, miss?'

'Twice. I was taught that if one fires, one should always fire twice.'

'That is prudent, if one's intent is to bring the target down, whether it is a Cape buffalo or a man,' Lieutenant Coetzee said.

'It was my intent to bring the target down, sir. It was my intent to save Mrs Mason's life,' Gitte Damgaard said, unflinching.

'And so it seems you accomplished both your objectives, miss. Was anyone, other than the malefactor, Mrs Mason, and yourself, witness to these events?'

'No, sir, although I would hardly call Mrs Mason a witness, since she was unconscious with a cloth bag over her head and a rope around her neck at the time I shot the filthy mongrel.'

'And were you acquainted with this, as you say, filthy mongrel?' Coetzee appeared almost disinterested as he asked the question.

'He had been a driver for me while touring for a day in Cape Town. And Mrs Mason mentioned that he had driven her and Mr Mason while the ship was in port there.'

Lieutenant Coetzee turned an inquiring eye in my direction.

'That's right,' I said. 'He drove us to Table Mountain.'

Coetzee returned to Miss Damgaard. 'Was he known to you before this trip?'

'No.'

The policeman then focused on Señora de Ribera. 'Were you on this excursion, too, madam?'

'Yes, I was,' the señora sniffed. 'But I was not present when the shooting occurred. I had walked in the opposite direction on the beach. I was returning when I heard two shots. I ran toward the sound and came upon Miss Damgaard standing over Willy, our driver, with a gun in her hand. Willy was quite dead, shot once in the neck and again in the chest. Mrs Mason was also on the ground, alive, moaning, with her head in a cloth bag and a rope around her neck. We, Miss Damgaard and I, freed her and assisted her to the car. Miss Damgaard drove us directly from the beach to the ship.'

Captain Dane spoke up. 'I can assure you, Lieutenant Coetzee, that I have become acquainted with each of these ladies during the course of this voyage. None of them has proven to be anything other than of the highest character. I take it, after formalities, all of them will be allowed to continue on with the ship.'

'That remains to be seen . . .' Lieutenant Coetzee began, when there was a slight commotion outside the door. Two more policemen stepped into the cabin and spoke to Coetzee in Afrikaans. After some back and forth, they handed him a folded paper and he dismissed them with a curt salute.

'You ladies are very fortunate,' he said. 'In the last two years, two female tourists have been found strangled with a bag over their head, and robbed here in Port Elizabeth. One victim was from an Italian liner docked in Cape Town, the second just returned from safari in Port Elizabeth. There was a third victim who survived and was able to provide a description to a sketch artist. Does this look like your driver Willy?' He unfolded the paper to reveal a drawing that looked remarkably like Willy.

'Oh, my dear God,' Señora de Ribera said. Miss Damgaard nodded affirmatively.

'That's him,' I said.

'This is the man the two officers found on the beach north of town.' Lieutenant Coetzee folded the sketch and buttoned it into his uniform breast pocket. 'Captain Dane, the *Columbus* is in port here until tomorrow evening, yes?'

'That is correct, Lieutenant.'

'I will work tonight and tomorrow to confirm my preliminary

determination that this killing was in defense of another in mortal danger, and was justified. If I am satisfied that this is the case, all passengers will be permitted to depart when the ship sails tomorrow evening.'

And we all did leave on time with the ship. The police even returned Gitte Damgaard's .45 automatic just before we cast off.

TWENTY-FIVE

> Mombasa is a typically Oriental city, with a maze of narrow and tortuous streets and lanes that run between blank-walled houses broken here and there by mosque and market.
>
> – *Round Africa Cruise brochure*

Mamie – March 11, 1939 – Mombasa, Kenya

It has been over a week and I can't lay up forever, much as I'd like to. My throat is almost back to normal. It still hurts to swallow, hurts like I'm trying to choke down a billiard ball, but not enough to return to the diet of soup or porridge spooned for me in the first few days by Bert or Steward Grap. The bruises have gone from purple to black to a nasty mottled greenish-yellow which I have been covering, none too successfully, with a silk scarf and face powder the last couple of days.

Bert has been more than solicitous, never moving from my side while I was out from Doctor Ehring's sedative, and only leaving occasionally to take a round on deck since then. The old shoe really seems to have been shaken by my near-miss. I guess that's not a bad thing but it's a hell of a way to get Bert to appreciate what he has, one that I'm not prepared to suffer again just to keep him opening doors and pulling out chairs for me.

Last night, at sea, I returned to the dining room for the first time since the incident, or attack, or whatever you call it. Bert and I ate with Bunky and Jack Olsen, a quiet meal with good plain food, roast beef and potatoes, no fancy Frenchified stuff, and I was OK with it. People stared and whispered, not at the table next to us, but a few tables farther away. I guess I was a touch jumpy. I let out a little yip when a wine waiter accidentally brushed my shoulder while refilling my glass. Bert shot him a look. For a minute I thought he was going to pummel the poor man.

Today my objective is to get out and move around the ship on my own. I want to go on the shore excursion by train to Nairobi tomorrow and that won't happen if I don't get out of this cabin. This morning I sent Bert on his way after breakfast, and told Steward Grap I could fend for myself unless he felt the need to button up the back of my sundress for me. The boy fled like I'd asked him to give me a sponge bath. I have been sitting here in the silence for an hour and I've not been this frightened since that scratchy bag was jammed over my head back in South Africa. I guess the only way is to bite the bullet and go out. Maybe I will find Bert and get him to join me for lunch.

My first impression of Mombasa as I stepped from the stateroom was that of heat. This place is hotter than Satan's house cat. Of course, I could say that about all of Africa south of Dakar. The port here is pretty plain: a collection of rickety docks, a railhead, and some ramshackle buildings along the shore and spreading up to the low hills. The hills themselves are a lush green, like rainy late spring in Ohio. You can tell this is a farming area by the ordered cultivation along the slopes. But the simple fact of the matter is that there's not much to Mombasa. It's just a way station where you begin a journey to someplace else, or return from such a journey.

The harbor waters were crowded with boats and ships, with the *Columbus* by far the largest. Other than a rust-bucket tramp freighter or two, most of the watercraft were river steamers, small coasters, and sailboats with swept masts that Grap says are Arab dhows. We were anchored in the middle of the harbor and I could pretty well make out what's happening on the docks, all just mobbed by Negro boys and men, some busy loading and unloading cargo but most looking for work. I didn't think it was possible for a place to have an air of prosperity and poverty at the same time but Mombasa sure does.

Walking along the Promenade Deck, every woman I met quietly nodded to me. The men all tipped their hats with exaggerated formality. I assume by now everyone on the ship knows what happened to me, although no one seems to want to speak to me about it. It was like I had some dreaded disease, seeing the concern, or maybe pity, in their faces but none willing to come close to me.

I wandered up to the Beach Club Deck, thinking Bert might be taking the air there, but found only the crowded pool, the throng splashing and thrashing like frogs being parboiled. Maybe they were, in this heat.

I finally got Bert in my sights in the smoking room. 'Whatcha doing, Bert?' I asked, even though I could see he was sitting in one of the oxblood leather club chairs, dozing.

'Thought I'd come here to get out of the heat,' he said. The room, all carved wood in a style Captain Dane called 'bar-oak', wasn't any cooler than the rest of the ship but it had the appearance of an English men's club. Maybe that made it seem cooler. To men, because that is where all men on the boat seemed to be.

One man made a beeline to us, the Aryan god, Lieutenant Haas. 'Ah, Mrs Mason, it is so good to see you up and about after your unfortunate circumstance.' His perfect blue eyes betrayed none of the concern that his words expressed. He had the same dead eyes when he got the news about the death of Major Heissemeyer. Do all Nazis have dead eyes? Dead souls behind them, too?

'Thank you, Lieutenant. I'm feeling much better now.'

'I understand the man was a psychopath, a mental defective,' Haas said.

'Where'd you hear that?' Bert asked. I could tell he was surprised.

'From Fräulein Schon,' Haas said. I wondered where she had heard that, but said nothing.

The lieutenant continued. 'In Germany, such defectives are being removed from society. Psychotics, pedophiles, homosexuals and other degenerates who do not conform to the German norm are taken to places where they will not infect the German people with their perversions.'

'It might be good for your country to get shed of the pedophiles, Lieutenant, but I can't see where those nancy boys are really anything but harmless,' Bert said.

'Nancy boys?'

'The homosexuals.'

'But there you are mistaken, Mr Mason,' Lieutenant Haas said, with something approaching intensity in his voice. 'The homosexuals waste themselves on each other, depriving the flower of German womanhood and the *Vaterland* of the children needed to propagate the Aryan race. In so doing, these degenerates strike a blow at the very heart of the Reich and its future. They are as much an enemy of our country as the Jew and the Communist.'

You can't even make a little small talk with these Nazis without it turning into some kind of twisted political, racial, pseudo-moral palaver. I could see that Bert was taken aback. He said, 'Well, there ain't that many of them,' probably hoping to end the whole thing right there.

'But there are, Mr Mason.' Haas lifted his chin. 'There are, and they must be done away with, even those who are otherwise good party members.'

'You're not saying that Willy fellow was a nancy, are you? Or a Nazi?' Bert asked.

'No, Mr Mason. He was probably another form of degenerate, do you not think? But we shall never know now, since Fräulein Damgaard has disposed of the evidence and the problem in one quick stroke.' The lieutenant's pale pink lips twisted into a wry smile. 'Disposition of the problem and the evidence in one quick stroke seems to be a characteristic of this voyage.' He nodded and left.

'What the heck was that all about?' I said.

'I don't know, Mamie. All I know is that he didn't seem to be talking about what happened to you.'

TWENTY-SIX

> The two-day excursion from Mombasa to Nairobi, the capital of Kenya, is like no other excursion anywhere in the world. It will leave Mombasa late in the afternoon by special sleeping-car train and next morning when passengers awaken will be skirting the edge of the Southern Game Reserve. For more than two hours the train will pass along this reserve and wild animals frequently may be seen from the car windows.
>
> – *Round Africa Cruise brochure*

Bert – March 12, 1939 – On the railroad near Voi, Kenya

It has been a while since I've been on a good old-fashioned coal-fired steam train. Most trains in the States use diesel oil now, but this beauty we are on today still belches gritty coal smoke, chugs and puffs, and has that air of drama about it that reminds me of the first train ride I took with my father in 1896, off to visit relatives in Michigan. The Kenya–Uganda Railway engine here is more modern – it was built in the Twenties – but the stoker still shovels and sweats, and the pitchy wail of the whistle as we left Mombasa hasn't changed since my first ride. It is still a call to adventure and the unexpected.

Our home for the 300-mile shore excursion to Nairobi consists of two first-class cars, a second-class car, a dining car, and an observation/bar car, all older, all meticulously maintained, with wood paneling, large windows, and carpeting in the aisles.

'More coffee, suh?'

'I'm good, Juma. Fine coffee, though,' I say when he looks disappointed as I decline a third cup of Kenya's bracing black richness. Juma is the bar boy, if you can call him a boy at the age of probably fifty-five; always smiling and good-natured, and always ready with another cup.

'So, Juma, how long have you been doing this?'

'I come with the train, suh, when I was a young boy. I don't know how old because my people don't keep track of the years, but I must have been nine or ten. My daddy and mama died from the Rift Valley fever and I made my way to Nairobi and started carrying bags at the station there. Porters took me in the train and it has been my mama and daddy ever since. I served coffee to Teddy Roosevelt in that chair you're sitting on in 1909. We had a platform then, on the front of the engine, so you could see the game. Ole Teddy rode up there most of the trip,' Juma said. 'Coffee, ma'am?'

'You bet, Juma,' Mamie said. The old girl has really bounced back since that crazy Willy tried to kill her. I think this side trip is doing her good.

'Good morning, Fräulein Schon. Care to join us?' Mamie said, looking past my shoulder. I had to tear my attention away from a flock of giraffes. Juma says a bunch of them together are called a 'tower', which makes sense but sounds silly to me.

'I would be delighted, Mrs Mason, if I am not imposing,' the fräulein said. She was dressed in a khaki safari outfit, bush jacket over a crisp cotton shirt, and mannish trousers. Her eyes had a lost air about them.

'How are you, dear?' Mamie asked. Mamie gets motherly with folks sometimes, especially now that the kids are grown, and she had felt that way towards Beatta Schon ever since we had met her. The younger woman took to it, I could see, and there was a bond between them.

'I'm fine, Mrs Mason,' she sighed. 'Well, I should be fine, but I'm not really. Can I ask you a question, confidentially?'

Woman-talk is not my strong suit but I was trapped between Mamie and the aisle in the close quarters of the bar car. I did the best I could, turning my attention out the window to a herd of hartebeests that had been spooked to a gallop by the appearance of the train.

'Sure, Beatta. Ask old Mamie anything,' Mamie said.

'Well . . . have you ever been in love, really in love?'

I slewed my eyes from the hartebeests to Mamie and caught her jocular smile. 'I might have been,' my bride of thirty years said.

'Oh . . . of course. I'm sorry, Mr Mason,' Fräulein Schon colored.

'Think nothing of it, child. It does the old girl good to have to publicly admit it every few years,' I said.

Fräulein Schon continued. 'You see, that proves I am not thinking straight.'

'What's bothering you, honey?' Mamie pressed.

'I think I'm in love.'

'With Lieutenant Haas?' Mamie said.

I made a show of returning my full attention to the hartebeests.

'Yes. He's wonderful, so strong and handsome. He's quiet, but when you get to know him, so nice.'

A nice Nazi. And I'd thought I'd heard it all.

'So how is that a problem, Beatta?' Mamie asked.

'I'm leaving Europe.' Fräulein Schon's deep brown eyes welled with the start of tears. 'It has all been so wonderful since Casablanca, being with him, laughing together. Even when Sturmbannführer Heissemeyer fell overboard, such a terrible thing, being there to comfort him was wonderful. But Kurt won't – can't – leave Germany, and I cannot go there or even return to Danzig, which is now just Germany by another name. I came on this train excursion to clear my head, to give myself some time to think, but all I can think of is him, and losing him, and how terrible that would be. Mrs Mason, is that love?'

'It's a symptom,' Mamie said. 'Does he feel the same way about you?'

'He hasn't said as much, but then neither have I to him.'

'That may not mean anything. After all, he's had a lot on his mind. Having your boss go overboard' – Mamie carefully chose her words – 'is no small distraction.'

'Maybe, but I don't think that has much to do with it.'

'Why, dear?'

'It's difficult to speak about . . .'

'You don't need to tell me if you don't want to, child.'

'No, no, I want to. And I should. It's just . . . it's not something that's talked about in polite circles.'

Mamie just nodded, encouraging the young woman to speak if she wished to. I tried to blend into the scenery, but I don't much look like a zebra or giraffe. Maybe a warthog.

Beatta Schon closed her eyes. 'Sturmbannführer Heissemeyer became Kurt's commanding officer just before they left on this trip. They had known each other only slightly, but one day about two months ago Kurt received orders transferring him to Sturmbannführer Heissemeyer's unit. As soon as he reported, the sturmbannführer named him as his aide-de-camp and informed him that he would be taking him on a special assignment aboard the *Columbus*.

'When they arrived, Kurt found out for the first time that they were booked into the same stateroom. He thought that was somewhat unusual, since bachelor officers in the SS usually have single quarters of their own. But he told himself it was just Sturmbannführer Heissemeyer being frugal, trying to save the *Vaterland* some money.

'Then the comments began. Comments about Kurt's appearance. Comments like a man would make as compliments to a woman, about Kurt's hair, his skin, even his lips. It made Kurt very uncomfortable but what could he do? He was aboard a ship at sea with a superior officer and there was no one to report it to.

'When I came aboard, Kurt was attracted to me and the situation between him and Sturmbannführer Heissemeyer only grew worse. We began spending time together and Heissemeyer was clearly jealous. The sturmbannführer began making negative remarks about me to Kurt, saying I was not a proper Aryan woman and that I was unsuitable for Kurt. You heard some of it. It was very upsetting to me.

'One day, Kurt and Sturmbannführer Heissemeyer had angry words about me in their stateroom and Kurt left, went out on deck, and walked around for a while until he thought the sturmbannführer would be asleep.

'When he re-entered the stateroom, the lights were out and Kurt thought he was sleeping, but as soon as Kurt closed the door, Sturmbannführer Heissemeyer switched on the lights. He was contrite, apologetic, told Kurt that he only wanted what was best for him. Heissemeyer moved closer and closer as he spoke, until he ended up very close to Kurt's face, speaking softly, and then . . . and then he kissed Kurt. On the lips, like a man kisses a woman, and told Kurt that he loved him and that he wanted to make love to him.

'Kurt broke away and spent the rest of the night outside, pacing the decks until dawn. That was the morning of the day we would cross the equator. Kurt worried all day what he would do that night and during the rest of the voyage. But then the sturmbannführer fell overboard that night and Kurt . . . felt bad that he was lost, but in a way he was relieved, too. Don't you see?'

To Mamie's credit, she had taken this all in without a flinch. Now she said, 'Yes, dear. I do.'

I thought then I should ask the obvious question but Mamie beat me to the punch, and just as well. I suspect the answer she got from Fräulein Schon was the absolute truth.

'Was Kurt with you on the night Major Heissemeyer was lost at sea, Beatta?'

The railcar swayed and the cups and glasses on the small table between Fräulein Schon and Mamie and me tinkled and rang against one another. Outside, a troupe of baboons gamboled through the green countryside.

'Yes,' the young woman said. 'Why? Why you don't think . . . Sturmbannführer Heissemeyer fell overboard. There was no foul play. No, no, and even if there was, Kurt and I were together, all day and all evening, until . . .' – and Fräulein Schon's brows knitted in a look of anguish – 'late. I remember drinking too much champagne. Both Kurt and I got very sleepy and he took me back to my cabin and laid me down on my bed. I remember pulling him down to kiss me and then falling asleep in his arms. He was such a gentleman. I woke the next morning, on my bed, still in my costume from the day before. He was gone.' She put her hand to her mouth, looked from Mamie to me and back, and fled the length of the car to the first-class car beyond.

'It appears we have another suspect,' Mamie said.

TWENTY-SEVEN

As recently as fifty years ago Henry Drummond described Zanzibar as a 'cesspool of wickedness, Oriental in its appearance, Mohammedan in its religion, Arabian in its morals.'

– *Round Africa Cruise brochure*

Mamie – March 14, 1939 – Zanzibar

I confess to being rattled by Beatta Schon's revelations on the train to Nairobi. Maybe it was me being sentimental about the two lovers in our midst. I just had never really focused on Lieutenant Haas as a prime suspect. To now think that Fräulein Schon's young beau might be the killer of Major Heissemeyer was uncomfortable, to say the least. But, then, having any killer in our midst was uncomfortable.

Bert convinced me to put it out of my mind for a couple of days. 'Nothing we can do about it away from the ship,' my sweet old cabbage said. He was right; the *Columbus* passengers had been divided into two groups for the shore excursion to Nairobi. Lieutenant Haas and most of our other potential suspects were with the other group, separated from us by a hundred miles on a second train. I set thoughts of murder aside to truly enjoy the green hills of Africa. Ernie Hemingway got it right – the country here is beautiful: rich rolling land, dark with canopied trees and coffee plants; acres of cotton and sorghum and okra; little villages of flimsy huts, populated with laughing children, their hardworking mothers always singing, their indolent fathers grouped together on haunches, smoking and gossiping.

And Bert has finally had his true African adventures. We've come face to face with tall Masai warriors, their flame-red robes cast elegantly over one shoulder with the panache of a New York runway model. We ate a picnic lunch in the deep shade of a croton tree, until some baboons stole our basket. We watched an assembly of Kikuyu women, bare-chested, with faces painted in intricate patterns of white dots, dancing in the firelight. We sipped tea and gin and tonics on the veranda of the Stanley Hotel in Nairobi, the white-jacketed waiters only a generation out of the bush. And we saw animals, the Big Five – elephant, lion, leopard, Cape buffalo and rhinoceros – as well as massive herds of zebras, giraffes, wildebeests, Thomson's and Grant's gazelles, and the comic relief of African fauna, ostriches and warthogs.

The end of several blissful days traveling to and from Nairobi found us back aboard the *Columbus*, snug in our cabin and rested after the time ashore. A tap on the door signaled the arrival of Steward Grap. 'Your cuppa joe, madam,' he said. 'And here is the program for your afternoon's entertainment.'

'What's that?' Bert asked. We were expecting to take in the bazaar along the waterfront and then motor out to Kizimbani to see the Swahilis, a tribe of mixed Arab and native blood with its origins in the region's trading roots.

'His Highness Sheikh Sir Khalifa II bin Harub Al-Said, the Sultan of Zanzibar, has graciously offered his band for a concert later this afternoon. We will delay sailing until the conclusion of the performance.'

'A real live sultan, Mamie! This just gets better and better,' Bert said.

'By all means have your day ashore,' Steward Grap said. 'But don't be late. The sultans have all been touchy since the loss of the war.'

'They sided with the Axis in the Great War?' I asked.

'No. The war I was speaking of was the Anglo-Zanzibar War of 1896. Fascinating. It was the shortest war in recorded history, thirty-eight minutes for the British to defeat the sultan at the time. England then forced a protectorate and deposed the belligerent sultan, who was only two days into his reign. The current sultan is of the same line and, even after forty-three years, they remain touchy and prone to exaggerate social slights, real or imagined.'

'We better get going, Mamie, so we can be back for the

concert. We don't want to create an international incident,' Bert said, laughing.

We took a tender ashore and idled most of the day away in the bazaar. Arab traders hawked spices and silk, as they had done there for centuries. The local police, fantastically garbed in tall tasseled fezzes, wool sweaters, white shorts, and black leggings ending in bare feet, kept order with ancient rifles. Bert bargained with a Masai man for his robes without success, finally settling for the cow-tail fly swisher with a beaded handle that the man carried. He spent the rest of the shore excursion ostentatiously swishing away at the many flies lingering around the market's stalls. 'Makes me look like one of the locals,' he said, looking about as local as one of the Masai men would have looked on the courthouse square back in New Philadelphia. It was a good thing negotiations for the robe failed, or Bert would have pranced through the bazaar in that thing, all knobby knees and flesh the color of a pink pig's tummy.

We were back to the *Columbus* by late afternoon. The sultan's band was already assembling on the Beach Club Deck, the clatter of cymbal and drum and the flat blast of horns marking their warm-up, buttoning their frogged green tunics despite the killing heat on the shadeless deck. After an eternity of fits and false starts, the band made its way through Ord Hume, von Suppé, and a trombone solo by Moss, finishing with an Africanized *Top Hat* medley, swaying tarnished tubas and battered clarinets in a manner surely never envisioned by Irving Berlin when he wrote the pieces for Astaire's movie. Their sweaty task completed, the band members peeled their tunics off to bare chests and drifted away in twos and threes toward the gangway.

Bert and I headed down the stairs to our cabin, where we found Steward Grap waiting outside our door, a tray bearing two icy lemonades in hand.

'I thought you might enjoy these after standing in the sun watching the concert,' Grap said.

'That's mighty thoughtful of you, Grap,' Bert said as he opened the door and stepped back for me to enter. Always the gentleman, that Bert.

I went in and almost stepped on an envelope on the floor.

'What's this?' I said. There was no writing on the outside addressing it, so I tore it open.

THE PURSER IS YOUR MAN

The message was written in block print on the single sheet of blue stationery inside the envelope. I handed it to Bert, who read it silently. I noticed Steward Grap, tray in hand, reading over Bert's shoulder.

'Grap, did you see someone slip this under our door?' Bert waved the sheet and envelope as he spoke.

'No, sir. What does it mean?' Grap's curiosity was, I thought, possibly beyond what was proper for a servant, but he was really more like a considerate friend to us now.

'Not sure,' Bert said. 'But I've got a theory or two I'll keep to myself for now. Say, Grap, this isn't ship's stationery. Do you recognize it from anywhere? Or the writing?'

'Neither, sir,' the steward said.

'Have you seen anyone around our door? And I mean in the last few days, not just today.'

'No, sir,' Grab answered. 'Not in the last few days and I've not been here for most of today since you both were away. I tidied your room after you left for shore. The envelope was not here then. After I finished tidying up, I worked on some of the other passengers' rooms to help the steward who had assumed responsibility for my old charges and took an hour to myself at mid-afternoon. When I heard the sultan's band had boarded, I came up to A Deck to be ready for your return. When I realized how hot it would be for you in the sun at the concert, I left to get the lemonade but I was only gone for ten minutes.'

'Long enough for someone to slip the envelope under the door.'

'Yes, sir.'

'Well, then, maybe it's time we spoke to Captain Dane. Can you arrange a time for us, Grap?'

'Happy to, sir,' he said, and bowed his way out the door, leaving the two glasses of lemonade perspiring on their tray atop the dresser.

TWENTY-EIGHT

> It is doubtful if any other liner of the *Columbus*' size or speed has made as many cruises to as many different parts of the world. She has already carried highly successful cruises repeatedly to the West Indies, round South America, and round the World and she promises to bring new standards of luxury and added prestige to the round Africa route.
>
> – *Round Africa Cruise brochure*

Bert – March 15, 1939 – At sea

The only thing I can figure is that Steward Grap told Captain Dane that a crew member might be involved. Otherwise, there would be no reason to schedule a meeting for midnight. And the captain would have had us come to his cabin through its bridge entrance, as he had done in the past.

Instead, at the appointed hour, Mamie and I followed an instruction from Steward Grap and slipped up two decks to a door marked '*Privat*'. Mamie turned the shiny brass knob and the door swung open to a hall lighted by a single caged bulb. At the hall's end was a metal stair and at the stair's landing, another door marked '*Privat*'.

'Turn the knob,' Mamie hissed. In the absolute quiet of the dim passage, it sounded like someone had rolled a wheelbarrow over a cat's tail.

I tried the knob but it was locked. A light two-knuckle tap on the wood, though, and the door popped open.

'Welcome, Mr and Mrs Mason. Come in, please.' Captain Dane greeted us in his full uniform, pants pressed, buttons polished, just as he had on the first day aboard when he had managed to exchange a momentary pleasantry with each passenger.

I stepped through after Mamie and saw that we had entered the captain's cabin through a spacious closet. We walked in six feet, shoulders touching the formal and everyday uniforms arrayed on each side, until we reached the cabin where we had met before.

'Please excuse the time and the means of ingress to our meeting, Mr and Mrs Mason. I felt it necessary since Steward Grap indicated the note you received implicated a member of the crew,' Dane said.

'That's all right, Captain,' Mamie said.

'May I see the note?' he asked. I handed it to him and he stared at the paper for a much longer time than was necessary to read it.

'Steward Grap tells me you have no idea how this found its way into your room.'

'That's right. Nor did Grap.'

'And you do not recognize the writing, nor are you otherwise aware of who might be the author?'

'Correct.'

'Have you or Mrs Mason spoken to anyone about it?'

'No.'

'Have you found anything, other than this message, to implicate Purser Blanck in Major Heissemeyer's murder?'

'No sir. We' – I gestured toward Mamie – 'have not even spoken to him concerning it. Until this note we had no reason to even consider the purser as a suspect.'

'Perhaps now you do, Mr Mason. At least sufficiently to have a conversation with him.'

'Of course,' I said.

'Do you have *any* suspects?' Dane asked.

'Yes. Some folks with possible motives.'

'May I ask who?'

I occurred to me that we were done discussing the message, and Purser Blanck, and had moved on to what was essentially a report of our progress. That report was going to be mighty thin. I had to remind myself that I wasn't working for this guy and the only reason I was doing this at all was to locate and neutralize someone who might want to harm Mamie.

'Herr Huber. Miss Damgaard. Señora de Ribera. Lieutenant Haas.'

Captain Dane had been as impassive as a headwaiter when I announced the first three names but I thought I detected just a twitch when I mentioned Haas. 'Your list is rather longer than I expected, especially when one adds Herr Blanck. You believe all of these persons had an animosity to Major Heissemeyer sufficient to make them want to kill him?'

I thought about it. Huber, yes. Haas, yes. Damgaard was a stretch, but she had that gun and some pretty shady dealings thus far on the trip; enough to keep her on the list. Señora de Ribera? Call it a hunch. No, call it something more than a hunch, given her fears of what the major threatened and what he might have done to her.

Mamie had no misgivings. 'You bet, Captain Dane. At least sufficient to put them on the list for now, until we can weed them out somehow. Leave it to Bert and me.'

'Very well, Mrs Mason. And Mr Mason, you are the professional on these matters so I must defer to your capable judgment,' Dane said. Mamie flicked a barely concealed eye roll my way on hearing the word 'professional' used in reference to my investigative skills. Maybe she was right to be skeptical.

The captain shifted topics. 'Part of the reason I asked you to meet in secret tonight relates to the upcoming shore excursion to Sudan and Egypt for which you are scheduled. My first obligation to you both is, of course, your personal safety. I am concerned that your participation in such an extended shore excursion may make it difficult to meet that primary obligation. This will be different than the short trip to Nairobi.'

'What do you mean?' Mamie asked.

Dane smiled a parsimonious smile. 'Several reasons exist for my concern. First, on such an extended trip I cannot begin to provide the protection, however limited, that has been accorded you on the *Columbus* and the train to Nairobi. Second, the area where you will travel is wilder, and more . . . lawless. Finally, there is the fact that the purser is one of the ship's officers assigned to go on the excursion.' He lifted a list he had written while we were speaking of suspects and studied it. 'And all of the other passengers you list as suspects are also on that shore trip, except Lieutenant Haas.'

I mumbled a 'hummm' and gave my head a scratch. The captain made a good point.

'Bert, sailing up the Nile was a big reason you wanted to come on this trip,' Mamie said. 'It would be a shame to miss it. And I don't think anyone who had designs against us would attempt anything on the shore excursion that they wouldn't as easily do aboard the *Columbus*.'

Captain Dane turned to me, a question on his face.

'Mamie's right,' I said. 'Besides, if I'm supposed to be investigating Major Heissemeyer's murder, I should be where the suspects are, not miles away on a boat.'

'Ship,' Dane corrected, his smile softening.

'Yes, ship,' I said. 'You'll have to excuse me, Captain. I'm just a simple farmer and ships and boats are out of my ken.'

'As farming is out of mine, Mr Mason,' Captain Dane said. 'I cannot say that I am disappointed with your choice. I would certainly like to solve Major Heissemeyer's murder, especially if one of my own crew members was involved. I appreciate your willingness to undertake the risk. And yours, Mrs Mason,' he said, turning to address Mamie. 'At the very least I can send Steward Grap along with the group to keep an eye on you. While the outfitters conducting the shore excursion have their own servants, we usually send along one or two stewards to assure the quality of service matches that aboard ship. As Grap knows the circumstances, he is the logical choice.'

'Much obliged, Captain,' I said. 'We've kind of become attached to the young fella.'

'Very well, then, Mr and Mrs Mason. Bring me the murderer and stay safe in the process.' With that, the captain shepherded us to his closet and the secret door.

As the door closed behind us and Mamie and I found our way along the passage, I wondered if it was possible to carry out one of those objectives without failing at the other.

TWENTY-NINE

> Leaving the *Columbus* at Port Sudan, we will cross the barren and desert-like section of the Anglo-Egyptian Sudan to Khartoum, just above where the Blue Nile and the White Nile join to become the Nile.
>
> – *Round Africa Cruise brochure*

Mamie – March 20, 1939 – Aboard a special train from Port Sudan to Khartoum and Omdurman, Anglo-Egyptian Sudan

Purser Blanck hardly seems to be a killer. He is cordial to all us ladies and affable to the gents. He always has a ready quip, often made more humorous by his clipped, German-accented English. He has solutions to all problems and answers to all questions. He is our shepherd on this shore excursion, the second ranking officer in our little band, with the third officer, Herr Kletz, he of acting fame from earlier in the voyage, nominally in charge. Herr Kletz appears satisfied to devote himself to transportation and logistics, his English being nowhere near as good as that of the purser.

We arrived in Port Sudan this morning after steaming for several restful days from Mombasa, around the Horn of Africa, and moving into the Red Sea. Steward Grap tells me that Port Sudan is a city of twenty thousand and is the only major port for miles around. It consists mostly of stone docks and warehouses, with a sad smattering of mud buildings petering out into the great desert beyond.

At noon, we transferred from the *Columbus* to what was rather generously called a 'special sleeping-car train' for the trip to Khartoum and Omdurman. Thirty-five *Columbus* passengers, together with Herr Blanck, Herr Kletz, Steward Grap and a callow steward named Stockfisch, made up the Anglo-Saxon component of the travelers on the train. We were housed in two sleeping cars, plus a dining/bar car. Appended to our 'special train' were two additional cars, filled beyond capacity with Arabs, Nubians, and various other native types and their baggage, which included livestock, produce, and assorted sundries. We must have made for a very colorful picture, the train's diminutive engine huffing across the scorching countryside, the dust-covered cars trailing scarves and unwrapped turbans out the windows.

'Look at this, Mamie,' Bert called for the umpteenth time during the morning, pointing out a rock formation or the sheer emptiness or yet another ostrich (how do those great gangly things live out in the middle of absolute nothing?).

'Yeah, Bert, I see,' I said, slapping dust from my cotton blouse. It comes off pretty well, where it hasn't stuck to the sweat. There is red dust everywhere, on the windows, in the sheets of the sleeper bunks, between my teeth. The local people even have a red cast to their skin, what you can see of it that isn't protected from the unblinking sun by robes or headdresses.

'*Salaam*, Mr Mason, Mrs Mason,' a voice in the doorway said. It was Suliman, our local guide, he of flowing robes, leathery skin and raptor eyes. 'Your compartment is to your liking?'

Suliman is into validation; his favorite English sentence always ends with '. . . is to your liking?'

'Fine, Suliman. Great views,' Bert said, while I scanned the microscopic chamber for one square inch that wasn't gritty with dust. Not that complaining would make any difference. What would Suliman do if I complained – move us to the one clean compartment they keep on the train for whiners? I don't think so.

Suliman was still nodding and bobbing in the narrow doorway when Gitte Damgaard appeared over his shoulder.

'Care to join me in the bar car for a drink?' she asked. Gitte had taken a shine to me now that she had killed a man on my behalf, and I have to say the same about my feelings toward her. We'd become fast friends. I'll also confess I didn't mind having someone with a gun, and who knew how to handle it, nearby on this trip after what Captain Dane had said.

'Count me in, Gitte. I could use a little dust-cutter,' I said. 'Gangway, Suliman.'

Suliman flattened against the other side of the narrow passageway to allow us to pass, his Mohammedan soul undoubtedly appalled by these two alcohol-crazed white women charging for the bar car and wondering why these sahib men hadn't learned to keep their wives in check.

'Gin-tonic,' Gitte said to the dust-coated barman as he polished the dust-coated bar with a dust-coated rag.

I looked at my watch. A quarter past noon, so the sun was over the yardarm and the drinking lamp was lit. 'Gin-tonic,' I said. My usual was bourbon with some water and a cube of ice, but I had learned that neither bourbon nor ice were to be found in any bar in East Africa. The Brits had been here too long and had ground their medicinal 'gin-tonic' into the very heart and soul of every barkeeper from Cape Town to, I suspected, Cairo. Ask for whiskey and the answer was always 'no whiskey, gin-tonic'. A glass of vodka? 'No vodka, gin-tonic.' So I adapted when we were away from the well-stocked bar of the *Columbus* – 'gin-tonic' was my drink of choice in the field.

And Gitte Damgaard's as well. Though it was served with no ice, and thus at a tepid eighty-five degrees, she took a long, luxurious swig, closing her eyes momentarily to relish that rarity in Africa, an almost-civilized libation.

'Ain't this train some kind of special?' I said, to get the conversational ball rolling. Too much silence and I sip too quickly, making for a long, fuzzy afternoon.

'I've seen worse. I've seen worse in Europe, in Germany,' she said.

'I thought Herr Hitler made all the trains run on time, and they were all so clean you could eat schnitzel off the floor.'

Gitte Damgaard's brown eyes seemed to go on a journey to a place very far away. 'Oh, the trains are very efficient and they run on time. But the train to the concentration camp is not clean. The cars are cattle cars, with used straw on the floors and slatted sides that let in the frigid wind off the North Sea.'

'Concentration camp?'

'Surely you have heard of them?' Gitte now spoke matter-of-factly.

'Yes, but . . .' I hesitated to ask what I desperately wanted to know. Gitte, however, had no hesitation in answering the unspoken question.

'How do I come to speak of them? Because I have been in one, Lichtenberg, near Merseburg in Saxony, carried there in a stinking cattle car with thirty other women.'

She stared at me directly, her expression not quite defiant, almost inviting questions. So I asked.

'Why?'

'I was labeled an undesirable, subject to a *Vorbeugungshaft*, a preventive detention order for habitual and professional criminals. Funny, I almost made it out of Germany. I was in Bremerhaven, with a ticket on a coastal steamer to Denmark for the next morning. A knock on my hotel room door by the Gestapo in the dead of night, an official shuffling of papers, and I was put in the cattle car for the trip across Germany by dawn.

'Ah, and the next question I will save you from asking, Mamie, though you are probably too polite to do anything other than think it – am I an habitual and professional criminal? Let's just say I am a woman who knows how to get by in the world and who must make a living somehow. I'm no worse than most men, and a lot better than those swine who imprisoned me. I was in Lichtenberg from February 1937 until September of last year. All during that time they were after me, the guards and the officers. "A favor for us, Fräulein, means a favor for you." I never gave in, and there were plenty of other women there willing to engage in the exchange of favors, so I came out untouched. I hear now that the Gestapo men no longer offer to trade favors, they just take what they want. I was lucky to get out when I did.'

'How did you get out?'

'They released me, finally deciding after eighteen months that there was no evidence of any criminal status. I suspect I was released simply because they required my space and I had not obliged to vacate it by dying, as so many others did.'

Gitte raised a furtive index finger to the barman. Thirty seconds later he placed another one of his signature warm gin-tonics before her. She took it, swigged a healthy swallow, and stared at the table.

'He was there, you know.'

'Who was there?' I asked.

'That monster Heissemeyer. He was in charge of the guards' battalion at Lichtenberg while I was there. I thought at first when we met aboard ship that he recognized me, but maybe not. I was blonde then, much thinner, and had a different name. And there were thousands of women in the camp, so he could not know them all. Not that he tried what the other guards did. No, he liked the boys. I heard that was why they sent him there, to a camp of all-women prisoners, to present him with all that willing female temptation and wean him off his boy habit. He was a favorite of Himmler, you know. That is why they did not shoot him outright for being a homosexual. Plus, he was such a good sadist they could not bear to thin him from their ranks. I saw him separate mothers from their children, torture confessions from inmates. His favorite was to sentence newly arrived young women to thirty days in the isolation cage in the middle of the camp parade ground. It was open to the elements, unbearably hot in summer and freezing cold in winter. No one could survive a month out in the weather with only a skimpy prison shift for protection and, after a week, even the strongest realized that. That was when Heissemeyer would have them brought into his office and tell them he would commute the remaining weeks of their time in the cage to a night in the guards' barracks, provided they were sufficiently obliging to his men. Most agreed, and lived with the rape, never the same afterward. Two women, I remember, refused his offer. They died in that cage, before our eyes, begging for food, or a blanket, or just to be shot to end it all. The bastard even returned a girl, a beautiful dark-haired Roma girl, to the cage because she had not been "sufficiently cooperative" when she served her "commuted sentence" in the guards' barracks. They found her frozen to death the next morning after an early season snow. I saw him laughing with his second in command as they watched a work group of prisoners try to extract her body, frozen to the ground, from the cage.'

Gitte was in another place now, I could see, her eyes not seeing the barren desert through which we passed, but rather that frigid late autumn morning many months before in the camp in Germany. I had to ask.

'Did you push him overboard?'

'No. I should have.' She was almost wistful. 'I wish I had. No, I wish I had taken my automatic and leveled it between his eyes and made him get down on his knees and beg for his life the way he made that Roma girl beg for hers, made him cry, and plead, and debase himself, and then I wish I had shot him. But, no, I didn't push him overboard,' Gitte said. She shook her head and abruptly rose and walked out the entrance of the bar car, passing Bert on the way in.

'What was that all about?' he asked, joining me after Gitte brushed quickly by him.

'Just some girl talk,' I said.

THIRTY

> Once the Mahdi capital and the scene of wild orgies and atrocious cruelties, Omdurman, which lies across the Nile from Khartoum, is now a quiet native city of mud houses.
>
> – *Round Africa Cruise brochure*

Bert – March 21, 1939 – Omdurman, Anglo-Egyptian Sudan

When Mamie told me Gitte Damgaard was made so upset by 'girl talk', my reaction was, 'Says you.'

'OK, Bert, I'll come clean. After all, I only owe the dame my life,' Mamie said. 'Here's the truth. Gitte got a little deep into the giggle water . . .'

'This time of day?' Bert said.

'Bert, remember, we're all on vacation, and she *has* been shooting people. She's entitled to a stiff one or two. And, don't worry, I haven't been matching her.'

Maybe so, but it wasn't because Mamie couldn't. I once saw her drink an Irish longshoreman under the table at a wedding party in Cleveland where the booze was free and there wasn't much in the way of entertainment.

'OK, so?' I said.

'So, the poor bunny is hard as nails on the outside but she's been through a lot. She was in a German concentration camp for a year and a half and guess who the head man there was.'

'Not Major Heissemeyer? On the level?'

'Yeah, Heissemeyer,' Mamie said. 'On the level. And she hated the guy, said she would have killed him, given the chance.'

'Did she say she did it?'

'No.'

'Did she say she didn't?'

'Sure. Do you believe her?'

'No. Do you?'

'Yes. At least, I want to believe it,' Mamie said. 'Why would she spill to me about her past if she did kill him? If I was in her shoes and had killed the guy, I sure wouldn't go around advertising that I had a motive, whether I'd had two drinks or ten or none.'

'Maybe she has a guilty conscience and needed to talk to someone and you were the safest person for that. She did save your life, after all.'

'One thing I'm sure of, Bert, is that she has no reason to have a guilty conscience. From what I've learned about the sadistic little worm, I wouldn't have had a guilty conscience about tossing him into the drink myself.'

The conductor, in a battered cap, dusty (of course) jacket, and bare feet, came into the car just then, bawling 'Khartoum, next stop, Khartoum' like there was any other stop on this line. Shoot, we had not seen so much as an outhouse since we left Port Sudan, yesterday. I tossed a silver ten piastres coin on the table for Mamie's drink and we headed to our sleeper compartment to pack up.

When we reached our car, Steward Grap was hustling along the swaying passage in our direction. 'Ah, Mr and Mrs Mason, I was trying to locate you. We're about to enter Khartoum.'

'I know, Grap. The conductor announced it like we were entering Grand Central Station. We're on our way back to pack.'

'Very well, sir. I will be back for your bags shortly. I've got my own tab to settle in the dining car.' He dashed down the passage.

'I don't know when the young fellow would have had time for a drink,' I said. 'He always seems to be around . . .'

I stopped short in the sliding doorway of our compartment. There, on the floor just inside, was a light blue envelope with 'MRS MASON' written on the front. The envelope was the same type of stationery which had been used to transmit the earlier anonymous message about Herr Blanck. I examined it for any identifying marks and, finding none, slit it open with my penknife. The message inside read:

WILLY WAS HIRED TO KILL YOU

There was no attempt to disguise the block-printed lettering on the pale blue sheet. The handwriting looked to be the same as on the earlier missive.

'What's it say?' Mamie asked.

I handed her the paper. She turned a shade or two paler than she had been, and then straightened and tossed back her shoulders.

'I guess we'll need to be more careful for a while,' she said.

Khartoum itself is not a bad-looking town, if you like the desert. There's still the dust but you can look out on the waters of the Blue Nile and the White Nile and know you wouldn't die of thirst here. The Brits have straightened out the old winding alleys into an orderly grid, and modern steel trestle bridges span each of the lesser rivers before they merge into the great Nile. Modern buildings and a ribbon of shade trees line the riverbanks.

Our accommodations at the Grand Hotel, a venerable British holdover from the last century, are first class. The hotel is situated on the main drag, Nile Street, so we are close to the action. That action is mostly a parade of old men driving pack strings of donkeys, and a smattering of colonials passing in the few automobiles in town. The place has a very civilized air to it, one that won't do for me. I came on this trip for *less* civilization. I can get all the civilization I want at home in New Philadelphia.

That is why I am writing this at a café table in Omdurman, across the Nile from Khartoum. This place is everything Khartoum is not – all low mud-brick buildings and winding streets, the growl and fart of camels in my ears, the stench of garbage, tanneries and spice merchants' shops in my nose. The memory of the Mahdi and his frenzied followers visiting monstrous atrocities on the colonials seems fresh here. I love it.

Mamie took a pass on this expedition, claiming fatigue from the train ride and a desire to nap in a bed that isn't moving for the first time in weeks. I can't say that I blame the old girl. She's been through a lot for me on this trip. When she said she was not coming with me, I told her that I wouldn't leave her alone, but she insisted I go without her, that she would be all right. Steward Grap agreed to watch the door of our room, and the hotel even has a house shamus, a wiry expat with a mustache like that English actor from *Dawn Patrol*, David Niven. I slipped the dick a ten-pound note and asked him to keep an eye on the room while I was away. He raised his eyebrows, pocketed the cash, and settled into a chair at the opposite end of the hallway from Grap. With two guards, I think Mamie's safe while I'm away exploring.

After traipsing around Omdurman's open-sewered streets for the afternoon, inspecting the rugs, gold jewelry, and scimitars for sale, I let myself be led by a pushy tout to this place, thinking I'd have a pick-me-up. What I had in my mind's eye was a cold beer in a frosty mug, but the waiter, he of baggy *jalabiya* and stained apron, told me beer is *haraam*, forbidden in the *Qur'ran* and not served. I ended up with coffee so black it almost came in chunks, made palatable only by the mottled brown sugar cubes the waiter produced when I took my first sip and made a face. At his insistence, I also tried a sweet cake called *basboosa*. It was passable but I wouldn't serve it at a wedding.

I was taking in the street scene and sipping my gritty coffee when a familiar face happened by. Señora de Ribera was accompanied by a local guide, and looked the worse for wear. When she spotted me at the café, she invited herself in. Her guide, a thievish-looking fellow, immediately went to the proprietor and got into an argument, I suspect, over whether he had produced the señora as a customer and was thus entitled to a kick-back. The señora was oblivious to the commotion, dropping gracelessly into the other seat at my table and ordering 'anything cold'. She was dog tired and it didn't help her mood when the waiter appeared with her order, a smudged carafe of tepid *karkadey*, a tea made with hibiscus flowers.

'Is there not one ice cube in this entire country?' she said, her face contorted following her first sip of the cloudy liquid.

'Nary a one, nor a drop of hooch, either,' I said.

'So I understand. Pity. A glass of wine and relaxing at a café as the world parades by is one of the pleasures I miss about my home. In America, we have the wine but no sidewalk cafés. Here there are cafés but no wine. Ah, well, as in all of life, one can't always get what one wants.'

'I pretty much have everything I want in life,' I said. It sounded funny to me when I said it, because nobody spends much time realizing how grateful we should be for what we have. Maybe it's something we should spend more time doing.

'You Americans. You should be satisfied. You have everything.'

'I thought you were an American now, too,' I said.

'Not by choice. Oh, America is fine when you are a European but it is not the same as home. I'm sure most Americans would find Europe less to their liking than the United States, though they could make a life there.'

'Many do,' I said.

'And most of those who do are misfits in America. The ones who are not . . .' Her voice trailed off.

'Never leave? You left Spain, Señora. Did you consider yourself a misfit?'

'No. Nor did my husband, an Argentine by birth and a German by heritage, consider himself a misfit in Germany. We both loved our countries, loved living in them, until they were co-opted by the fascists. We were forced to leave, you see,' she said. 'Leave or die.'

'It can't be as bad as all that,' I said. 'Spain and Germany are civilized countries, not tribal backwaters in Africa.'

'Do not be mistaken, Mr Mason, by the thin veneer of civilization in places like Germany, Spain and Italy. Those places today are no better than the worst tribal fiefdom, run by barbarians and beasts. I know; I have lived in them. You should know, as well, having seen Major Heissemeyer at his best before he met with his accident.'

'He didn't seem so bad. A little full of himself, maybe,' I said, for the second time, following Mother Mason's admonition to never speak ill of the dead, even when they so richly deserved it.

'He lived to threaten and intimidate, relished it, and backed it with brutal force, I can assure you.' Señora de Ribera looked directly in my eyes. 'He threatened me, you know.'

'Mamie told me that,' I said. 'But don't you think it was just an idle threat, just bluster or, as you said, intimidation?'

'No, Mr Mason, I don't think it was mere bluster or intimidation. His kind are capable of anything and one must be prepared to defend oneself against them.'

'No longer,' I said.

'True, the threat has been removed.' She was hard now, as hard or harder than the man who had threatened her and was now dead. 'A fortunate accident.'

Señora de Ribera seemed to have revived rather nicely, whether from the rest, her cloudy tea, or the thought of her vanquished antagonist, I don't know. She rose, tossed piastres in the saucer on the table and crooked a finger to her waiting guide.

'It has been a pleasant respite, Mr Mason. Do give Mrs Mason my regards.'

'Of course, Señora. Good day,' I said.

She moved off serenely, her guide trailing in her wake. Was her serenity a product of Major Heissemeyer's demise? More importantly, I wondered if she was responsible for it.

THIRTY-ONE

> We leave Khartoum late in the afternoon, by special sleeping car train for Wadi Halfa.
>
> – *Round Africa Cruise brochure*

Bert – March 23, 1939 – Wadi Halfa, Anglo-Egyptian Sudan

'It is here that the Pharaohs had their gold mines. From here, below the second cataract of the Nile, the gold was moved to the ancient cities to be worked and turned into the jewelry and the household pieces of Egypt's rulers.' Kashif, our *halfawe* guide, swept his hand to take in the broad expanse of rock-tumbled desert as he said the words. Here and there one could see a worked stone or a tip pile, but the real evidence of the Pharaohs' mine was a broad shallow pit that marred the otherwise unbroken face of the desert.

'Think of doing all of this by hand, Mamie,' I said. 'Just picks and shovels and a man's back to do the work.'

'Sounds like farming to me, Bert.'

'Except they were growing gold,' I said.

'Yes, *ra'us*. And it was the gold from this place that made the riches and the greatness of the Pharaohs,' Kashif said. The words were proud, in a place where there hadn't been much to be proud about since that time.

Suliman, an Egyptian, hissed some sharp words to Kashif in Arabic. The Nubian *halfawe* smiled, and nodded, but his eyes were not smiling.

'What did he say?' Mamie asked of our statuesque local guide. God forbid she let this minor tiff between the two men pass without adding fuel to it. The woman has to know everything.

Kashif, whose English was twice as good as Suliman's, smiled again and said, 'He said that before the Egyptians came, the Nubians were grubbing in the banks of the Nile for worms to eat, and, after the last Dynasty, they returned to the practice until the British came and saved them.'

Suliman grimaced and growled at Kashif, maybe embarrassed that his demeaning words had been translated to the foreigners who were the source of his tips, but he stopped there. Kashif was armed, a slender foot-long dagger sheathed on his belt and an ancient Martini-Henry rifle slung across his broad back. Most of the *halfawes* carried arms, rifles and various pig-stickers, as there was really no law in the area and differences were settled the old-fashioned way.

The weaponless Suliman knew when to quit. He returned to his fallback when dealing with his charges. 'This outing is to your liking, Mr Mason?'

'Indeed, it is, Suliman,' I said. To Kashif, 'Your part of the world is filled with dramatic beauty and wondrous history.' The Nubian beamed. Both guides' egos appropriately massaged, or at least diverted from what I worried might turn into a blood feud, I got to what was really on my mind. 'But I think it may be time for us to return, before the heat of the day.'

'Before?' Mamie said. 'I thought it was already here. It must be ninety-five degrees.'

'Perhaps so,' Suliman said. 'But the full heat is not yet upon us. Perhaps we should return to your camp, if it is to your liking?'

It was to both Mamie's and my liking, so we piled into Kashif's rattletrap Model A, a desert veteran, and crept the ten miles back to Wadi Halfa. Half of the party from the *Columbus* was ensconced in the only hotel in town, a mud-brick way station with string beds, dirt floors, bucket showers and a pedigree reaching back almost to 'Chinese' Gordon's 1884 expedition against the Mahdi. The place had a derelict air about it, enhanced by its clientele of Egyptian traders, desert dwellers waiting for the weekly boat down the Nile to visit relatives or obtain medical care, and a handful of desiccated Westerners who looked like they wanted to be anywhere but where they were.

With the hotel half full when we arrived, Suliman and the crew members from the *Columbus* were confronted with how to house us for the two days before the steamer for the trip down the Nile returned. In efficient German fashion, Herr Blanck had brought along six spacious and clean wall tents for such an eventuality, I suspect because it had happened before.

The ladies were given the first opportunity to bunk in the hotel. Mamie chose not to do so. 'I ain't staying in that chicken coop,' was her response to the offer to share a room with Gitte Damgaard and Beatta Schon. Mamie's response was prescient; by the second day, Señora de Ribera, Miss Damgaard and Fräulein Schon were rightly complaining of drafty nights, sullen service and threadbare bedding lively with the local insect population.

The tent-dwellers, consisting of Mamie and me, Bunky and Jack Olsen, Stewards Grap and Stockfisch, Suliman, Purser Blanck, Herr Kletz, and two other couples not well known to us, had an Arabian Nights experience. Our tents were commodious, warm in the desert night and pleasantly shaded by date palms in the daytime heat. The camp was outside town, slap on the bank of the great Nile. Suliman procured a local cook, a giant Nubian woman who had mastered cooking over the open fire she kept burning day and night. She fed us with a constant outpouring of fried Nile perch, a kind of bean dish she called *fuul*, bread baked in an ingenious oven she constructed using nothing but mud and water, and dates from the very trees under which we were camped. Suliman supplemented her services with three camp-boys, who toted water, brought firewood, served meals and saw to our every need.

The stewards and Herr Blanck supervised at first but soon, seeing our needs effortlessly met by the cook and camp-boys, lapsed into a hang-about-camp lethargy. After the first day, when the mid-morning heat struck, they could be seen lounging like the rest of us against goat-skin pillows on the thick-carpeted floors of their tents, idly eating dates and drinking tea from glass-and-silver cups.

'This place isn't so bad, Bert,' Mamie said on our last night. We were sitting in two camp chairs near the crackling fire to ward off the gentle crispness of the early evening. The stars were a swath of diamonds overhead. Down by the river, the giant cook washed our dinner dishes, singing a throaty tune with no distinguishable words.

'No, Mamie, it ain't. It's pure Arabian Nights, is what it is,' I said. 'The only thing missing is a genie. I already have my Scheherazade.'

'You are a smooth talker, Bert. This Africa stuff seems to suit you . . .' she began, only to be interrupted by a man's voice shouting from one of the nearer tents, followed by the short snap of a pistol shot.

I got up from my chair and ran to the sound of the gunfire, Mamie close on my heels.

THIRTY-TWO

> This day will include the camp where the Bisbareen have their tents.
>
> – *Round Africa Cruise brochure*

Mamie – March 23, 1939 – Wadi Halfa, Anglo-Egyptian Sudan

No one was more surprised than me when Bert shot the purser. True, you could not have knocked me over with a feather this time because it was the second time I had seen him do it. But, unlike the first time, this time it was real.

I knew it was real when I saw Herr Blanck drop to the carpeted ground, clutching his hand to his chest, just like he had done when Bert shot him with the funny little starter's pistol and he was playacting. Only this time, fresh crimson blood seeped between his fingers. This time, he shuttered and choked, and foamy spittle, pinked by blood, painted his agonized rictus. This time, the radiance of life faded swiftly away, leaving unseeing eyes.

I wanted to cry out but I could not; my scream caught in my throat at the sight of Bert clutching the shiny automatic, still smoking, that he had picked from the floor of the tent and used to shoot Herr Blanck.

Bert turned to me, standing behind him just inside the tent. The flap had dropped closed after I had entered. 'I had to do it,' he said. 'He was about to stab Grap. You saw it, didn't you, Mamie?'

I had seen it. When Bert ran to the sound of gunfire, I ran after him, grabbing at him and trying to pull him back from his rush toward unknown danger like any good wife would. He pulled away and I stumbled and fell and then was up and in the flap of Herr Blanck's tent right behind Bert. Herr Blanck had Grap down on the floor and a knife with a heavy, grooved blade raised above him. When the purser plunged the knife, Grap parried it with his hands, and the knife missed. Herr Blanck raised the blade for a second thrust, and it was then that Bert bent, picked the automatic from the carpet and fired in the same motion. If Bert hadn't shot, Herr Blanck would surely have stabbed the prone steward. Bert had acted in defense of Steward Grap's life.

There was the sound of confused voices off in the darkness. Steward Grap jumped to his feet. 'Listen to me, Mr and Mrs Mason. This is very important and we only have a moment. Herr Blanck was a Nazi agent, a spy. I am a British agent. Herr Blanck discovered my identity and was trying to kill me. You did the right thing by shooting him. You saved my life. But if we tell the truth about what happened, my status will be found out and I will be imprisoned when we return to the ship. We must tell the same story about what happened – that we heard a shot, and came here to find Herr Blanck dead by his own hand. It appeared he was cleaning his gun when it discharged. Indeed, it discharged a second time when Mr Mason picked it up from beside his body just now. There are no authorities to speak of here. If we all tell the same story, they must believe it.' Grap looked anxiously from me to Bert. 'You saved my life just now. Please, please save it again.'

Nothing moved for a few seconds that seemed like forever. I could hear the blood pounding in my ears. The voices outside drew near. Finally, Bert said, 'OK, Grap.'

The steward-spy looked to me.

'OK,' I said.

Grap rushed to Bert and took the gun from his hands, careful to handle it with a handkerchief. He racked the slide to eject the unfired shell in the chamber, palmed it, and withdrew the clip which carried the remaining ammunition. He placed the gun, clip and the single bullet back on the carpet at Bert's feet. He moved quickly to the purser's body, picked up the knife and, with a practiced motion, slipped it into his boot. He then rummaged in Blanck's small valise and came out with a metal box, opened it and spilled the contents – some cloth patches, a short metal rod with a wire brush on the end, and a small screwdriver – next to the body.

'Herr Blanck, are you all right?' a quavering voice called from just on the other side of the tent canvas. I looked to Steward Grap, who nodded. I drew back the tent flap.

Outside stood Steward Stockfisch, clad in a hastily donned shirt and pants, his feet bare. He was trembling like a puppy. Suliman was behind him, interested but hardly as rattled, and careful to place Stockfisch between him and any danger, in the form of gunfire or other peril, which might remain in the tent. There was a general hubbub in the camp as others emerged from their tents, drawn by the shots and the shouting.

Steward Grap took the initiative. 'Herr Blanck has been shot. He has a gunshot wound to his chest. He is dead. It appears he was cleaning his gun when it discharged. Mr and Mrs Mason and I heard the shot and arrived here at the same time. We called for Herr Blanck and, when he did not respond, we entered.' Grap flicked his eyes almost imperceptibly toward Bert. Bert said nothing.

Stockfisch's voice squeaked when he said, 'I will get Herr Kletz.' He dashed off into the night.

'This is a most calamitous event, Mr Mason,' Suliman said to Bert. 'But it appears there is nothing that could have been done to prevent this accident.'

'That is, sadly, true,' Steward Grap said, providing Suliman with his needed validation and cementing the story of the death as an accident. Suliman executed a slight bow, incongruously, satisfied to be absolved of even peripheral responsibility. No one mentioned the fact that there had been two shots.

Herr Kletz, as third officer the youngest and least experienced of the *Columbus*'s officer corps, ran up breathlessly, trailed by Stockfisch. Mere steps behind them, Kashif walked purposefully, his Martini-Henry at port arms, his eyes those of a man who had moved to the sound of gunfire before and was prepared for whatever it now brought.

To his credit, Herr Kletz did not hesitate, rushing to where the purser lay and checking for a pulse. Finding none, he turned to the small knot of onlookers gathered at the tent door and said, 'What happened?'

Steward Grap repeated the story he had told Stockfisch moments before, with precision and just a touch of manly emotion in his voice, upset but willing and able to do his duty. He was one cool customer.

As was Bert. He stayed silent, shook his head affirmatively at the correct times to confirm Grap's tale, and was otherwise composed.

As was I. It was almost as if it was all a clever play like the one put on during the first days aboard the *Columbus*. I wondered, too, if Bert and I had just participated in the first skirmish of the war to come, with Herr Blanck as the Third Reich's first casualty. And whether we had unconsciously chosen the side on which the United States would later participate.

One of the group of onlookers – Kashif – proved more astute than his companions in the tent doorway. 'I heard two shots,' he said. I noted that his rifle was still at the ready position.

Grap was quick to squelch the Nubian's curiosity. 'The second shot came after the Masons and I found Herr Blanck,' he said. 'I was checking Herr Blanck for signs of life and asked Mr Mason to secure the gun – which was still in Herr Blanck's hand – and unload it. As he was doing that, the gun discharged a second time. See here,' – he pointed to a tear in the canvas wall of the tent – 'the bullet exited here. We were very lucky that a second person was not hurt. I remember Herr Blanck mentioning that the automatic had a hair trigger and that when we returned to New York he intended to take it to a gunsmith to see if the trigger pull could be adjusted.'

Kashif took in the information without comment and with precious little concern. I wondered if he saw the death of this stranger to his land as anything more than an inconvenience.

Herr Kletz, returning to cognizance of his role as ranking officer, said, 'We must notify the local police. Suliman, who do we contact?'

Suliman, satisfied that no fault for this foreigner's death would fall on him, was quick to pass the buck. 'Kashif will know the proper authorities.'

'Indeed, I do. The governor-general in Khartoum is Sir George Stewart Symes,' Kashif recited.

'No, Kashif, the local authorities,' Herr Kletz said.

'Mistah Orde Jameson is the governor-general's representative from the Sudan Political Service in Wadi Halfa. He is the magistrate here.'

'Good,' the third officer said. 'Send one of the camp-boys to fetch him.'

'Mistah Jameson is not here. He was taken sick with malaria and left for the hospital in Cairo on the last steamer north, last week. There has been no replacement for him sent yet.'

'What about police?'

'There are no police. The Sudan Defense Force garrison in town administers order. Lieutenant Allen is in charge.'

'Send a boy for him, then.'

Kashif dispatched two camp-boys, dashing into the velvet midnight. Two hours later, one returned with word that, as the victim was already dead and the shooting was purely accidental, Lieutenant Allen would arrive in the morning. Apparently an interrogation of the camp-boys had satisfied Allen that there was no need to rush.

'It makes no sense for you to stay up all night waiting, Mr and Mrs Mason,' Herr Kletz said upon hearing this news. 'Try to get some sleep. Steward Grap can see to anything you need. Steward Stockfisch and I will stay with Herr Blanck's . . . remains.'

Steward Grap trailed Bert and me out of the tent and into our own. Once inside, he whispered, 'I am sorry you became involved in this. And I am grateful that you have chosen to protect me. I owe you my life, Mr Mason.'

Bert had been calm about the events of the night until now, but when he raised his hand to his brow I saw that it was trembling.

'Here, Bert, sit down,' I said, steering him to the side of one of our cots. Then, to Steward Grap, 'You have some explaining to do. And it better be good.'

'Of course,' Grap began, and I couldn't help but notice when he spoke that his accent made a subtle shift from its previous guttural German bent to a more British English. How much of that was for the benefit of the story we were about to be told, I wondered. Or was it just nervousness?

THIRTY-THREE

> We have arranged an extensive program of Sightseeing Drives and Shore Excursions, including trips overland.
>
> – *Round Africa Cruise brochure*

Bert – March 24, 1939 – Outside Wadi Halfa, Anglo-Egyptian Sudan

I was pretty shook up. I'd never shot a man, and now I had killed one. Sure, it was for the defense of another man's life, and justified, but saving Steward Grap didn't lessen the impact of what I had done to Herr Blanck. And the story Grap told in those few seconds before the others in the camp arrived – I didn't know what to think or believe. I was kind of numb and I went along with it. It sank in fast when we got back to our tent. I was glad Mamie was along and took the bull by the horns.

'You want the story. Here it is, the unvarnished truth,' Grap said, lowering himself to sit on the cot opposite Mamie and me. 'I am a British agent, an operative of Section D of the Special Intelligence Service. I was placed aboard the *Columbus* to monitor its movements and to determine the sympathies of its officers and men in the event of a war between Great Britain and Nazi Germany.'

'Why ever in the world is that important enough to kill or be killed for?' Mamie asked.

'When the war comes,' Grap said, 'and it *will* come, despite the prime minister's pap about peace in our time, the movement of the large numbers of troops necessary for its prosecution will take place by sea. The existing warships and troop transports of both Germany and England will be insufficient for the task. The slack will be taken up by civilian ocean liners pressed into naval service. There are a mere handful of such civilian ships available to Germany, among them the *Columbus* and her sister ships *Bremen* and *Europa.* Denying a few or even one of these ships to the Nazi war effort could mean the difference between success and failure. If troops cannot be transported to the battlefront, there is no need to defeat them.

'My job is to report the whereabouts of the *Columbus* so that her return to her home port can be prevented if she is caught outside Germany at the start of the war, and, ideally, to create a situation where her crew, or those of it with the correct sympathies, might even deliver the ship to Great Britain to be used on the British side.'

'Why don't you simply travel as a passenger?' Mamie asked.

'In the event of a conflict, the passengers would probably be disembarked at a neutral port. The crew, on the other hand, would be needed to operate the ship. Even stewards such as myself.'

'Well, what did poor Herr Blanck have to do with this?' Mamie said.

'He was a Nazi agent, doing on the German side what I was tasked to do for Mother England. He was also supposed to locate and eliminate any British agents aboard the *Columbus.* He was about to do just that when Mr Mason saved my skin.'

'How did he manage to find you out, Grap?' I said.

'That I don't know, Mr Mason. I just know that he confronted me this evening as I walked by his tent on the way back to my own. He invited me in, a sure breach of command protocol on board ship, but out here . . .' Grap shrugged. 'I played the subordinate and stepped inside. It was then that he drew his pistol and confronted me about being a spy. He had the evidence. He had been in my footlocker in my tent. It has a false bottom where I kept a codebook. He had it, showed it to me.

'I knew I was done for. It would either be transportation back to Germany and prison for espionage, or a midnight walk along the Nile with a bullet to the back of the head and a shove into the river. The latter was not a pleasant prospect and the former not much better, really only a delay in the ultimate result.

'So I took a chance, made a lunge for his gun and was able to knock it away from him as he tried to shoot me. That was the shot that brought you and Mrs Mason to his tent. I had my own weapon, a boot knife, and managed to draw it while we grappled, but Blanck, or whoever he was, took it away and . . . well, that was where the two of you came in.'

'Not smart, Grap, bringing a knife to a gun fight, and then having even that taken away from you,' I said.

The steward-spy hung his head. 'I was one of the worst in my training group when it came to hand-to-hand combat. But I excelled at deception and clandestine operations.'

'Or so you thought,' Mamie said. 'It looks like Herr Blanck found you out completely.' Her eyes narrowed. 'Any chance he wasn't working alone?'

'Most operatives work alone. I suppose there could have been someone assisting him but it is unlikely. After all, the Nazis already had someone keeping a very public eye on the *Columbus*.'

'You mean Major Heissemeyer?' No flies on Mamie.

'Yes. And Lieutenant Haas.'

'Do you think they knew about you?'

'Truthfully, no,' Grap said. 'If they had found me out, there would have been a public arrest with a lot of show. Major Heissemeyer couldn't have passed up that opportunity.'

I thought about that for a minute and decided he was right. And, if Major Heissemeyer had known Grap to be a spy, the odds are he would have clued in Lieutenant Haas. I considered whether Steward Grap might have been the one who pushed Major Heissemeyer over the side and decided he had not. Major Heissemeyer wouldn't have confronted Grap without plenty of muscle, in the form of Lieutenant Haas, backing him up. And Grap was not on the *Columbus* to kill people, at least not pompous majors who, when you got right down to it, were not vital to the Nazi cause. No, the young steward hadn't shoved Heissemeyer into the drink.

Mamie, God bless her, bore in like a terrier with a rat. 'OK, suppose we buy all that. Why should we help you and what happens from here?'

'As I said, the next war is coming.' Grap, or whatever his name was, studied Mamie's face and then mine. 'It will be the second World War. Make no mistake, the United States of

America will be fully involved in it. Isolationism, behind a wall, a border, or an ocean, is a thing of the past. America will have to pick a side. You heard the Nazi philosophy from Major Heissemeyer. Is that your side? Or do you belong with Britain, the home of your forefathers? You fired a shot, Mr Mason, maybe a shot unknown to the world, and probably not the first shot in the upcoming war, but you picked a side when you fired it. The right side. The just side. The side of light, of democracy, of humanity. Continue on that road. Help me complete my mission.'

Steward Grap never took his eyes from mine as he waited for my answer. With more information and more time for reflection, I found my answer was the same as it had been a few hours before. I nodded affirmatively.

'Good,' Grap said. 'Now, Mrs Mason, here is what comes next. In the morning—'

'Just one thing, Steward Grap,' Mamie interrupted.

'Yes, Mrs Mason.'

'If you didn't kill Major Heissemeyer, and I don't think you did, then the killer is still among us, here or on the *Columbus*. The killer, it seems, wants me dead. I want to come out of this vacation, and I use the term loosely' – a sidelong glance in my direction – 'alive.'

'Yes, ma'am?'

'You can get information.'

'Ma'am?'

'You can get information about people, can't you? Through your intelligence network?'

'Not here, no.'

'But in port. In the ports yet to come, in Cairo, Villefranche, Naples, Gibraltar?' Where was Mamie going with this?

'I suppose I could. If it was essential to my mission. I suppose I could cable to the section offices for information.'

'Consider it essential to your mission, Steward Grap or Mr Mata Hari or whatever your name is. When we get to Cairo, Bert and I will give you the names of a number of persons we suspect of killing Major Heissemeyer, and you'll cable your spy home office for information on each of them. And when you get the goods, you'll share everything – and I mean everything – with Bert and me. Or we can share the information about who you are with Herr Kletz and the soldier boy coming over to investigate Herr Blanck's untimely demise. What's his name, Bert?'

'Lieutenant Allen,' I said.

'That's right. Lieutenant Allen of the Sudan Defense Force.'

Grap was one cool joe. 'I can assure you, Mrs Mason, that a lieutenant of the Sudan Defense Force is not going to turn an SIS operative over to the Germans.'

'True. But your cover would be blown and your mission over. You would have failed.'

'Point taken, Mrs Mason. All right, you shall have your information, however much I am able to obtain. I assume then that I shall be able to keep my cover intact.'

'And Bert won't be implicated in the shooting of Herr Blanck to save your neck,' Mamie said.

'Correct.'

Mamie smiled. 'Then we have an understanding, Steward Grap.'

Sometimes the woman truly frightens me.

THIRTY-FOUR

> We leave Wadi Halfa by steamer for a leisurely voyage down the Nile.
>
> – *Round Africa Cruise brochure*

Mamie – March 24, 1939 – Outside Wadi Halfa, Anglo-Egyptian Sudan

Dawn broke cool, desert clear and dazzling blue, a stunner of a day that would have had me excited to begin the steamer trip down the Nile if I hadn't been so worried about Bert. As it was, I just hoped nothing wrong would slip out of Grap, or Bert, or me to delay our departure, or worse, cause us to be put in custody. I knew a man was dead, but he had it coming, being a Nazi and being about to kill Steward Grap on top of that. I just wanted to get as far as possible away from Wadi Halfa.

Bert and I had both drifted off to sleep in the late wee hours, and had slept in our clothes. Steward Grap had slipped away while we slept but returned at dawn, stubble-chinned and red-eyed but otherwise none the worse for wear, with my cuppa joe. He was back to being a deferential steward, his spy persona shed sometime in the mystic hours before sunrise, as a mamba sheds its skin.

I sat inside the tent, drinking down the bitter Arab brew, and trying to puzzle out the man who had brought it to me. There were some things that didn't quite make sense. Why was Grap at one point afraid to be returned to the *Columbus* and be carted off to a German concentration camp, and then, only an hour or two later, certain that the as-yet-to-appear Lieutenant Allen of the Sudan Defense Force would never let him be taken away by the German wolves? I supposed that when he first worried, he was unsure if the local gendarmerie would be Brits, or some more casual, and bribable, locals. He did, nonetheless, want to avoid giving the truth about the circumstances to Lieutenant Allen, even when he saw Allen as providing a safety net in the event the Germans learned of his true identity.

In the end, I put it down to a spy just being a spy and wanting to maintain his cover in all events, even when dealing with those who could be counted upon to be friendly to his cause. That was how we had left it, just before four in the morning, when we three had confirmed, and thrice-confirmed, the story we would tell today.

The big Nubian cook had just dished out a breakfast of millet porridge, fresh-baked bread from her trusty clay oven, and dates when the long-awaited Lieutenant Allen arrived.

I must say, after all the preparation work we three had done, Lieutenant Allen was a disappointment. He shambled into camp, trailed by two tall native soldiers carrying even taller rifles. The soldiers were in shabby wool tunics, short pants, and, as it seemed with every native policeman and soldier on the continent, were barefooted. Lieutenant Allen matched the panache of his underlings, sporting long, dirty pants, scuffed boots, and a half-buttoned bush jacket which exposed a gray singlet underneath. He had tried to shave, evidenced by the hacked flesh on his face covered by bits of that rarest of commodities in the Sudan, toilet paper. The failure of his efforts was doubly confirmed by scraggly wedges of whisker along his right jowl and by his Adam's apple.

'Right, now, where's the poor bugger who shot himself?' Lieutenant Allen said by way of introduction, followed by, 'I say, is that fresh bread I smell?'

'Would you and your men care for some, sir?' Steward Grap asked. He was still in obsequious-servant mode.

'I would. Can't speak for the fuzzy-wuzzies. Never know what's going on in their heads.' Lieutenant Allen seated himself at the breakfast table, leaving his men momentarily confused until they reverted to parade rest on their own.

'Who saw what happened, then?' Lieutenant Allen said, chewing with his mouth open. The flower of the British officer corps, I surmised, must end up in places other than Anglo-Egyptian Sudan.

'I did,' Grap spoke up. 'Together with Mr and Mrs Mason here.'

'Well, spill, lad.' Lieutenant Allen made a boarding-house reach for a bowl of dates at the far corner of the table.

Steward Grap did just that, launching into a ten-minute recitation of the story which had its beginnings in those first moments in Herr Blanck's tent, with the pistol shot still ringing in our ears, and which had been refined to believable perfection in the hours before dawn.

When the steward-spy finished, Allen turned to Bert. 'Is that what happened?'

'It is,' Bert said. His somber eyes were bloodshot, I noticed.

Lieutenant Allen did not notice, or did not care. Nor did he care to question me, not even bothering to glance in my direction. 'Bad business,' he said. 'Poor bugger. Well, he's not the first, nor will he be the last to be shot by his own weapon handled in a careless manner. What do you plan to do with him?'

Apparently the investigation, or inquest, or whatever it might be called, was over, with the verdict being accidental death.

'Do with him?' Herr Kletz, until now silent, asked.

'The remains, man. The body. Do you intend to take it with you? No refrigeration on the steamer, you know, and not enough ice in Wadi Halfa to pack around him for the trip downstream. Hell, not enough ice for a cool gin-tonic in the whole bleedin' town, if it can be called that.'

Herr Kletz looked to the two stewards, and then around the table, hoping someone would make the decision for him and realizing no one would. 'I guess he will have to be buried here,' he finally said.

'Fair enough.' Lieutenant Allen pushed himself up from the camp table. 'I'll need his passport, for my report. There are no Christians here, so if anyone's to say words over him, it'll need to be one of you. The cemetery is west of town. I'm sure your camp-boys can do the necessary digging. Thanks for the breakfast.' After Herr Kletz turned over Blanck's passport, Allen rose and turned to go.

Herr Kletz, momentarily panicked, said, 'Wait.'

'Yes, sir?' Lieutenant Allen said, turning back to the third officer.

'Is that all? I mean, a man is dead.'

'I know. Men die here. They die of Rift Valley fever, malaria, drowning, river blindness, accident, fighting, and drunkenness. They die from snake bite, from scorpion sting, from robbery, and dysentery. They die of heat exhaustion, of loneliness, of sheer boredom and of despair. They die by their own hand, by the hand of others, and by the hand of God. This is Africa. Men die here. Good day.' The lieutenant walked out of camp, his two soldiers following, rifles at port arms.

We buried Herr Blanck in the rubble-strewn cemetery of Wadi Halfa at ten that morning. Herr Kletz said a few words in German over the body and the camp-boys began shoveling rock and dusty soil over it as soon as we turned our backs to leave.

The steamer from Aswan arrived at noon.

We departed Wadi Halfa at one in the afternoon.

Pia de Ribera, Gitte Damgaard and Beatta Schon decided that the hotel in Wadi Halfa was not so bad after all. At least no one had been shot and died there, although they all had a healthy dose of fleas, to be cured only by a fumigated laundering of all their clothing. And a vigorous washing, I assume, of their hair and . . . other parts in the tin washbasins provided in each of their cabins.

Now we four sat at a wicker table beneath the canvas sunshade on the fantail of the Nile steamer *Sudan*, sipping tea. We were somewhere south of Abu Simbel. Bert, now loath to separate himself from me for even a short time, was dozing on a deck chair just out of conversational earshot. When he first sat down, he was out of the sun, but the *Sudan* rounded a bend in the river and, for the better part of an hour, most of his face had been in the intense Egyptian sun and had turned a mottled red. If he didn't wake soon, I would need to rouse him or he'd be burned badly and I'd have to listen to him whine about it.

'Did you know that this boat was the model for the steamer in Mrs Christie's *Death on the Nile*?' Señora de Ribera said, lifting a cucumber sandwich from the platter in the middle of the table.

'What is *Death on the Nile?'* Gitte Damgaard asked.

'Why, a mystery novel published in the US last year.'

'I had no time for novels last year,' Miss Damgaard said with a thousand-yard stare out over the motionless river. Green cane lined the banks in this area, the wild vegetation a contrast to the usual cultivated fields of cotton, barley and wheat. For the first time since leaving Wadi Halfa, there was not a farmer behind a plow drawn by oxen in sight. I expect this is how much of the Nile appeared in the time of the Pharaohs.

'I adore novels, so filled with romance and exotic places,' said a dewy-eyed Beatta Schon. Her beau, the reptilian Lieutenant Haas, had stayed with the *Columbus*, so Fräulein Schon had found time to be with the rest of us ladies. I understood it. I was young once, too.

'*Death on the Nile* was about romance. And murder.' Señora de Ribera spoke the last word with a certain relish.

'Thank God we've had no murder on this voyage. Death, sadly, yes,' Fräulein Schon said. 'The accidents suffered by Major Heissemeyer and Herr Blanck were tragic enough, but at least they were not murder.'

Gitte Damgaard huffed.

'What does that mean?' I asked.

'Two tragic "accidents" and an attempt on your life, Mrs Mason, in such a small group of people and only a few weeks apart?' Damgaard said. 'That is a great deal of tragedy.'

'Are you saying that they were not accidents?' Fräulein Schon asked.

'We know that the attack on Mamie was not an accident.'

'But that was a . . . a madman,' Beatta Schon protested. 'The incidents involving the *sturmbannführer* and the purser were clearly accidental.'

Unless you saw them, like I had.

Gitte Damgaard could not be dissuaded. 'How could a man as short as Major Heissemeyer accidentally fall over the ship's rail? He would have been hard pressed to climb over it.'

'So you think it was foul play, that someone killed the major?' Señora de Ribera asked.

'He didn't engender warm feelings among his fellow passengers,' Gitte said.

'Oh? Who, for instance?' Pia challenged.

'Herr Huber, for one. Candidly, myself. You as well, Señora.'

'I can assure you that I did not have anything to do with Major Heissemeyer's death.' The señora peered down her aquiline nose at Gitte Damgaard. I wasn't sure if it was anger or mere self-assurance in her eyes. 'I can also guarantee you that Herr Huber is likewise without fault. Now, can you say the same about yourself?'

Fräulein Schon's head swiveled from Pia de Ribera to Gitte Damgaard, eyes wide. My head probably did the same, without the wide eyes. I'd seen a few cat fights before. This looked like one in the making, but there was no reason to go all googly-eyed over it. Stay calm and learn something, I said to myself.

'The assurance I can provide to you, Señora, is that if I wanted Major Heissemeyer gone, my methods would have been much more direct. Like the method I used on Willy the driver back in South Africa.' When she spoke, Gitte Damgaard was as motionless as the Sphinx we were drifting down the Nile hoping to see.

Tension sibilated in the morning air.

'Ladies, ladies.' I was surprised to hear Beatta Schon inject herself, verbally, between her two sparring elders. 'The deaths of Major Heissemeyer and Herr Blanck are tragic enough, without compounding the tragedy by allowing it to create an unseemly rift between us. And on this fine morning.' As she spoke the last words, she swept her arm across the prospect, her gesture taking in the ice blue of the river, the green cane on the banks, and the endless tan of the far horizon. It was a feeble effort but it broke the tension.

'Of course, you are right, Fräulein,' Señora de Ribera said. Gitte Damgaard nodded assent. I, a non-belligerent, looked on in neutral disappointment.

'More tea?' Fräulein Schon moved to pour.

Damn, just when it was about to get good.

THIRTY-FIVE

At Luxor there will be sightseeing with automobile drives.

– *Round Africa Cruise brochure*

Bert – March 25, 1939 – Luxor, Egypt

Sometimes I think Mamie will be late for her own funeral. I know, yesterday was a tough travel day, beginning with our third day aboard the *Sudan*, passing the Philae temples with the first real glimpse of the glories of the Pharaohs, now half submerged by the embankment dam at Aswan. Then the long walk across the dam to the automobiles, the sightseeing trip to the stone quarries and the obelisk, massive, incomplete and forlorn in its hole in the desert, and the final, baking train ride to Luxor. The night at the hotel where we are now was none-too-comfortable, with a small fan in the room the only cooling, and one threadbare blanket for the two of us once the night chill set in.

Today should be a full dose of old Egypt at its finest. Seeing the country as it is now, poor, with its few buildings broken down and its people living hand-to-mouth, makes it hard to imagine what could have happened to bring this country tumbling from where it stood at the apex of the ancient world. What we have seen of the remains of that time is astounding, massive in scale, imposing in structure, monumental in the truest sense of the word. The places we are to see today are supposed to be the finest examples of that past world – Thebes, Karnak, Luxor, and the Valley of the Tombs of the Kings.

If Mamie gets a move on. I guess I can't fault her for luxuriating when she has a chance. There's been no opportunity for a bath since Khartoum; I know I was getting a tad gamey. I cured that with a cold-water sponging in the hotel room's metal tub last night. Mamie, however, insisted on hot water.

That's not an easy thing to acquire anywhere in Africa. It is a particularly alien concept in Egypt. I finally ended up slipping the bellman a pound note early this morning, which resulted in a bucket-brigade of boiling-water-toting urchins shuttling from the hotel kitchen to our room until the tub was full. Now Mamie has been in there for an hour.

'Come on, old girl!'

'Hold your horses, Bert. Sometimes a girl's just got to get clean.'

We sure got our fill of it today, clambering over toppled columns, walking stone streets worn smooth by four thousand years of bare feet, hearing tales of the grandeur and glory of Egypt from guides dressed in rags, and who may not have had a square meal in their entire life. At least they looked like they hadn't.

At Luxor, even I started to give out. Mamie and I found a spot in the rare shade and sat on a tumble of stones that had once been a temple lintel. Soon others from the group joined us. Then up comes Steward Grap, and danged if the fellow didn't produce lemonade in a real, and clean, glass. With ice. In the middle of the desert. He shared out the precious liquid among his charges, arriving at us last, having reserved a generous portion of the ice and lemonade for Mamie and me.

'Sorry, ma'am. Not a cuppa joe but it will have to do,' he said, smiling as he handed Mamie a bedewed glass of clinking cubes and sugary elixir. She pressed the glass against her forehead and sighed with gratitude.

Steward Grap and I had kept things at the master-and-servant level since our long conversation on the night I shot Purser Blanck. But now, as he poured a stream of lemonade on to the cracked ice in my glass, I caught his eye. I had been thinking about some things, and Mamie and I had spent the late hours in our cabin talking about the commitment she had extracted from Grap. I decided it was time we had a further conversation about that commitment, and Mamie's and my involuntary careers as murder investigators. And Grap's career as a spy. 'Thanks, Grap,' I said, then, more quietly. 'Let's talk. Later.'

'Of course, sir,' he said, unblinking. Spy school must teach you that. 'I will be stopping at your compartment on the overnight train to make up the bunks.'

'Perfect,' Mamie said. The lemonade had revived her nicely, and myself as well.

The sun was dropping lower and we passed the rest of the afternoon pleasantly, walking among the ruins.

I could tell we were getting closer to real civilization by the quality of our transportation. The train from Luxor to Cairo, while still drawn by an elderly steam locomotive, was made up of modern Pullman Wagon-Lits, painted yellow. The upholstery on the seats wasn't worn and the gritty desert soil had yet to populate every crack and crevasse in the spiffy railcars.

We boarded and immediately had dinner in the dining car, a plate of something called *kushari* that seemed to have every starch known to man in it, and *kofta*, balls of unidentified ground meat. By now even Mamie had learned not to ask what the meat was when the world-weary waiter placed the food before us.

Mamie had just popped off her sturdy walking shoes and was rubbing her tired toes when Grap tapped on the door. 'I take it you are settling in comfortably, Mr and Mrs Mason,' he said after sliding the compartment panel closed behind him.

'We're fine, Grap,' I said. 'But we'll be back on the *Columbus* soon and I thought we should speak before then.'

'Very well, sir. If you mean about the incident at Wadi Halfa, I assume Herr Kletz will provide his report to Captain Dane. I may be questioned by him or one of the other officers about what occurred, and I intend to provide the same . . . information . . . as I did to the authorities in the Sudan. I assume you and Mrs Mason will, too, if asked.'

'Yes, Grap, we'll stick by you, but that's not what we wanted to talk to you about.'

'What is it then, sir?'

'You made a commitment to Mrs Mason and me that you would obtain information on some of the passengers and crew when we get to Cairo.'

'Mr Mason, I am not certain just how much information I

can obtain for you, let alone whether I should be doing that,' Grap began.

'Steward Grap, I remind you that I saved your hide just a couple days ago and while in the process I didn't stop to decide whether I should be doing it. And I thought you had one of the world's finest intelligence networks at your beck and call.'

'It is. I do. Point taken, Mr Mason. But you do know it will be at some risk to myself, and the need for the information may be questioned by my superiors.'

'I'm sure you'll think of the right words to put them at ease about your request,' Mamie chimed in. I wouldn't have expected her to be a tenth part so diplomatic. 'Now, Bert and I are going to give you the names.'

Steward Grap, knowing by now that Mamie was not to be crossed, took down the names as she recited them to him. 'I can send a cable at Cairo, before we board the *Columbus*,' he said. 'But I probably won't have any response before we arrive in Naples, or maybe even as late as Gibraltar.'

'Do what you can, Grap.'

'Yes, sir.' He turned to leave.

'And, Grap,' I said. 'You are the one who slipped the two notes under the door, on the *Columbus* and on the train from Port Sudan, aren't you?'

The steward-spy stopped in his tracks. I could feel more than see him weighing whether he should lie to me. It only took him a moment to decide.

'Yes, sir,' he said, and continued, to provide his justification. 'You see, sir, I believed Herr Blanck had killed Major Heissemeyer as a part of his mission on the *Columbus*. Ever since the Nazis gained power, there has been infighting between the SS and the other German intelligence agencies. The SS, the Abwehr, elements of the SD inside the SS, and even the Gestapo – they all hate each other's guts and aren't above killing one another in various twisted efforts to show their loyalty to their Führer. I thought Herr Blanck, on behalf of a rival agency, had done in the major as part of the latest episode of that infighting. And as for his hiring Willy to kill Mrs Mason . . . well, that was only my speculation.'

'But you were willing to point us in Blanck's direction, despite it being only speculation,' I said. 'I take it from now on we'll have direct conversation about your suspicions and speculations, rather than anonymous notes under our door, Steward Grap.'

'Yes, sir.'

I wish I could say I believed him.

THIRTY-SIX

> At Gizeh, on the edge of the Libyan desert, rise the most celebrated symbols of ancient Egypt – the Pyramids and the Sphinx.
>
> – *Round Africa Cruise brochure*

Mamie – March 26, 1939 – Cairo, Egypt

After all the backwater ports, desert villages and unpopulated ruins we had visited for the last ten days, Cairo reminded me what a country girl I had become. Even rolling into the Cairo railway station was an assault on the senses. While the station was only somewhat over forty years old, it seemed to contain a full four thousand years of Egyptian culture under one roof. Steam trains hissed, camels bellowed, hawkers cried the sale of dates, fake antiquities, and pornographic postcards. Fine European ladies in the latest fashions strolled by legless beggars in rags on the platform. The smells of frying oil, sewage, coal and incense waged a battle for possession of the station's air, the result being nothing remotely breathable inside its walls or for blocks on its exterior. The crowds on the platforms and in the main terminal building jostled, pushed, stroked and grabbed, the local men emboldened by the crowding to cop a feel of any unaccompanied Western woman. Bert and Steward Grap flanked me and several of the ladies to escort us from the platform after Señora de Ribera, importuned by a fat, greasy lecher, slapped the man hard enough to cause exclamation from those in the immediate area. Good for her. I hope his ears are still ringing.

'Had I a switch, I would have beaten him,' the señora huffed. I shudder to think what might have happened if the porcine troll had accosted Gitte Damgaard and her handy, dandy Colt .45.

'Hey, Suliman, let's get out of here before one of us gets arrested,' Bert said.

'I can assure you, Mr Mason, that the transportation and the guides for this afternoon will be much to your liking,' the guide said, non-sequitur, and reassuring to no one but himself.

Once outside the raucous confines of Cairo station, and within the confines of the half-dozen new Packard Super Eight touring cars assigned to us, our little party settled down. The short drive from town was pleasant, if warm and dusty. Maybe I was just becoming accustomed to dust and heat but when I saw those Pyramids and the haunting profile of the Sphinx, it all seemed worth it. Maybe Africa has gotten under my skin and into my soul after all.

Turned loose at the foot of the great monuments, we climbed on their limestone blocks for a story or two. We had our photograph taken in front of the Sphinx by a smooth-talking pitchman with one cloudy eye, an ancient camera, and a promise to have a developed print to the *Columbus* before we sailed. Bert put the odds of that happening at 10 per cent, and gave only even odds that there was any film in the camera at all. We rode a mange-ridden, braying camel for a hundred yards before it dropped to its knees and shook us off. In short, we had a terrific time.

Our companions did as well. For the first time in as long as I can remember, none of them made comments about the others, or fought, or, God forbid, shot or stabbed anyone. They were all just tourists, Bert and I were just tourists, on holiday, with no murders, or Nazis, or threats, or assaults, to concern us.

Steward Grap did not travel to Giza with us. Maybe his absence made it easier to forget all that had transpired on the trip until now. He had parted from us at the Cairo rail station, ostensibly to ready our cabins on the *Columbus*. But, as he was turning from the rank of touring cars at the station entrance, I made sure to remind him of his promise to obtain information on Bert's and my list of suspects in Major Heissemeyer's murder, and to reiterate the specific names for him.

'Of course, ma'am. I shall visit the cable office and make the request of my superiors before I return to the ship,' he said, as sincere, I supposed, as a spy could ever be.

The eye of Ra, that is, the sun – see, I did learn something from all the jabbering Suliman did during the ride to Gizeh – was lowering in the hazy western sky by the time the column of Packards approached the docks of Port Said, and the welcoming profile of the *Columbus* came into view. After the tents and the train cars of the many days of our desert expedition, the navy-blue-hulled ship looked like home to me.

'Old man,' I said to Bert. 'It's gonna feel good to kick off these sensible brogans and spend a couple of days staring out at blue water instead of tan dust.'

'That is the truth, ain't it, Mamie? But you go on without me when the car stops at the gangway. I've got business to take care of before we sail.'

'Business? What business?' The king of the jungle was suddenly all about business?

'I have to send a cable.'

'A cable? To who?'

'Just back home, to Polish Katie. Something I forgot before we left.' Bert evaded about as well as he always evades. I decided to let it pass. It had been a long day and, if he wanted to spend the end of it wandering off to the telegraph office to wire crop instructions to the help, he could have it.

'Fine,' I said. 'I'm going to soak my feet.'

THIRTY-SEVEN

> With Naples, the very brightness of the sky and sea seem to have produced in the city not merely a merciless contrast of light and shadow, but a brilliancy of color, and a noisy and exciting animation that makes of its streets a pageant that cannot be matched elsewhere in Western Europe.
>
> – *Round Africa Cruise brochure*

Bert – March 29, 1939 – Naples, Italy

I am going to miss Africa. The sights – the wine-violet tinge of the slope of Table Mountain in the setting sun, the lush surroundings of Mombasa, the stark, barren desert beyond the Nile. The sounds – the call of the muezzin, the grunt and bleat of a lagoon full of contented hippos, the cadence of drums in the night. Even the smells – rank rivers in the dull heat of the afternoon, the perfume of forest blooms, the unwashed funk of the crowded warrens of the few cities.

I will definitely not miss some things Mamie and I encountered in Africa – the death, the danger, the terror of an assault, and the horror of killing a man, no matter the necessity and the justifiability of that killing. I resolved to leave those things behind when we cleared the harbor entrance at Port Said, and thought I had until Mamie and I received a summons from Captain Dane, through his usual messenger, the bewhiskered Herr Lau.

So, while the *Columbus* steamed across the moonlit Mediterranean, and our fellow passengers slept off the rigors of a month on the Dark Continent, Mamie and I made another midnight pilgrimage along the now-familiar corridor to the closet entrance of Captain Dane's cabin. Our knock was answered by Herr Lau, who escorted us to the captain.

Captain Dane skipped the formalities. 'You and Mrs Mason

have a very unlucky tendency to be nearby when death visits this cruise, Mr Mason.'

'I can assure you that it is not by choice, Captain,' I said.

Dane nodded and turned to Mamie. 'My apologies, Mrs Mason, for what must have been a most upsetting experience for you.'

'I think I'll get through it,' she said, melted to a puddle of jello by Dane's soulful eyes. At least, she tells me they are soulful.

'You must forgive me for bringing you in like this tonight,' Dane continued. 'It concerns Herr Blanck's tragic death. While I have the reports of the crew members on what transpired on your shore excursion, and have spoken directly with Steward Grap and Herr Kletz concerning the incident, I wanted to confirm their accounts of the matter with you.'

'Of course,' I said, and proceeded to repeat the story Grap, Mamie and I had agreed on in the tent at now-far-away Wadi Halfa. I was getting good at it, so good that – when I finished – it didn't feel like a lie. For a few seconds.

When I was done, Dane said, 'Is that how you remember it, Mrs Mason?'

'Yes.'

'That comports with what Steward Grap said, as well.' Dane shook his head. 'A sad and unfortunate occurrence. Herr Blanck was a good officer and an amiable companion, though this was only his second cruise on the *Columbus.* I suppose the one consolation is that it appears he did not have any immediate family. A search of his effects on board revealed no correspondence, no information about next of kin, no connections ashore of any kind. Ah, well, I wired the Norddeutscher Lloyd line home office before we left Port Said. Perhaps they will have some information about him and be able to find his family. A shame, though, to consign him to a lonely grave so far from home and country.'

Mamie and I returned to our cabin, and she was asleep when her head hit the pillow. I tossed and turned, thinking about old Blanck, or whoever he was, below that pile of stones out in the black cold of the Sudan desert.

* * *

The docking of the *Columbus* still holds a fascination for me, even though I have seen it numerous times on this voyage. Maybe it is the delicate maneuvering it takes to get the big lady so neatly into her berth. Maybe it is the promise of a new port and a new land to explore that each landfall holds. Or maybe, as in this morning, it is a way to rush along the beginning of a new day and cut short a night of fitful sleep punctuated by unhappy dreams.

At five in the morning in the early Mediterranean spring, there was more darkness than light, a hint of gray in the east being only a suggestion of the approaching dawn. More light came from lamps on the quay, illuminating figures scampering to catch the *Columbus*'s lines. Shouts in Italian from the dock were answered in German or English by the ship's deck crew, neither understanding the other and neither needing to, each so well trained in their respective roles that the entire process resembled an intricate folk dance, with lines and hawsers as props for the tale the dance told.

'The men on deck, they know their jobs, do they not?' a voice on my left said in German-accented English. 'Though you cannot let them know that or they will begin thinking they are better than my engine room boys, which certainly is not true.'

Turning toward the voice, I recognized the hulking figure as one I had not seen for nearly a month. 'King Neptune! What brings you to the surface from your watery realm?'

'Not King Neptune, sir, except for one day of each southern voyage of my dear *Columbus*. Heinrich Becker, sir,' the chief fireman said, extending a great paw of a hand to me.

'Bert Mason, former polliwog,' I said as we shook.

'I usually do not see passengers out and about at this hour, Mr Mason.'

'Couldn't sleep. And I like to see the crew handle the ship.'

'Professionals all, Mr Mason. Most of the boys aboard *Columbus* were in the Kaiserliche Marine in the last war, at least the old salts. Let us all hope we are spared from the next.'

'Do you think there will be a next war?'

'There is always a next war, Mr Mason. Yes, I think the

next war will come soon. There are those in Germany who lust for war, who see it as the only way to undo the injustice of the last.'

'Do you think that?'

'No. But it does not matter what I think. The Nazis are going to do the thinking for all of us on that issue. Little pricks like Sturmbannführer Heissemeyer are going to have us at war within a year, mark my word. And there is no way to prevent it, unless we can get them to all walk the plank like Heissemeyer did.'

I was beginning to think my suspect list was about to grow by one, but Chief Becker cut that thought short.

'I should not say that,' Becker said. 'A few of them are good sorts, good Germans, if misguided. Take that young Haas, for instance. You are acquainted with him, no?'

'Yes, I met him on this trip. Do you know him?' My antenna went up.

'Not well but well enough. I never met the young man until the night of the equator-crossing ceremony. Drank with him all night, until the man overboard alarm was sounded. Once he was in his cups, it turned out he was no more a Nazi than me, and I am damn sure not one. He is just ambitious, and could not get ahead without joining the party. Doesn't believe any of their tripe, just parrots it to get ahead. Germany could use a few more like him, instead of all the shit-heads like Heissemeyer. Say, look at the sun coming up over Vesuvius!'

The chief fireman pointed east, and it was glorious, a canvas of orange, pink and yellow. We watched in silence for a time, each alone with our respective thoughts. Mine were that one of my primary suspects was a suspect no longer and not even the Nazi he appeared to be. Something told me, though, that the chief's information on Haas might lead Mamie and me to the real murderer.

I just didn't know how.

THIRTY-EIGHT

> Through winter and spring, the Riviera's fashionable seasons, trim white yachts dot the blue harbor at Villefranche, the port of Nice. On shore the red roofs of luxurious villas emerge from masses of foliage.
>
> – *Round Africa Cruise brochure*

Mamie – March 30, 1939 – Villefranche-sur-Mer, France

When Bert told me what he had learned about Kurt Haas, I must confess that I was somewhat relieved that the boy wasn't a true Nazi, and even more relieved that he wasn't the one I had seen shove Major Heissemeyer overboard. It was a good thing Chief Becker spoke up, because until then I was considering the lieutenant a prime suspect. Of course, Haas and the chief's drinking bout left Beatta Schon without an escort and an alibi at the time of Major Heissemeyer's death, and she rose higher on the list of possibles. Still, she is such a little thing, and so nice, that I did not consider it within her capabilities or her nature to kill a man, even a man as small and nasty as Major Heissemeyer.

Macht nichts aus, as the Germans say, because Bert and I decided that our return to the civilized world in Naples should be a celebration. So we painted the town red, walking up and down the cobblestone streets, visiting shops and just gawking our way around, glad to be back in a place where no one rode camels, and where there were no lions outside of town and no crocodiles in the river. Bert bought himself a fine pair of handmade shoes that a cobbler put together in an afternoon. I got some lace that will look nice draped across the tea table in the parlor. We had a lunch of grilled sardines, pasta *al forno*, and red wine from an earthenware pitcher at a hole-in-the-wall joint on a side street with balconies covered in flowers and drying laundry. We didn't talk, or think, about murder, spies, or Nazis for the entire day. It was heaven.

Now that we are on the French Riviera, I am hoping for another day of the same. Well, not exactly the same. Maybe sidewalk cafés instead of holes-in-the-wall, bottles of crisp Viognier instead of jugs of hearty Piedirosso, white tablecloths instead of checkered red. Riviera serene instead of Napoli rough-around-the-edges.

Mid-morning found Bert and me at one of the sidewalk cafés on Rue du Poilu. Steward Grap, who said he would meet us there, told me that '*poilu*' means 'hairy' in French. I wondered why someone would name a road 'hairy', but then Grap explained it was an honored term among the French, referring to their common soldiers in the Great War, the 'hairy ones'. Those frogs, they have some odd ideas.

One idea they have exactly right, though, is the café thing. Bert has taken to it like a duck to water, and I have too, basking in the spring sun, watching the swells and their chic ladies stroll by, staring out across the cascade of terra-cotta roofs down to the cobalt harbor filled with fishing smacks and sailboats. Bert especially likes the coffee they call espresso, which comes in tiny cups, with water and a cookie on the side.

'Fine coffee, Mamie,' Bert said. 'Even if the portions are a mite small.' He was on his third cup and seemed particularly lively this morning, bright-eyed and talkative.

'Here comes Grap,' I said, as the steward approached with a sheaf of cable flimsies in his hand.

'Enjoying the view, Mr and Mrs Mason?' Grap seated himself with his back to the harbor. Without waiting for an answer, he waved the flimsies and said, 'The background information you wanted on your fellow passengers.'

'OK, Grap, spill,' I said.

'Yes, then, where to start? Señora de Ribera, I guess. Much about her you already have. It is confirmed that her husband is Jewish. Much of his and his family's business holdings and real property in Germany have been confiscated, so obviously there is no love of the Nazis on his part or hers. About the only surprise is that the señora is a . . . well, to put it delicately, if she were a man, she would be called a philanderer.'

'A what?' Bert asked.

'A skirt-chaser, Bert,' I said. 'Whatever the equivalent is for a dame. An adventuress, I suppose. That right, Grap?'

'Precisely, Mrs Mason. The information is that she travels for the purpose of indulging that, er, predilection.'

'OK, Grap. Roundheels de Ribera, I get it. What else have you got?'

'Gitte Damgaard is a grifter and a thief, with a penchant for jewels and jewelry. She's bounced around most of the continent, been arrested here and there, was deported from Belgium and has most recently been incarcerated in Germany. She was released shortly before this cruise began, as a matter of fact.'

'I know that. Tell me something new.'

The steward flinched a bit at that. 'That is about it for Miss Damgaard.'

'What about Herr Huber?'

'Herr Huber's story is exactly as he related to you. He has no criminal past but no love of the Third Reich, either.'

'OK. Next.'

'Lieutenant Haas, confirmed Nazi . . .'

'You can skip him, Grap,' I said. 'Unless he has ties to one of the others we haven't heard about. And we've got eyes, we know about his shipboard romance with Fräulein Schon.'

'There are no known ties to any of the others you listed, Mrs Mason.'

'OK, Grap,' I said. 'Let's move on to Herr Blanck . . .'

'Blanck . . . he's dead, Mamie, in case you hadn't noticed.' Bert's expression went sour as he said this.

'I know, Bert, but that doesn't necessarily mean he wasn't Major Heissemeyer's killer.' I turned back to Steward Grap. 'What have you got?'

'Not surprisingly, a pretty plain vanilla report. No criminal past. Steady employment aboard a number of ships since the war. Honorable discharge from the Kaiserliche Marine. And, of course, nothing showing up about his career in espionage, else I would not have found myself in the awkward position I did at Wadi Halfa. My superiors were as surprised about his affiliation with the Nazis as I was.'

'I guess that leaves Beatta Schon,' I said.

'Who is the most squeaky clean of the lot,' the steward said. 'Age nineteen. No criminal record. Trained as an actress but works as a stenographer in a law office. Apparently the acting comes from her mother, now deceased, who was a fairly well-known stage performer in Danzig. The name of her father is unknown. She was born out of wedlock and was raised by an aunt, her mother's unmarried sister, after her mother died when she was three. Her mother was Jewish.'

'That matters,' Bert said. 'That matters a lot given what has been going on between her and Lieutenant Haas.'

'I don't think so,' I said. 'And nothing on her father, you say?'

'No, ma'am. The name of the father was left blank on her birth certificate.'

'OK, Grap. You've kept your end of the bargain. We each have.'

'My thoughts precisely, Mrs Mason. Now, if you will excuse me, I am due back at the ship in fifteen minutes.' Grap stood, gave a nodding bow, and left.

'Whadda ya think, Bert?' I asked as Grap rounded the corner.

'I think, Mamie, our hunch might be right.'

THIRTY-NINE

The Town of Gibraltar, which lies along the water front, is unmistakably English, yet there is little that is actually English in its aspect.

– Round Africa Cruise brochure

Bert – April 1, 1939 – Gibraltar

Our last landfall before returning to New York is also the first where the North German Lloyd line has seen fit to leave us to our own devices, with no scheduled tours, programs or performances. I guess they figure after a month in Africa we ought to be able to manage the staid English personality and balmy Mediterranean climate of Gibraltar without a wet-nurse.

Mamie is off on a mostly ladies' expedition to see the macaque monkeys and explore the famous Rock. I was more than a little dubious about her going with the gaggle, but since the party involved Miss Schon, Señora de Ribera, and Miss Damgaard, leavened and spiced with Bunky Olsen, and with Herr Huber as a male escort, I figured Mamie had the benefit of safety in numbers. She promised not to go off alone and they promised not to allow her off alone, and this isn't, after all, the wilds of Africa.

Gibraltar appeared to be yet another effort by yet another group of transplanted Englishmen to make yet another far-flung outpost of the mother country as English as England, if not more so. As I wandered along Main Street, I saw the Union Jack and its related color scheme displayed at every storefront, sometimes in multiples and often paired with the local ensign, a red castle on a red and white field. There were Morris automobiles in the streets, red telephone booths on the corners, pubs in the alleys, and a changing of the guard, though it takes place at something called the Convent, instead of Buckingham Palace.

My destination was the telegraph office and I found what I had hoped for there. Polish Katie had come through, far more than I had ever expected. It turns out she has a sister in Danzig who was able to provide some extensive background dope on Fräulein Schon. Mamie will be mighty interested in the cable she sent.

Mamie hustled in the cabin door just as the *Columbus*'s horn signaled one-half-hour before departure.

'Did you acquire anything besides sore feet and a sunburn?' I asked as she gave me a pecking kiss and kicked off her brogues at the same time. The cruise had given her a healthy tan. Maybe it was just the short separation of an afternoon apart after spending so many full days together, but I'd missed her. And I saw now that she appeared younger and more vital than she had at the start of the voyage. Who knows, maybe I appear younger than I did at the start, too. Her Jane, me Tarzan.

'You bet your life I did. I thought this was going to be a trip for biscuits, just another sashay around another port town eyeballing monuments and churches,' Mamie said. 'Leave it to Bunky, though. She's no wet sock. She had the girls roaring at lunch with this game – truth, dare, double dare, or promise. It's really a kids' game but Bunky egged us on, calling us a bunch of stodgy old biddies. So we played along with her, right at the café table over sangria and sandwiches. I double-dared Bunky that she wouldn't say a vulgar word and she said "damn" so loudly that the waiter came and hushed us. Then I had to do it, because it was a double-dare, and the maitre d' threatened to throw us out. Then came Señora de Ribera's turn and she chose "truth". So Bunky asked her if she had entertained any gentlemen friends in her cabin during the trip.

'As Bunky says, you could have heard a thousand pins drop. Young Miss Schon sucked in her breath but that was the only sound. I thought the señora would slough it off or simply refuse to answer, but the ice queen just looked right across the table at Herr Huber and said, "Yes. Every night since the equator-crossing ceremony. We have a love of good wine in common. And a taste for a few other good things."

'I tell you, Huber turned so red I thought he was going to pop a cork. Then he jumped up from the table, excused himself, and took off down the street, almost at a run. Señora de Ribera stared after him and said, "Why is it that timid men make the best lovers? I guess because they do what you tell them to do." And just like that, without a flinch, she said, "My turn. Miss Damgaard, truth, dare, double-dare or promise."

'"Truth," Gitte said.

'"Very well, I pose the same question to you as was asked of me."

'Gitte was no flincher, either. She said, "I have entertained no men visitors in my stateroom during the voyage as yet. But I shot a man. Does that count?"

'It shows how on edge everyone was when that remark got us all laughing and broke the tension. At that point Fräulein Schon said she couldn't play the game, and the lunch broke up. I spent the afternoon with Bunky and the fräulein.'

'So what do you think, Mamie?' I asked. 'Was Señora de Ribera telling the truth about her and Huber?'

'If it would have been up to me to decide by reading her face, I couldn't have told you. But no one can fake a flush like the one that came over old Huber. So, yes, I think they've been doing the horizontal hula since the night we all got sworn into Neptune's social club.'

'So that means . . .'

'Both of them are off the list of suspects.'

'So, not Lieutenant Haas,' I said. 'Not Señora de Ribera. Not Herr Huber.'

'And not Gitte Damgaard,' Mamie said. 'If she was the one who pushed Major Heissemeyer over the side, the last thing she would do is kill Willy the driver when he was busy trying to strangle the only witness to the crime.'

'Herr Blanck?' I asked. 'I don't think so. A Nazi agent wouldn't kill a Nazi officer. First off, he didn't have a motive that we know. And, second, why risk his cover – and maybe his mission – to kill Heissemeyer, even if he had a motive. I just don't buy Grap's theory that he was settling scores among the German spy agencies. No, it can't have been him.'

'Who does that leave on our list of suspects, Bert?'

'Only Fräulein Schon, the one you say is too small and too nice to be the killer,' I said. 'Or someone who isn't on the suspect list we made and should have been. Like we were thinking.'

FORTY

> Along with the careful provision for comfort and pleasure there is everywhere the impressive North German Lloyd efficiency.
>
> – *Round Africa Cruise brochure*

Mamie – April 2, 1939 – At sea

As the pink of dawn painted our stateroom, I sat in my dressing gown, wondering if I should put on clothes and get my cup of joe for myself. For the first time since leaving New York, Steward Grap's gentle knock had not come to signal the beginning of the new day.

I needed that steaming eye-opener and decided it was time to act. 'Bert. Bert, are you awake?' I said.

'I am now.' For a farmer, Bert can be grumpy in the morning.

'Where's Grap?' I needed that joe.

'How should I know?' Bert dragged the bedclothes over his head. 'Maybe he has the good sense to still be asleep.'

Right then, something happened. I know, that's not very definite. Shoot, it's loose as a goose for describing what occurred. But it is accurate – *something* happened but you couldn't hear it. It was more like an absence of sound. *Something* happened but you couldn't feel it. It was more like a cessation of movement that you'd barely known was there in the first place. Then I recognized what it was from our port visits. The massive twin screws that propel the *Columbus* had stopped turning. It had happened each time we anchored or docked but it had never happened in open water like now. We were somewhere beyond the Azores, miles from any coastline.

'Bert, wake up.' I shook his shoulder and got a sleepy growl in response. 'I think the ship is stopping.'

The bedclothes parted like the Red Sea and Bert sat bolt

upright. 'Why would we be stopping in the middle of the ocean?' Without waiting for an answer to his question, he held his hand up for silence. 'You're right, Mamie. The screws have stopped. Better get dressed.'

We threw on clothes and popped out the door, nearly colliding with a running Steward Stockfisch, our old traveling companion from the Sudan. Stockfisch slid to a halt, mumbled a distracted, 'Excuse me,' and started to bolt.

Bert was too quick for the boy, snagging him by the arm. 'Whoa, Stockfisch. What's going on?'

'There has been an accident in the engine room.'

'And?' Bert said, not releasing his grip.

'Steward Grap has been hurt.'

'Take us there,' I said.

Stockfisch hesitated. 'You should not go.'

'Take us. Now!'

Stockfisch turned and rushed for the nearest stairwell, with Bert and me on his tail. We plunged deep into the bowels of the ship, down stairwell after stairwell, until we came to a knot of crewmen struggling with a stretcher on the steep incline.

Captain Dane had already arrived and had charge of the situation, leading the stretcher bearers. Herr Doktor Ehring showed up a second or two after we did. The bearers halted on a grated landing. I saw then that the form on the stretcher was covered from head to toe with a greasy blanket. A white shoe protruded from one corner of the blanket, drenched in what appeared to be blood.

Doctor Ehring lifted the corner of the blanket nearest the head and winced at the sight revealed to him. As in the vignette during our eastward Atlantic passage, he said, '*tot*.' Dead. Only this was no playact.

Captain Dane heard me gasp at the doctor's pronouncement, turned to see Bert and me, and said, 'Please, Mr and Mrs Mason, you must leave here. There has been a terrible accident in the engine room.'

'What's happened?' I asked.

Captain Dane knew he had to answer. 'Steward Grap has been killed.'

'How?' Bert stammered.

'We are not certain, but it appears he was caught in the main engine's crankshaft. Now, please, Mr Mason, go. This is no place for Mrs Mason.'

My knees wanted to buckle at the thought of young Grap twisted and ground up in the crankshaft, but I resolved not to let it happen. As it turned out, Bert was not much better off than me. We leaned heavily on each other until we found our way up to the sea air on the Promenade Deck. We leaned against the rail and stared out at the Atlantic, the morning sun a slash of molten gold against the deep blue of the fathomless ocean.

'Oh, dear God, Bert. That poor, dear boy. What an awful way to die. What a horrible accident.'

Bert's eyes were on the horizon, his face grim. 'What makes you think it was an accident, Mamie?'

FORTY-ONE

The attentions of an expert and solicitous cruise staff will help make the days at sea, as well as those on shore, pass pleasantly and rapidly.

– *Round Africa Cruise brochure*

Bert – April 7, 1939 – At sea

We hashed it out for the next few days, Mamie and me. When we finally had it to the point we were sure, we asked for a meeting with Captain Dane. He scheduled it for our usual hour of midnight. We were due to arrive in New York on the same day, today, at noon.

Herr Lau's bristly face greeted us at the door to the captain's private passage to his cabin. As we walked through the captain's closet, the ordered rows of dress uniforms were missing one, marked by an empty hanger whose occupant adorned Captain Dane as he waited for us at his chart table.

The captain nodded to his first officer. 'Thank you, Herr Lau. That will be all.'

The silent Lau went out the door to the wheelhouse, leaving us alone with a cordial Captain Dane. 'Please, Mr and Mrs Mason, be seated. Would you care for a cognac? A short drink to the memory of Steward Grap and to the end of this ill-starred cruise?'

'I could use a belt,' Mamie said.

'Thanks, none for me, Captain,' I said. I wanted a clear head and I can't hold my liquor like Mamie.

Captain Dane moved to a corner cupboard and returned with two snifters of caramel-colored liquid. He placed one before Mamie, seated himself behind the chart table, and silently raised his glass in salute. He and Mamie drank.

'So, Mr Mason, you asked that we meet,' the captain said. 'To what do I owe the pleasure of your and Mrs Mason's company on this last night of our voyage?'

'You asked that I investigate the death of Sturmbannführer Heissemeyer and find his killer. Mamie and I have done that, and we have a theory as to who the killer is. Of course, only you are in a position to see to the arrest of that individual and his delivery into the hands of the proper authorities at the conclusion of the cruise.'

'Of course. Though I must admit, I am somewhat surprised that you are coming to me at this late date. I had assumed that you had been unsuccessful. Please tell me how you arrived at your, as you say, "theory".'

'Well, Captain, I really didn't have much investigative experience during the short time I served as a sheriff's deputy.'

'Come, now, Mr Mason. You are too modest.'

Mamie put in her two cents. 'No, Captain, he's not. He really didn't conduct any investigations while he was a deputy. He didn't know where to start when you asked him to investigate the major's death. Neither one of us did. So I suggested that the first thing to do was just talk to people, passengers and crew, and see if we could find someone who held a grudge against Major Heissemeyer. And it wasn't hard to do. In fact, it was so easy and the number got to be so large that we had to make a list to keep everybody straight. I have it here.' Mamie held out a handwritten list to Captain Dane, who took it and scanned it briefly.

'You have many persons on your list, Mrs Mason. Do you have evidence against any of them?' he asked.

'Well, you know, Captain, there's not a great deal of evidence to be had,' I said. 'Major Heissemeyer was shoved or thrown overboard, so there was no murder weapon to be examined. Mamie was the only eyewitness and she, as you know, didn't see much. And, with so many people with a motive, it looked to me like the crime might be unsolvable. For a time we thought we might have a perfect crime here, at least from the criminal's standpoint.'

Mamie spoke over her snifter of cognac. 'That's what my dear old Bert said at first, that it might be unsolvable. But I told him we should keep our eyes open, think, and the killer would show himself to us.'

I took up the narrative. 'So we tried to eliminate suspects

from the list. Some were easy. Take Gitte Damgaard. With a little digging on our own and a little help from Steward Grap, we found out that she was basically a criminal and had been imprisoned in a camp where Major Heissemeyer was in charge. She hated Heissemeyer and she didn't try to hide it after his death. In fact, she spoke about it openly. And then there is her continuing criminal career. She may or may not be smuggling jewels on this trip. Major Heissemeyer was the closest thing to a policeman aboard ship, and having him out of the way would not have hurt her chances of success, if she was smuggling.'

'But she was the one who plugged Willy the driver and saved my skin in South Africa,' Mamie said. 'Since I was the only witness to the major's murder, it would have been in the killer's best interest to have me dead. I figured if Gitte Damgaard was the murderer, she would have minded her own business and let Willy finish what he had started. And I wouldn't be drinking this fine cognac with you.'

'That makes sense,' Captain Dane said. 'What of the other suspects on your list?'

'Pia de Ribera and Matthias Huber, both who had a motive, were otherwise occupied at the time Major Heissemeyer was murdered,' I said.

'Otherwise occupied?'

Mamie rolled her eyes. 'Doing the deed, Captain. Taking a roll in the hay. Making whoopee. Dancin' the horizontal shag.'

'Ah, I understand. Having sex,' Dane said.

'Well, if you want to be vulgar about it,' Mamie huffed.

Ignoring Mamie, Dane said, 'I see you have Lieutenant Haas on your listing. You suspected him of killing his own superior officer?'

I felt sheepish explaining this; something about discussing pansies, though I got nothing against them. Mamie had no such compunctions.

'Major Heissemeyer made passes at the young lieutenant. Romantic passes. Plenty of them, we found out. Haas kept putting him off. Then, when the lieutenant fell for Beatta Schon, Major Heissemeyer started to make noises about her ancestry, that she was Jewish and not good enough for an SS man or any self-respecting Nazi. Haas was worried sick about what Heissemeyer could do to him and to Fräulein Schon. Heissemeyer's murder made both those problems go away. So, yeah, he was our prime suspect until your chief fireman, Becker, made it a point to let Bert know that he had spent the night of the murder drinking with Lieutenant Haas. And also that Haas wasn't a real Nazi after all, just a poor misguided youth. I thought this was kind of strange, but checked out the drinking story with the bartender on the Beach Club Deck and a couple other crew members. It was true, so Lieutenant Haas dropped off the list. As did Chief Becker, if he was ever even on it. That moved the lovely and gentle Fräulein Schon right to the top of the list as a result.'

'Surely not the young lady . . .' Captain Dane began.

'That's what I said, too, Captain,' Mamie said. 'Too nice, too young, too petite to muscle a man, even a man as small as Major Heissemeyer, over the rail against his will.'

'Mamie raised good points about Fräulein Schon, all of them,' I said. 'But there was still something that made me uncomfortable about her, a hunch that told me that the more we learned about her, the closer we would be to learning the identity of Major Heissemeyer's killer. So we called in a favor, Mamie and me. A favor that had been obtained at the expense of a man's life.'

'A man's life . . . *mein Gott.*' When Dane said this he barely whispered it.

I took a deep breath and let it out slowly. 'I am going to tell you about it now, Captain, but it doesn't leave this room. And if you do tell anyone I spoke to you about it, I'll deny it and so will Mamie.'

'You bet your ass I'll deny it, Captain.' Thus spake the ever-supportive Mamie. I love the old girl.

'And there was a thorough and extensive investigation of the death by the authorities in Anglo-Egyptian Sudan, resulting in a finding that it was accidental,' I continued.

'Very thorough,' Mamie chimed in.

Captain Dane eyed me coolly. 'Herr Blanck? I underestimated you, Mr Mason.'

'It's not what you think, Captain,' I said. 'We heard a shot and, following it up, walked in on a struggle between Herr Blanck and Steward Grap. Blanck had a knife and was about to stab Grap. I shot Blanck with his own pistol, but it was in defense of Grap.'

'Then why the story about it being an accident, all that gun-cleaning nonsense?' Dane said.

'Steward Grap was a spy, a British secret agent he said, tasked with making sure that, if a war began between Germany and Great Britain, the *Columbus* would not return to Germany. He told us that the purser was a Nazi agent, placed on the *Columbus* to ferret out spies and to make certain the ship would return to Germany on the outbreak of war. Grap said if the truth about the fight between him and Blanck came out, his cover would be blown and he would either be imprisoned or shot. The story about Herr Blanck accidentally shooting himself was to protect Grap. Mamie and I decided to go along with it.'

'So the story . . .' Captain Dane said. 'But what of the favor?'

'In return for our silence, Steward Grap, or whoever he actually was, agreed to cable his superiors for information on the suspects on our list. He got the responses back at Villefranche and reported them to us. One important bit of information was that Fräulein Schon's mother was Jewish, meaning the fräulein was considered to be a Jew as well. Her mother was an actress who died when Fräulein Schon was very young. She was raised by an aunt. According to Grap's report, nothing was known about her father, with her father's name left blank on her birth certificate.'

'What can be the significance of this small fact, Mr Mason? Surely she is not implicated in Major Heissemeyer's death merely because his suspicion that she was Jewish was confirmed.'

Mamie took the ball. 'The information that Beatta Schon was Jewish was important, but only as confirmation of something we suspected was true anyway. The most important fact that Grap provided was that her father was unknown. It got us to puzzling over who he might be.'

'And,' I said, 'we were also puzzling over the two spies

aboard ship and what they might have to do with this. One German agent and one British agent. Which of them would want to kill Major Heissemeyer? Not the German agent. You don't kill your own people, even if they are nasty martinets like Heissemeyer. And not the British agent, either. Why? Spies aren't assassins, at least not the spies on the *Columbus*. They weren't put in place to kill. They only kill to protect themselves. And if Major Heissemeyer had found out a spy, he wouldn't have confronted him alone. The man was all bluster and no courage. Even I could see that. No, if Heissemeyer had thought Blanck was a British spy, there would have been an arrest with a lot of show and a lot of force. So Mamie and I concluded it wasn't Herr Blanck or Steward Grap who killed Major Heissemeyer.'

'That threw us, once it all hit the fan in the Sudan.' Mamie couldn't resist a smirk at her own doggerel verse. 'We were diverted for most of the trip down the Nile, trying to pin the murder on one of the spies. But neither Grap nor Blanck had been on our original suspect list. So we went back to the original list, worried over each of the names on it for hours, talked and argued, and got nowhere. Then it hit me . . . the entire list was a clue.'

'The list was a clue? Whatever do you mean?' Captain Dane was good, so good. Even at feigning ignorance.

'The list was all the best suspects, but it was also something else. It was a list of the regular guests at the captain's table. It was a list of red herrings designed to divert us. It was a list put together by you.'

FORTY-TWO

> The seamanship of the Lloyd officers and sailors is of the highest type and has been a tradition for generations.
>
> – *Round Africa Cruise brochure*

Mamie – April 7, 1939 – At sea

'Coincidence,' Dane said, still cool as a cucumber. 'Recall that the group at my table was in place well before Major Heissemeyer was lost overboard.'

'We considered that,' I said. 'I wanted to believe that, like I'm guessing any of the ladies on this cruise would have wanted to believe. But Bert couldn't get by it. He finally decided that it was part of a contingency plan – a plan put in place in the event the major had to be removed from the ship. So Bert did some digging on his own, sent a cable back to Ohio that really panned out.'

'Panned out? I am not familiar with the expression.' Captain Dane looked earnestly at me with those eyes of his. I nearly forgot where I was.

'It was very successful,' Bert explained.

'Sure was,' I said. 'You see, Captain, we have two groups of workers back in the greenhouse in Ohio – a man's crew with a male foreman and a woman's crew with a woman in charge. Bert won't admit it, but the women's crew regularly outworks the men's crew.'

'I'll admit it,' Bert said.

'At last,' I said. 'Anyway, the woman in charge of the women's crew is from the Old Country.' A quizzical look from Dane. 'From Europe. We call her Polish Katie. She's a Pole from a place near Germany, and she still has a whole passel of relatives back there.'

'I knew the odds were long,' Bert said. 'But there was no

other way that I could check on what I suspected. I knew Polish Katie was from Danzig, so I cabled her and asked if her relatives there could do some bird-dogging for me. I thought it was a pretty big town, and it is, but it turns out that, like most places, it's a small town when it comes to rumor and scandal. By scandal I mean things like notable local actresses giving birth out of wedlock. One of Katie's sisters there remembered the stir it caused when our Fräulein Schon was born. The whispers then were that the father was a ship's officer. Unfortunately, that was all she remembered.'

'Interesting, but a rumor from many years ago is not much solid evidence for your "theory", Mr Mason,' Captain Dane said. I noticed he was toying with a letter opener that was on the chart table. Maybe that was a tell of nervousness, a crack in the inexorable facade of the great captain.

'You know, Captain Dane, I didn't think much of it either,' Bert continued. 'But the North German Lloyd line helped me out some on the rumor. I guess you know they put a little safety brochure in each stateroom. It explains about lifeboat drills, where to find your life vest, that sort of thing. And you must know that it also includes a few paragraphs about the captain and the first officer, to show their extensive experience and to put folks' minds at ease. It said that you and Herr Lau had both served in the Kaiserliche Marine in the Great War, as shipmates aboard the battlecruiser *Lützow* at Jutland. And, of course, I had already learned that Chief Becker served on the *Lützow* as well.'

'Yes,' Dane admitted.

'And you served together after the war on several ships of the Baltic American line, including the SS *Polonia* from 1920 until late 1922.'

'Yes, that is correct.'

'What was the *Polonia*'s home port?'

'Danzig,' Captain Dane said, evenly.

'It must have been difficult. First, her mother's death, and then all the years having her grow up without you.'

Dane's face took on a wistful expression. 'It was very difficult.'

'And then to see her in danger from the Nazis these last few years just because her mother was a Jew.'

Dane's eyes hardened. 'The Nazis are fools. I, we, so many of us thought them such fools and buffoons as to hardly be dangerous, but they have proven us wrong. Now they will take us into another world war that, like the last, cannot be won.'

'So you decided to get her out of the way before it began.'

'Yes. Are you a father, Mr Mason?'

'I am.'

'Then, as a father, you must know.'

'I can understand.' Bert was gentle now with his questions. 'She had taken up with Lieutenant Haas before this voyage, hadn't she?'

Dane sat back in his chair. His voice dropped to nearly a whisper when he answered. 'Yes. They met in Danzig. Kurt was a naive young man, like so many, and fell in with those beasts. He began to see them for what they actually were only after he was too deeply involved.'

'And she wouldn't leave Europe without him?' I asked.

Captain Dane shook his head negatively.

'But an opportunity presented itself when he was assigned to be aboard this cruise?' The tick of Dane's desk chronometer was a roaring drumbeat compared to the timbre of Bert's voice as he posed the question.

Dane sighed. 'Had they been able to stay apart for the duration of the voyage, Major Heissemeyer might not have been a problem. But they were in love and they couldn't stay apart. They thought they could carry off the fiction of a shipboard meeting and romance, and that Heissemeyer would simply wait for it to die out on the return to Europe. That is, until the major started meddling.'

'You did it to protect her,' Bert said, speaking as one father to another. 'It was then that you were forced to put your contingency plan into action, wasn't it, Captain?'

'I will admit that is your theory,' Captain Dane responded. 'But that is all I will admit.'

'And the *Columbus* will never return to Germany,' I said. 'You and your comrades from the last war on board will see to that.'

'Why do you say this, Mrs Mason? We are all loyal Germans. Do you, like Mr Mason, have a theory on which you are working?'

'As a matter of fact, I do. I wasn't sure about it until Steward Grap suffered his accident but I'm pretty confident of it now. Grap told us he was a secret agent aboard to make sure the *Columbus* ended up in the possession of the right side if war broke out, but he lied to us in one respect. He said he worked for the British, but he was actually a Nazi agent. Or what I guess the professionals call a double agent, at least as far as his representations to us were concerned. And now, Captain Dane, you are going to look innocently at me and ask how I could possibly conclude he was a Nazi agent. That is a simple one, Captain. Why would Herr Lau and Chief Becker, your shipmates from the *Lützow*, take him to the engine room and do him in if he wasn't a Nazi?'

'But, my dear Mrs Mason, I thought you and Mr Mason believed Herr Blanck to be the German agent aboard.'

'We did, until Grap was done away with. Such a nice boy, too.' And I meant it.

'So Herr Blanck was a British agent, the opposite of what Steward Grap had led you to believe?' Dane asked.

'C'mon, Captain,' Bert said, obviously fed up with the pussyfooting. 'You knew that. The man had been working on you since he joined the crew of the *Columbus* two cruises ago. I'm almost sorry I shot him.'

'Almost?'

'Well, he did try to have Mamie killed. To protect you. I take it you knew that.'

'Only after the fact, I assure you,' Dane said. 'After the failed attempt, I chastised him, but I could never be sure he might not try again to eliminate Mamie as the one witness who might identify me. Speaking only in the theoretical sense, of course.'

'Of course,' Bert said.

Captain Dane rose from his seat at the chart table and drank off the remainder of his cognac in one swallow. 'This has all been very interesting. Those are quite the intriguing theories you have come up with, Mr and Mrs Mason. I am certain that you are disappointed that there is insufficient evidence to warrant taking your theories to the authorities when we land in New York City. Not that they would be in the least interested in a man, a Nazi, falling overboard from a German ship off the coast of Africa, in any event.'

'Any more than they would be in the death of a man in a gun accident in the Sudan,' Mamie said.

'I see we all understand the situation clearly,' Captain Dane said. 'Now, Mr and Mrs Mason, you will have to excuse me. We are about to make landfall and I have obligations on the bridge. The passengers will be excited to reach the end of such a long cruise. Some exceptionally so. Fräulein Schon, for instance, and Lieutenant, soon to be Mister, Haas, seem to be particularly enthralled to be reaching their new home.'

'I hope they appreciate the captain's efforts on their behalf,' Bert said.

A momentary darkness passed across Captain Dane's eyes. 'I hope they do, too. And, Mr Mason, let me express my appreciation for your and Mrs Mason's efforts, as well. Fräulein Schon and Lieutenant Haas's future happiness must be attributed, in some part, to you. Now, I must go. I would say, "*Auf Wiedersehen*", but I doubt very much that we are likely to encounter each other again. I daresay the coming storm will see to that.'

And with that, Captain Dane clicked his heels together and gave a brief bow as he showed us out the door.

EPILOGUE

Mamie – December 20, 1939 – Hills Corners, Ohio

I thought that Bert had finally settled back into his old routine, no small feat after two months of wild beasts, dancing natives, murder plots, and spies, in Africa. The autumn crop was ripening, just in time to allow all the well-to-do in their New York mansions to have fresh tomatoes on their Christmas salads. The men's and women's greenhouse crews would get a couple extra days off at Christmas. Polish Katie had brought over a plate of raspberry, prune and cherry *kolaczki* she had baked for us to have as dessert after Christmas dinner. Bert had stopped talking about the bazaar in Dakar, dinners at the captain's table, and the rough camp at Wadi Halfa, and had started talking about making seed for the spring crop, the Elks Christmas party, and who the Republicans would run against Roosevelt next year.

Until he unfolded this morning's paper.

'Mamie, look at this!' he said as I put his breakfast, a rasher of bacon and two poached eggs, before him.

'I don't have my reading glasses, Bert. Can't it wait till after breakfast? I'll read it then.'

'No. No, it's about the *Columbus*. She's gone down. I'll read it to you:

LUXURY SHIP BURNS

***Special to* The New York Times**

The US cruiser *Tuscaloosa* flashed word to the Navy Department today that the German liner *Columbus*, which left Veracruz, Mexico, five days ago on a race through the blockade to Germany, had been scuttled by her crew and was sinking. A British destroyer was standing by.

> **Later, Captain Henry Bodt of the *Tuscaloosa* informed the department that 579 survivors, including nine women, had been taken aboard. Two engine room crewmen, and the *Columbus*'s captain, Wilhelm Dane, are missing and presumed to have gone down with the ship. The *Tuscaloosa* is steaming to Ellis Island in New York harbor with the survivors.**
>
> **The *Columbus* was returning to New York from a Caribbean cruise when hostilities commenced in Europe on September 1. The ship disembarked her passengers at Havana, and, shortly after, steamed to the neutral port of Veracruz where she had remained until beginning her run for Germany. It is presumed the sinking of the *Columbus,* if necessary to avoid capture, had been ordered by Berlin before the liner set sail to run the British-French blockade. The appearance of the British destroyer apparently caused the German crew to scuttle the liner.**
>
> **As the United States maintains its position of neutrality in the European conflict, the crew of the *Columbus* are considered 'distressed seamen', having survived a maritime disaster, and will be turned over to the German Embassy for registration when that becomes possible.**

Bert lifted his eyes from the paper. 'Quite a ship, the *Columbus.* It's hard to believe something that large, that graceful and elegant, is gone. And Captain Dane gone with her. Quite a man, that Dane. He made some difficult choices, right down to the end.'

'I think there are going to be a lot of difficult choices made in the Old Country in the next few years,' I said. 'I'm glad the United States is staying out of it.'

'Me, too,' Bert said. 'What goes on in Europe is none of our concern, no matter how much the folks there try to pull us in. It disappoints me, though, that this new war will keep us from going back to Africa anytime soon. There's a lot of peril in crossing the Atlantic these days. But, Mamie, have you seen this advertisement in the paper about a cruise to South America in February? It really looks like a keen trip. Think of it – the Amazon, Buenos Aires, the pampas, you and me, Mamie, togged to the bricks, dancing in the moonlight in Rio. Whadda ya say, old girl?'

AUTHOR'S NOTE

While the characters and the story in this book are fictional, the SS *Columbus* was a real ocean liner and did make a sixty-three-day round-Africa cruise beginning in February, 1939. And, like her fictional counterpart, the real *Columbus* was scuttled and sunk off the coast of New Jersey shortly before Christmas that same year.

Unlike the fictional Captain Dane, the *Columbus*'s real captain, Wilhelm Daehne, was sympathetic to the Nazi cause. At the outbreak of hostilities on September 1, 1939, the *Columbus* was in the midst of a Caribbean cruise. Daehne diverted her to Havana, Cuba, offloaded her passengers, and continued on to Veracruz, Mexico, where she remained until December.

Ordered to make a run for Germany, she met the British destroyer *Hyperion* off the US coast. Captain Daehne opted to scuttle her rather than have her captured by the British. She was burned at sea, and her crew, less two casualties, was taken aboard the US Navy cruiser *Tuscaloosa.* Captain Daehne, unlike the fictional Dane, did not go down with the ship.

Thus began a long and unusual odyssey for the *Columbus*'s crew. With the United States still neutral, they were treated as distressed mariners. They were taken to Ellis Island in New York, and later moved to Angel Island in San Francisco Bay, where they waited for almost a year to be repatriated to Germany. During that time, a small number of the crew actually made it home by way of Japan, Siberia, and the Eastern Soviet Union, but a blockade and diplomatic efforts by the British prevented the rest from leaving the United States. The 410 crewmen who remained were then moved to an abandoned Civilian Conservation Corps camp near Fort Stanton, New Mexico.

Captain Daehne and the crew devoted themselves to rebuilding and improving the camp. They constructed additional barracks and officers' quarters, barber and tailor shops, a kitchen and mess hall, a library, soccer fields, tennis courts and even a swimming pool. As they were not technically prisoners, they had freedom to hike in the surrounding desert, and visit the nearest town. They even participated in a rodeo with the local citizens.

Their status changed in 1941 when Germany declared war on the United States. As enemy aliens, their liberties were curtailed, and guard towers and fencing were erected around the camp. New internees, including the officers and crews of other German merchant ships, were brought in to the camp. Captain Daehne remained in command throughout the rest of the war, and was sent home to Germany with the last of the crewmen to leave after the war's end in 1945.

– At Westlake, Ohio, June, 2022

ACKNOWLEDGMENTS

Many thanks to friend and fellow author Ed Duncan for all of his wisdom, support and counsel on all things "author" related to this book and all through my brief career as a writer.

Much gratitude to Rachel Slatter, my super-special editor, for her judgment, perspicuity and enthusiasm. There is no better boost for an author than an editor who regularly uses the word "fab" in her emails to him!

Thanks to the many people at Severn House who have pulled all these words together into a book, especially Tina Pietron, for correcting my sometimes-errant German and leading the later phases of editing; copy editors Penelope Isaac and Sara Porter, for a precise and flawless job on the details; and Martin Brown, for steering publicity and marketing.

And, of course, the greatest thank you to my enchanting wife, Irene. As first reader and a relentless booster of Mamie Mason, she never allowed this manuscript to be put on a shelf and forgotten. She is why you have the pleasure of reading it today.